Tara Sue Me wrot[...]e. Twenty years later, after pen[...] ne decided to try her hand at something spicier and started work on *The Submissive*, and she soon followed that with *The Dominant*, *The Training*, *Seduced by Fire*, *The Enticement*, *The Exhibitionist*, *The Master*, and *The Exposure*. The series has become a huge hit with readers around the world and has been read and reread millions of times.

Tara kept her identity and her writing life secret, not even telling her husband what she was working on. To this day, only a handful of people know the truth (though she has told her husband). They live together in the southeastern United States with their two children.

Find out more about Tara on her website www.tarasueme.com, or visit her on Facebook www.facebook.com/TaraSueMeBooks and on Twitter @tarasueme.

Praise for Tara Sue Me's breathtakingly sensual Submissive series:

'I HIGHLY recommend *The Submissive* by Tara Sue Me. It's so worth it. This book crackles with sexual lightning right from the beginning . . . It has heart and the characters are majorly flawed in a beautiful way. They aren't perfect, but they may be perfect together. Step into Tara Sue Me's world of dominance and submission. It's erotic, thrilling, and will leave you panting for more' *Martini Reviews*

'For those *Fifty Shades* fans pining for a little more spice on their e-reader . . . the *Guardian* recommends Tara Sue Me's Submissive Trilogy, starring handsome CEO Nathaniel West, a man on the prowl for a new submissive, and the librarian Abby, who is yearning for something more' *Los Angeles Times*

More praise for Tara Sue Me:

'Unbelievably fantastic! . . . Nathaniel is something special, and he has that . . . something "more" that makes him who he is and makes me love him more than all the others. Beneath the cold and detached surface there is a sweet and loving man, and I adored how Abby managed to crack his armour a tiny bit at a time . . . I can't wait to continue this beautiful story' *Mind Reader*

'Tara Sue Me's *The Submissive* was a story unlike anything I'd ever read, and it completely captivated me . . . It's an emotional, compelling story about two people who work to make their relationship exactly what they need it to be, and how they're BOTH stronger for it' *Books Make Me Happy*

'I am awed by Tara Sue Me . . . a very powerful book written with grace and style. The characters were brought to life with a love story that will leave you wanting for more' *Guilty Pleasures Book Reviews*

'Very passionate . . . The characters are very easy to relate to and there is a depth to their feelings that is intriguing and engaging . . . intense and very, VERY H-O-T' *Harlequin Junkie*

'This is the kind of erotic writing that makes the genre amazing' *Debbie's Book Bag*

'Titillates and captivates from the very beginning' *Romantic Times* (top pick)

By Tara Sue Me

In The Lessons From The Rack Series
Master Professor

In The Submissive Series
The Submissive
The Dominant
The Training
Seduced By Fire: Partners In Play
The Chalet (e-novella)
The Enticement
The Collar
The Exhibitionist
The Master
The Exposure
The Flirtation

MASTER PROFESSOR
TARA SUE ME

HEADLINE PUBLISHING GROUP
An Hachette UK Company

Carmelite House
50 Victoria Embankment
London EC4Y 0DZ

www.headline.com
www.hachette.co.uk

HEADLINE
ETERNAL

Published by arrangement with Berkley,
An imprint of Penguin Random House LLC

First published in Great Britain in 2017
by HEADLINE ETERNAL
An imprint of HEADLINE PUBLISHING GROUP

1

Cataloguing in Publication Data is available from the British Library

ISBN 978 1 4722 4270 9

Offset in 10.4/15.68 pt Fairfield LT Std by Jouve (UK)

Printed and bound in Great Britain by CPI Group (UK) Ltd, Croydon, CR0 4YY

MIX
Paper from
responsible sources
FSC
www.fsc.org   FSC® C104740

Headline's policy is to use papers that are natural, renewable and recyclable
products and made from wood grown in well-managed forests and other
controlled s   :ted
to confo

*To anyone who's ever had to decide between perfect
and almost perfect, but not quite.*

There's something altogether freeing about writing a new series. You don't have to remember what color someone's eyes are or if they said something three books ago that doesn't jive with what you have them doing now. You get to create an entirely new universe and YOU GET TO DO ANYTHING YOU WANT IN IT.

But as freeing as it is, it's also daunting because you have to decide what color everyone's eyes are and you have to try to imagine if what the characters do now will come back to kick your ass three books from now. Plus you have to create an entirely new universe and when you get to do anything you want, sometimes, you're afraid to do anything at all.

But if you're very, very lucky, you'll be surrounded by incredible people like I have been. Here are a few:

To the people of Portland, Oregon: You guys are the best. You are welcoming and friendly and don't mind us curious East Coasters. I love you and your city and can't wait to see you again.

To Elle Mason, my travel in crime partner: I still can't remember if it was "Bitches off grid" or "Off grid, bitches" but either way, it was a blast. Let's do it again Real Soon. Deal?

To Tiffany Reisz: You have no idea how much our chat over veggie burgers helped me. I owe you one. Or five. Maybe ten. Probably twenty.

To Mr Sue Me: Thank you for two thousand things it would take another book to cover.

CHAPTER
One

In the history of dumb and stupid ideas, Andie Lincoln couldn't shake the feeling that her current endeavor was the dumbest and most stupid of them all. She stood beside the arched glass window in her Portland, Oregon, hotel and wondered when exactly she'd lost her mind.

She shouldn't even have been in Portland. She should have been spending her summer interning as a chef in a Seattle restaurant like she'd told her parents. It still bothered her that she'd lied to them. But seriously, what was the alternative? There was no way she could tell them she was entering an exclusive BDSM school or that she'd begged Terrence to find a way to get her in.

Hell, half the time, she didn't believe it herself.

And they would never believe that it was her idea. Oh no, they'd think he had somehow brainwashed her into going. They would never have understood that she actually wanted this. Wanted to be trained in the BDSM world as a submissive. Even Terrence had only agreed to talk to his friend, who was also the headmaster, because she'd asked him to do so. Repeatedly.

Her phone rang, pulling her away from the window and thoughts of her parents. She smiled when she saw the display.

"Hey, Terrence," she said.

"How's my girl?" he asked.

The multiple voices in the background confirmed he was still on set. He must have had a break and used it to call her.

She sighed. "I can't believe I'm here on the West Coast—finally, I might add—and you're on location in Pittsburgh." Since he lived in L.A. and their hometown was Atlanta, usually she was the one on the East Coast.

He laughed. That softly seductive sound that never failed to make his audiences swoon. She pictured him raking his fingers through his blond hair and her heart sped up.

"I swear, if it wouldn't upset the production team and put the entire thing behind schedule, I'd be in Portland with you right now." His voice was deep and determined and she had no doubt he was speaking the truth.

"I understand," she said, because she did. "Besides, it's not like I'm going to be here long anyway. Tomorrow morning I head over to the academy."

"And how awful is it I'm not there for you?" He sighed. "Damn it, Andie. It's not right."

She loved it when his protective side came out. The side of him she knew would always put her first. It was a big part of the reason she asked to be trained for him.

They had been friends forever. When she was seven and he was nine, his family had moved across the street, and before too long, they were inseparable. Even after Terrence left for Hollywood and became a household name at nineteen, their friendship remained strong. And as time went on, it grew into something more. He said he loved how she wanted him for him and not for his celebrity status. And she loved him because he was kind and patient and made her laugh. But still, they were just friends.

Then, six months ago, during her winter break, *that* night had happened. The night they went shopping for a Christmas tree and went out for coffee after. He'd disguised himself with an old hat and baggy clothes, and they were laughing at a shared memory. He took her hand and looked in her eyes, and the laughing stopped as they both realized that something had changed.

To this day, her stomach got all fluttery when she remembered the way he'd lightly stroked her cheek and then leaned in for a kiss. It was then they both knew that not only had things changed, but there was no going back.

They went out a few more times and though it was nice, getting to know him in a way she hadn't before, she couldn't shake the feeling he was hiding something from her. It was in the way he'd start to say something and then stop himself. Or the look of intense concentration he'd get.

Finally, one night she confronted him, asked what was wrong. He looked momentarily taken aback before he'd sat her down and said he had things to tell her. Things he must tell her before they went any further.

He'd confessed he was a Dominant and wasn't going to give up that part of himself. She'd heard of the term, but had no idea what it really meant, so later, when she was alone, she did her own

3

research and gave her vibrator a workout and a half. It wasn't a lifestyle she'd considered before, but once the initial shock wore off, it sounded hot as hell.

"You can't help it," she assured him. "I know you'd be here if you could and I completely understand why you aren't."

"It still doesn't sit well with me that I'm not the one to train you."

"In that case," she teased, "I'll allow you to make it up to me the next time you see me."

"That I'll do." He laughed. "Call me tomorrow when you get settled."

"I will."

"How are you feeling? Are you nervous?"

That was another thing; ever since he'd brought up being a Dom, he was always asking how she felt and what she was thinking, like all the time. About everything. It took some getting used to. At first she thought he was asking just to be nice or because that's what he was supposed to do. Eventually, though, she realized he really wanted open communication.

She let out a deep breath. "I've moved beyond nervous but I'm not quite at the scared-shitless stage. It's just hard to wrap my head around the next few months. I mean, I'm not a prude, but I am a virgin. And when I think about what enrolling at the academy will mean . . ."

Another one of those *what the fuck am I doing?* thoughts hit her, but she shook it off. When she took the time to really think about enrolling in the academy, she was more excited than anything else. Thoughts of submitting to Terrence fueled her fantasies. She dreamed of the day she could give her whole self to him.

She and Terrence had agreed that while she was at the academy, she should feel free to explore her sexuality with no strings attached. That was when she brought up remaining a virgin. She'd never planned to be a virgin at twenty-three; it had just sort of worked out that way. But, she told Terrence, she didn't want to lose her virginity at a BDSM academy, so they agreed that would be the one thing that was off-limits. Terrence said he knew that in order for the training to work, she couldn't feel inhibited or guilty about what she would be doing. She appreciated the freedom, but it made her feel a bit apprehensive as well. Would she feel like she was cheating on him the entire summer?

She'd asked Terrence what would happen if she ended up hating being a sub. He said they'd worry about that if it happened. But she was pretty certain that would be the end of their relationship.

"Are you having second thoughts?" he asked, concern in his voice. "You don't have—"

"I know. I want to." How many times would she have to reassure him? "I think it's completely normal to feel anxious, but I'm not having second thoughts."

"I've known Lennox for years," he said, speaking of the academy owner and headmaster. "He's a great guy, and I trust him and his staff completely. I'd have to or else I'd never even think about you being there."

She twisted the curtain covering the window. "I know. And it makes me feel safe and protected when you say that."

"That's my job," he said. "Even though we're apart, I want you safe and protected."

There was a slight murmuring over the phone and she knew before he spoke that break time was over.

"I have to get back to the set," he confirmed. "I'll call you tonight before it gets too late."

"Okay. I'm going to go for a walk and grab something light for dinner." Maybe she'd call her parents, too. Assure them she was fine and everything was covered. That way maybe she could go a few days without calling again. She didn't want them to suspect anything.

They said their good-byes and Andie slipped her phone into her purse, determined not to let her nerves get the best of her.

FULTON MATTHEWS KNEW he was going to have to tread carefully with his boss, Lennox MacLure. After all, the man had just promoted him a month ago. At the time, Fulton had been thrilled with the new responsibilities, but he was starting to see they came with their own set of problems.

The door to Lennox's office opened and his boss waved him inside. "Come have a seat, Master Matthews."

Without waiting to see if he'd listen, Lennox walked over to his desk, sat down, and templed his fingers. Fulton crossed the room and took a seat in the leather chair across from his boss.

"I know why you're here." Lennox nodded toward the papers Fulton had brought in. "Those are the papers I gave you yesterday, aren't they? Andie Lincoln's application packet."

"Yes." And that was one of the questions he had. He was in charge of the new enrollees who would be arriving tomorrow and one of his duties was to create a tailor-made curriculum for each student. Why had Lennox waited until the last minute to give him the information?

"Go ahead," Lennox said.

He was a smug bastard—Fulton gave him that. Of course, he had reason to be. He'd single-handedly made the academy into what it was today: an elite BDSM learning center, known and respected throughout the kink world. Lennox himself was just as respected, although Fulton had never seen him participate in a scene. He'd once asked another staff member why that was and the person shook his head and told him to leave well enough alone.

"My first concern is why I was only given this yesterday," Fulton said. "The other enrollees have had their curriculum set for months."

"I have my reasons. And I know you'll have her curriculum ready by the time she arrives tomorrow."

Not if I can help it. But he kept that thought to himself.

"What else is bothering you?"

"To be perfectly honest, I'm wondering why she's here. She's not our typical student and several red flags came to mind when reading through her file."

"You've heard of Terrence Knight?"

Fulton frowned. "The actor?"

"Yes. Terrence and I go way back. Miss Lincoln is to be trained to be his submissive."

The situation was worse than he thought. He tried to think of a way to discreetly tell Lennox he had a potential fucked-up mess on his hands, but he couldn't come up with one. Not one that wouldn't get him fired, anyway.

He decided on: "It appears to be a really bad idea."

"Which part?"

"All of it." He took a deep breath. If Lennox wanted reasons, he was going to give him reasons and damn the consequences. "Miss Lincoln is a virgin with zero BDSM experience. And apparently she's only interested in submission because her Hollywood hotshot boyfriend is a Dominant."

It was a disaster waiting to happen and he feared the fallout when it struck. To take on someone who might not be submissive? Fulton's thoughts ran from harassment lawsuits to worse.

"Is that all?"

Was that all? Hell, he was serious. "Isn't that enough?"

"No, unfortunately, it's not." Lennox pushed back from his desk. "Miss Lincoln arrives tomorrow. I want you to do her initial interview and assessment. And I'd like to see the curriculum you design for her by five o'clock today."

And just like that, he was being shown the door. Heading to his own office, he resisted the urge to crumple up the papers he still held in his hand.

CHAPTER
Two

Though Andie had seen pictures of the academy, they in no way prepared her for seeing the real thing. It was a castle, for lack of a better word, located on a private island. Terrence told her RACK Academy was known internationally as an elite BDSM training facility. Whenever she felt anxious about actually stripping down and participating in BDSM scenes with strangers she reminded herself that it was considered an honor to be selected to attend.

She knew there would be no penetrative sex, and that fact brought her comfort. Her enrollment would require touching, but she told herself it would be clinical and feel sort of like going to the doctor. To be honest, she didn't think she would enjoy it at all.

The entire place had an eerie feel. She tried to attribute it to the low fog that surrounded the boat taking her to the island, but it was more than that. It was almost as if it were in the very air.

A representative from the school had met her at the docks this morning, after she'd checked out of her hotel and taken a cab to the coast. She'd read that there would be other students at the academy, but so far, she hadn't met anyone else. That probably wasn't helping the creepiness factor.

She stepped away from the boat railing and sat back down. The representative, who had introduced herself as May, was busy on her laptop, and the only other person on the boat was the captain. He didn't look like he was in the mood to chitchat.

She checked her phone for the twelfth time in thirty minutes only to verify that there had been no word from Terrence. And since she'd sent him a text when she checked out of the hotel, she didn't want to send him another for fear of being *that girl*.

He was busy filming. She didn't want to be a distraction. With a sigh, she put her phone down and tried to comprehend that the imposing structure before her was going to be her home for the next three months.

"When we arrive," May said, making her jump, "I'll take you inside and show you to Master Matthews's office. He'll take over from there." The other woman looked down at her watch. "I have to go pick up more students."

"How many are you picking up?"

"Three more today and five tomorrow. There're ten in your group, five men and five women. You're the second to arrive today."

"Do you pick us all up individually?"

May nodded. "Except, of course, for the couples. You'll have three couples in your group."

Andie drank in all the information she could. Out of ten, six were couples. It made her feel better knowing there would be other singles. Although technically, she wasn't single. She resisted the temptation to reach for her phone again. Probably didn't get good reception out here anyway.

"Is it always this creepy?" Andie pointed out to where the fog nearly touched the water.

May gave a half smile. It was the most emotion Andie had seen yet. "Yes, actually it is. Master MacLure said he bought the property for that very reason."

Master MacLure sounded like a nut job, but Andie kept that opinion to herself.

"The island is a rectangle," May said. "Almost a mile on the long end and a little over half a mile wide. While there are a few private homes and a lighthouse, most of your time will be in the castle."

They fell into silence as the boat approached the academy's dock. Andie couldn't take her eyes off the building. It looked even bigger up close. *Massive* might have been a better word. Built with gray stone and solid wood, it looked every bit like something she'd find in a history book.

The low fog hugged the dock and she almost felt she could get lost in it, it was so thick. As the boat came to a stop, she had to tip her head way back to look at the castle. Two turrets rose to the sky, but she couldn't see the tops because they were obscured by clouds. This was going to be her home for the summer?

"Wow" was all she could say.

"It does have that effect on people," May said. "Just wait until you see the inside."

11

* * *

ANDIE KNEW SHE should stop gawking, but she couldn't help it. Everything about the inside of the academy was just as awe-inspiring as the outside. The walls were covered with rich tapestries, expensive rugs lined the hardwood floors, and from what she could tell with an untrained eye, most of the furnishings were antique.

Shortly after she walked through the front door with May, a bellman appeared to whisk away her luggage. He didn't even ask her anything, but rather raised an eyebrow at May and waited for her nod.

"Come with me," May said. "I'll take you to Master Matthews."

They walked down a long hallway and finally came to a stop outside an open door. May stuck her head inside.

"Miss Lincoln's here."

"Send her in," said a low voice from inside.

May shook her hand. "Welcome to the academy, Miss Lincoln. Master Matthews will take it from here."

Andie nodded and stepped inside.

And froze at the sight of the man standing in front of a desk, arms crossed in front of his chest. His rock-hard, muscular chest. His T-shirt looked like it was practically painted on. He had to be over six feet and if his chest was any indication of the rest of him . . .

Damn.

She tore her gaze away from his abs to find two ice blue eyes staring at her. Two *ice-cold* blue eyes. And he was frowning. With those eyes paired with his thick, dark hair, he should have been incredibly handsome. But that frown of his? It changed everything.

"Andie Lincoln," he said. It wasn't a question, but she nodded anyway. "Sit down."

She sat in the leather chair that was much too close to where he stood. He towered over her, invading her personal space. She almost pushed her chair back, but the look in his eyes stopped her.

"Tell me why you're here," he said.

"May said you would take over my arrival procedures."

"Not here in my office," he said. "Here at the academy."

Wasn't that obvious?

"I want to be a submissive."

His nostrils flared. "One does not wish to be a submissive. One is either a submissive or one is not."

"I think I'm a submissive, but I want to be trained. I guess I want to find out for sure." What if she wasn't? She was so afraid Terrence wouldn't want her. This just had to work.

"You *think* you're a submissive? You *guess* you want to find out for sure?" He mocked her with her own words.

"Why are you being so mean?" She knew she was sounding like a child, but she didn't like this Matthews guy, no matter how good-looking he was. She hoped the rest of the staff was more like May and less like him.

"Miss Lincoln, there are ten people enrolled here this summer. Ten. Do you know how many people applied for those ten spots?"

She shook her head.

"You will answer me with me words so I know you heard and because I require a verbal response."

"No, I don't know how many people applied."

"No, *Sir.*"

Yes, he was truly an ass. Something must have flashed in her eyes, because his steely gaze grew considerably colder.

"Or Master Matthews," he said. "Either one will do, but when addressing a Dom here, especially one on staff, it is always 'Sir' or 'Master.'"

"No, *Sir*," she ground out. Damned if she was calling him *Master*. "I don't know how many people applied."

"Six hundred and twelve. And out of those six hundred and twelve, how many do you suppose *thought* they *might* be submissive, dominant, or a switch? How many do you think *guessed* they wanted to find out?"

"I don't know, Sir."

"One. You." He reached to his side to pick up a stack of neatly piled papers and dropped them in her lap. "Those are the applications of the six hundred and two that didn't get in. I need you to prove to me you're worthy of being here instead of them." Under his breath, he mumbled something about her being a virgin.

"I don't know how to do that, Sir." Tears pricked her eyes, and she cursed herself for being such an easy crier. She had the sinking feeling that maybe she shouldn't have begged Terrence to find a way to get her enrolled. And she bit back the apology she almost gave for being a virgin. What reason was there to apologize? The situation had never been right for her to have sex.

"Then I suggest you figure it out. Because unless you do—and soon—May's taking you back to your hotel when she returns with the next student."

Andie's throat was tight with her tears. She couldn't talk, so she simply nodded.

"Get out of my office."

* * *

ORDINARILY, FULTON WOULD have felt badly treating a student the way he had treated Andie Lincoln. There had been nothing out of the ordinary about her at first. Sure, she was gorgeous, but he'd taught plenty of attractive women.

She was also petite. Just the way he liked his subs. With long dark hair that had his hands itching to reach out and pull. And she was spunky. He liked that, too. But then she'd answered his question and said she *thought* she was a submissive. All of a sudden, his fantasies had come to a halt and he remembered she was playacting for her Hollywood boyfriend. Playacting. For her Hollywood boyfriend. Lennox had lost it.

But still, he could have handled that better. After all, she was a student—he had no business having fantasies about her.

"Whoa! What'd you do to the new student?"

He turned back to the door to find the academy dance instructor and a staff submissive, Mariela, glide into his office.

Talk about petite. Mariela couldn't have been much over five feet, but she was all firecracker.

"Hey, Mariela."

"Seriously, I said hello and welcome and she burst into tears."

"She shouldn't be here."

"And you determined this on the first day? After Master Mac-Lure made the decision to admit her? Don't make me regret voting to approve your promotion."

She was right. He knew it. Lennox would not be pleased with the way he had handled the situation. He sighed and ran a hand through his hair.

"I went too far," he admitted. "It's just, she shouldn't be here."

"It's not your decision."

"Maybe it should be."

She closed his office door. "I know what you're getting at, but don't. Don't go there."

Belatedly he realized anyone walking by could have heard everything he said. "Don't you think someone needs to?"

"Maybe, but I don't think it'll be you."

He studied the petite woman before him and knew by the rigid way she held her spine that she wasn't going to change her mind. In fact, she raised an eyebrow, almost daring him to try to make her.

He finally grinned at her. "You're a tough one for a sub."

"That's what makes me so good," she confirmed with her own smile. "Now, before I forget why I came in here in the first place—we'll have to move next week's dance class to the gym. They're going to be painting the ballroom." She held up a hand, anticipating his protest. "Don't say it. I know you don't like dance. Too bad, so sad. We're not canceling."

He nodded his head toward the door. "Fine. We'll dance in the gym. I'll catch you later. I'm going to see if I can find Miss Lincoln."

Mariela said her good-byes and slipped out the door. He picked up the discarded applications from where Andie had left them and had just put them into a neat pile when he was interrupted by a knock on his door. Probably Mariela, he guessed. If he knew her, she'd most likely come back to ask him if he'd be willing to do some sort of dance demo.

He'd turned around to tell her *no fucking way in hell*, but his words caught in his throat when he saw it wasn't Mariela.

Standing in his doorway was Andie Lincoln. Her eyes were red and wet, but her chin was raised in a defiant manner that reminded him of Mariela. It was so striking, he wondered for a second if he'd been wrong in saying she was only playacting at being a submissive.

"May I come in, Sir?" she asked.

He stood to the side and let her pass. She didn't sit down like she had before, choosing instead to stand in the middle of the room.

"I can't prove to you why I should be here instead of those other six hundred and two people," she said. "In fact, I'm fairly certain most of them probably should have had my spot."

He almost interrupted her to tell her it was okay and that he wasn't going to make her leave. But he got the impression that, for whatever reason, Andie needed to finish what she came to say.

"But," she continued, "the fact is I *am* here, and so obviously someone thought it was a good idea. I won't lie and tell you I know for a fact that I'm a submissive, but I suspect I am." She paused, thinking. "Terrence gave me a few basic commands and once he made me keep my hands behind my back while he kissed me." Her cheeks flushed; she'd liked being restrained. She looked back at Fulton. "The fact of the matter is, this is the best way for me to know for sure. So I promise you, if you let me stay, no one will work harder than me. I'll give you everything I have for the next three months, and I promise when my training is complete you won't regret letting me stay."

She took a deep breath and for just a second, her bravado faltered. But just as quickly, her expression settled into ironclad determination. And something deep in his soul ignited.

"I'm not going to send you away," he said.

Relief flooded her face. "Thank you, Sir. I promise you won't regret it."

"See to it." He crossed the room to his desk and sat down. "Have a seat, Miss Lincoln. We have some items to discuss."

She hurried to sit down in the chair she'd occupied before, and he didn't miss the wary glance she gave the pile of applications he still had on his desk. He chose to ignore those for the time being and took her information from the smaller pile on the opposite site.

"What's your current occupation?" he asked, glancing over the forms she'd completed and noticing the empty fields.

"I'm not employed at the moment. At the end of the summer I hope to find work as a chef."

A chef. That was certainly interesting. The academy had gone through a series of unsuccessful chefs. Too bad she was here as a student and not a potential employee. If she were here as an employee and didn't have the actor boyfriend . . .

He shut that thought down before it had time to grow. He scanned her medical history and raised an eyebrow. "You have asthma?"

"Yes, Sir."

"I assume it's under control and you brought your medications with you?"

"Yes, Sir."

"You may find the climate here beneficial."

"I'd heard that, Sir."

He looked over her checklist. For show really; he'd gone over it yesterday. "I see you filled out a checklist detailing your limits as well as what you would enjoy. We'll have you fill out another one once you start on the more physical aspects of your training."

"How soon . . . I mean, when will . . . the information I had was unclear."

He narrowed his eyes at her. God save him from virgins. This he didn't need. "It varies. Of course, you're a special case since you indicated you're a virgin and we're to keep you that way." He didn't add the *at your boyfriend's request.*

Her cheeks flushed again.

"But," he said, "you're still not to play with yourself or make yourself come." An image of her naked and in bed, legs spread as she used a vibrator, popped into his head. He shifted uncomfortably in his seat as his cock stirred to life. "You have played with yourself before, right? You've given yourself an orgasm?"

Her cheeks turned a deeper shade of red and she glanced away. "Yes, Sir."

"Look at me." He was going to have to do something about her inability to discuss anything pertaining to sexual contact without blushing. She reluctantly looked his way. "Embarrassment or shame has no place here. We're all adults and the fact is, you're here to be sexually trained. You need to become comfortable with your own body as well as talking about it."

She gave a halfhearted nod.

Unacceptable.

"Stand up and close the door, Miss Lincoln."

She slowly got to her feet and closed the door.

"Go stand in the middle of the floor and strip."

"What?" Her face was completely red. Hell, he bet her entire body was flushed at this point.

"I don't believe I stuttered. Off with your clothes. Now."

Not only was she flushed, but her hands trembled as she undid her pants and slipped them down. She tugged her shirt over her head and dropped it to the floor. She looked everywhere except at him. And though she was lovely in her lacy white underthings, she was still overdressed.

"All of your clothes." He pointed to her bra and panties. "I want you nude."

"I thought there would be nothing physical for at least a month?"

"I'm not going to fuck you. I'm not even going to touch you. I simply want you naked for the time being."

She didn't want to do it. That much was obvious. Too damn bad. There was too much for her to learn to be embarrassed about being naked.

"You're going to find yourself naked probably more than you think." Once again, he bemoaned the fact that she was here. What the hell was MacLure thinking? With nine other students, he didn't have time for virginal shyness. "Seriously, Miss Lincoln. You had to know you'd be getting naked."

"I didn't think it would start until the physical training started. I thought I had more time."

"Consider yourself an advanced student." And to prove they weren't moving on to anything else until she obeyed, he leaned back in his chair and crossed his arms over his chest. "You'll soon learn patience is not a virtue of mine. Especially once I give a command. And just for the record, I have your boyfriend's approval to turn you over my knee and give you a bare-ass spanking, the likes of which you can't even imagine. Either use the academy safe words or get completely naked. You do know the safe words?"

She glanced down as she slipped the strap of her bra off her shoulder. "Yes, Sir. Red, yellow, green."

"Eyes on me," he said.

He wondered if deep inside he was pushing her to quit. But when she reluctantly met his gaze, he found an unexpected strength. For the first time since she'd walked through his door, he thought she just might have it in her to make it after all.

MASTER MATTHEWS WAS an ass.

If she focused on that, maybe it wouldn't be so bad to strip for him. Besides, he probably did stuff like this all the time. More than likely, this wasn't out of the ordinary at all. For him, anyway.

Your virgin's showing, she chided herself.

She reached behind her back and unhooked her bra. She forced herself to keep her focus on him as she stepped out of her panties. Only then did he break eye contact, and his gaze roamed down her body and back up.

She took the time to appraise his body and noticed the sizable bulge in his jeans. Had she done that? She rather liked the idea of drawing such a reaction from him.

"Very nice, Miss Lincoln. You have a beautiful body."

"Thank you, Sir."

"Now tell me, why submission? What is it about kneeling before your boyfriend that turns you on?"

She appreciated his mention of Terrence. Thinking of him refocused her mind on where it needed to be. She was doing this for him, for *them.* And for them, she could stand a little embarrassment from Master Matthews.

"I haven't knelt before him yet," she confessed. But she wanted to. She really, really wanted to.

"That's right." He mumbled something else under his breath. "Tell me why you want to kneel before him."

"Because I trust him and I want to experience the pleasure he can give me when I give up my control to him. And I want to be what he needs."

He nodded. "Good answers. But what if you can't be what he needs? What if you discover that you hate submitting to anyone?"

"I'll cross that bridge if I get to it." And really, she didn't want to think about it right now. Not when she'd only arrived today and was standing naked in a stranger's office.

"What if you find you like being the one in charge?"

She frowned. She hadn't thought about that. "I don't think that's going to happen."

"Why?"

"Because in my fantasies, I'm not the one giving orders. I'm taking them."

"Close your eyes. Tell me."

She closed her eyes as she remembered the one she'd thought up the night before.

Master Matthew's office chair squeaked and she heard his footsteps as he came toward her. "Tell me, Miss Lincoln. Tell me what you fantasize about when you're alone in bed."

"I don't think—"

"Exactly. Don't think. Just talk."

She took a deep breath. This was probably a test. She really wanted to pass.

She'd always had an active fantasy life, but the one last night had been different.

She was blindfolded and kneeling in his bedroom. He'd been waiting for tonight to finally take her and make her his. She felt a little nervous and hoped she didn't forget or mess up. The night needed to be perfect.

Footsteps echoed in the hallway and she adjusted her position. He's finally coming. Finally.

But he didn't say anything when he entered the room. He crossed the floor silently and stopped when he was in front of her. She'd pulled her hair back in a ponytail and he took it out. He combed her hair gently, but just as quickly, his touch grew rough and he pulled her head back by her hair.

"You like it rough, don't you?" His voice was hard and the sound of it made her want him even more.

"Yes, Sir. Please."

"So polite." His grip tightened in her hair. "Are you ready for me to make you mine?"

"Yes, Sir." She was so ready, she nearly hummed with need.

"I've waited so long to have you. You have no idea of the things I want to do to you."

She didn't think it was possible, but his words made her want him even more. He only had her hair in his hands; how would it feel to have those hands all over her body?

"You're going to take anything I give you, aren't you?"

"Yes, Sir."

"And you know why?"

She had a good idea, but she shook her head anyway.

"Because you're my little slut."

Andie felt her cheeks heat as she told that part of the fantasy. "That was new last night."

"What was?" Master Matthews asked.

"When he called me his slut." She swallowed. Her mouth was so dry. "I've never had him do that in my fantasies before."

"And how did it make you feel?"

She couldn't understand why it was easier to talk with him about such things with her eyes closed. Especially considering how she was still naked. But she didn't hesitate to reply.

"I liked it." She licked her lips. "I liked it a lot."

"Open your eyes, Miss Lincoln."

He was close. So close. And when she opened her eyes, all she could see was him. His eyes were dark with an emotion she couldn't name. But his voice was remarkably calm when he spoke.

"There now, that wasn't so bad, was it?"

"No, Sir," she said, and she was acutely aware her voice was nowhere near as calm as his. *It's just because you were thinking about your fantasy. That's all. It has nothing to do with Master Matthews.*

"You may put your clothes back on." He walked to his desk and took a packet of papers and a room key. "This is your schedule for the first block of courses. Classes start the day after tomorrow. Once you're dressed, you can head up to your room and get settled. Your roommate will be arriving soon."

He didn't face her again, but instead sat down at his desk and started working on his computer. She wondered if she'd said or done something wrong. It didn't seem likely. From what she could tell, he had no problem letting anyone know how he felt. Maybe he had to get ready for the next student. May had said there were more to arrive today.

She slipped her clothes on quickly and since he was still working when she finished, she simply said, "Good-bye, Sir," on her way out.

And though it was faint, she heard his "Good-bye, Miss Lincoln" in reply.

Three

She went slowly up the stairs, taking the time to think about what had just happened. She had stood naked in front of a near stranger. Not only that, but she'd told him about her fantasies. And though she'd been a little embarrassed, it wasn't as bad as she'd feared. Maybe she was cut out for this submissive stuff after all.

At the top of the staircase, she turned to the right. Based on the information she'd been sent, her room was at the end of the hall. She opened the door, surprised to find her roommate inside waiting.

"Hi," the woman said. "You must be Andie." She held out her hand. "I'm Maggie."

Maggie was short, with shoulder-length red hair, eyes that danced with mischief, and a smile so infectious, Andie couldn't help but return it. When she'd first heard she'd have a roommate, she'd thought it sounded strange. She'd questioned Terrence and he'd told her the thinking behind it was to form connections and have someone nearby to talk with.

"I put your stuff over on that bed." Maggie pointed to the bed near a window. "We can change if that's not good."

Andie looked around the room. It was actually a lot larger than she'd anticipated. There was a massive sitting area, and the two beds, while in the same room, were separated from the living area by strategically placed furniture. The hardwood floor matched the flooring found throughout the rest of the castle, as did the rug.

"That bed's fine," Andie said. "This is a nice room."

Maggie followed her as she walked over to her bed to unpack. "It really is. I keep wanting to pinch myself, I can't believe I'm finally here. This was my third year applying for the summer session."

Master Matthews's words echoed in her head: *Do you know how many people applied for those ten positions?*

"Your third year?" she asked, making sure she kept her expression and voice neutral.

"Yes. I was starting to think they'd never take me."

"Wow."

"How many times did you apply?"

Andie stood up and faced her roommate. "Just the one time."

Maggie tilted her head. "Really? Huh. You must have sent in one helluva application."

Andie didn't want to tell her that it was Terrence who took the lead in getting her application into the hands of Lennox MacLure. She shrugged. "I guess."

"So are you with a Dom, or looking, or what?"

"I'm with a Dom." Her belly fluttered as she spoke the words. She was with a Dom. Terrence. He was going to be her Dom. "How about you?"

"I'm single. Just wanted to get trained by the best. I've been in the scene for five years. Thought it was time to take it seriously. Tell me about your Dom."

It was a reasonable request and one that, if she had been dating a noncelebrity, she'd have jumped at the chance to answer. But while it was certain that Maggie knew who Terrence was, he'd worked hard to keep Andie out of the limelight. So far the paparazzi didn't know who she was, though there had been rumors of his "secret girlfriend."

"He's great," she said, feeling the rush of warmth that always accompanied any conversation about Terrence. "His name is John. John Knightly."

It wasn't really a lie. John was his middle name and he often checked into hotels as John Knightly.

"Do you call him 'Sir' or 'Master'? I'm always curious about how different couples work."

Andie hesitated. She didn't want to tell Maggie she had zero experience. "Sir. I call him 'Sir.'" She cringed inwardly because *that* was a lie. The only person she'd ever called *Sir* was Master Matthews.

"I figured as much. I don't see a collar on you. Not that it means anything. He's probably waiting for you to finish your training."

She wasn't sure what Terrence's plan was. What Andie did know was that she needed to turn the direction of conversation away from personal BDSM discussions. "Did you check in with Master Matthews?" He'd said her roommate would be arriving soon. Andie had taken that to mean Maggie was his next appointment.

Maggie shook her head. "No, I got here earlier than expected. They said Master Matthews was busy. I guess with you. I met with Master MacLure."

"The owner?" Terrence hadn't told her much about the man, just that he was somewhat of a recluse.

"Right?" Maggie laughed. "I about died. Died! And everything you've heard about him is true. He's impossibly good-looking, but I think his face would crack if he smiled. And no joke, he put the tense in intensity. What's Matthews like? I heard he's hot."

"You did? Where?"

Maggie waved her hand as if brushing off the question. "There's a message board about the academy on one of the online groups I'm a member of. They said he's recently promoted, single, devilishly handsome, and a bit rough around the edges."

"That about sums him up."

"Just how devilishly handsome is he?"

Andie thought back to when she first saw him, standing in his office. His calculated stare. The way he looked over her body when she was naked. She shivered.

"That handsome, huh?" Maggie asked, obviously noting her response to the question.

"Yes, well, you know."

"It's okay. You have a Dom. You're not dead. You can still think a man is good-looking."

"Yes," Andie said as her phone vibrated with an incoming message. "He's extremely good-looking."

"Good. I heard he's going to be doing a lot of the lectures. I'll be less likely to fall asleep if I have eye candy to look at."

Andie smiled and checked her phone.

> **How are you? Everything okay? Haven't heard from you.**

Terrence. Damn. She looked at the time. It was almost one in the afternoon and she hadn't contacted him to tell him she'd arrived like they'd agreed and she'd missed his reply to her earlier text.

She typed quickly. **Sorry. Been so busy. Talking with roommate. All is well.**

> **So relieved. Have a dinner to go to in a few. Call you tonight?**

> **Yes! <3**

> **Talk soon**

When she looked up, Maggie had a knowing grin on her face. "John?"

She almost told her no, but then she remembered she'd given Maggie that name. "Yes," she confirmed. "He wanted to make sure I got here okay. I've been so busy, I haven't had a chance to contact him."

"Not good to keep your Dom waiting or make him worry."

Andie didn't think Terrence was like that. She might submit

to him in the bedroom, but she didn't think he'd expect any submissive behavior outside of that. "It's okay. He's cool."

"Not like he could do anything about it anyway, being so far away."

Again she heard Master Matthews's voice. *"I have your boyfriend's approval to turn you over my knee and give you a bare-ass spanking, the likes of which you can't even imagine."*

Had Terrence really told him that, or was it an empty threat on Matthews's part? And why did the thought of her being over a man's knee turn her on so much?

"I'm sure he could think of something if he thought hard enough." Andie's stomach rumbled. "Have you had lunch yet? Let's go find something to eat."

"Good idea!" Maggie walked to her bed and slipped her shoes on. "Master MacLure said there's a light buffet set up in the dining room. Want to head there?"

"Let's go."

ANDIE WONDERED IF she'd ever feel comfortable in the elaborately decorated castle. Everything was done in rich woods and lush colors. Antique furnishings were everywhere.

"I'm glad you know where you're going," she told Maggie, who was moving through the numerous hallways as if she'd been here for months.

"I'm friends online with several prior students. I've been studying this place like mad."

Hearing that only brought back Master Matthews's words, and once more, Andie felt like an impostor. She wondered what made Maggie so confident.

They made it to the dining room, though banquet hall seemed a much more fitting term for the grand room. A buffet line was set up in the far corner and several tables of various sizes filled the remaining space.

Andie took a plate and made a salad. The vegetables looked fresh and crisp, and she piled her plate high. The sandwich offerings of roast beef and ham didn't appeal to her, and neither did the lavish pasta bar, so she snagged a piece of bread and went to an empty table.

Maggie joined her moments later. Andie was getting ready to ask her where she was from when a group of staff members came in. At least, she assumed they were staff. Master Matthews was one of the men present.

Maggie leaned over. "Is that tall, dark-looking man with the abs Master Matthews?"

"Yes. And I take it the dour guy who looks miserable is Master MacLure?"

Maggie nodded. "It should be illegal to look that good and act that miserable."

Master MacLure was certainly handsome, but it was Master Matthews that captured her attention.

"Did any of your online friends happen to mention Matthews's first name?" she asked Maggie.

She nodded around a bite of sandwich. "Fulton," she said after she swallowed.

Andie risked a glance at him. Fulton. The name fit. As if he felt her gaze, he turned his head and caught her staring. The corner of his lip lifted and he said something to Master MacLure.

"They're coming over here," Maggie said.

Damn it. Why had she had to look at him? She plastered her best fake smile on her face and waited for the men to approach the table. "I wonder why?" she asked through clenched teeth.

But Maggie didn't have time to answer or even notice Andie's discomfort, because within a couple seconds the two men stood beside their table.

"Master MacLure," Fulton said. "This is Andie Lincoln. Miss Lincoln, this is Master MacLure, the owner."

Andie wasn't sure what the protocol was when Dominants approached your lunch table. If they were in a normal setting—or vanilla, as Terrence called it—she would remain sitting. Surely the dining hall was a neutral area. Surely, they didn't expect her to kneel on the floor. Besides, Maggie seemed much more experienced than she was and she didn't move from her seat.

"It's a pleasure to meet you, Miss Lincoln," Master MacLure said. He nodded at Maggie. "I trust you two are settled and found your room to your liking?"

"Yes, Sir," Andie said. "It's beautiful."

"And how's Terrence?" he asked.

Andie felt her face heat. Of course he would ask about Terrence. And of course he would use his real name. She didn't look toward Maggie to see if she noticed anything. She focused her attention on the man before her. "He's great. He's in Pittsburgh at the moment."

"Be sure to tell him hello from me next time you talk to him. I'll have to see if he's free for lunch when he gets back to the West Coast."

"I'm sure he would like that."

"Master MacLure!" A woman she had never seen before ran

up to the group. "Ms. Claremont cut herself and the infirmary says she needs stitches. What are we going to do about the rest of the lunch service? And dinner?"

"Meredith," MacLure said. "Take a deep breath. Good. And another. Good. One more."

The woman followed his directions and by the time he finished speaking, she'd pulled herself together.

"Now," he said. "Let me see if I understand. Ms. Claremont is getting stitches and cannot finish preparing lunch. And there's some concern she won't be able to do dinner either. Is that correct?"

The young woman smiled. "Yes, sir."

"Fulton," MacLure said. "How are your sandwich-making skills?"

It was unclear from the look on Fulton's face if he could make sandwiches, but it was very apparent he didn't want to. Before he could say anything, Andie answered.

"I can make lunch." She was actually itching to get a look inside the kitchen of the huge castle. But even more she wanted some time to avoid any questions about Terrence from Maggie. "I can help with dinner, too. I'm actually—"

"Thank you, Miss Lincoln," MacLure said, cutting her off before she had a chance to launch into her credentials. "That is very gracious of you, but you're a student here, not an employee."

"I really don't mind."

"Actually, Master MacLure, Andie is a chef." Fulton's relief was palpable.

"Is that so?"

Andie nodded. "Yes, Sir."

"I can't have you working in the kitchen by yourself. Insurance and all that. But if there's somebody in there with you, it would be okay." MacLure slapped Fulton on the back. "Kindly go in the kitchen with Miss Lincoln and assist her with anything she needs."

Andie had heard the expression *if looks could kill* but until that moment she'd never fully grasped the concept. Apparently, all it took was a certain alpha male forced to help her in the kitchen.

"Come on," he practically growled. "I'll show you where the kitchen's at."

He didn't ask if she was ready to go or if she'd finished lunch. But she wanted to make a good impression on MacLure. Obviously, Terrence thought highly of him.

She pushed her chair back and told Maggie, "I'll see you in a bit."

"I'll sit here with you," one of the other staff members said to Maggie. Andie remembered her from earlier in the day. The woman had been walking toward Fulton's office when Andie was walking out. Andie flushed as she recalled how she'd burst into tears when the lady asked how she was doing.

"Thank you, Mariela," MacLure said, and then he motioned to the last remaining member of the group. "Looks like it's just me and you for lunch, David."

"No problem, boss."

As the two men made their way to the buffet line, Fulton turned to look back at her. "You coming?"

Andie nodded, told Maggie bye, and followed Fulton out of the dining hall and into the kitchen.

Though the rest of the castle was furnished with antiques, the kitchen was thoroughly modern. All the commercial appliances were new and high-end. She could have wept for joy at the huge island, perfect for prepping. She immediately started exploring the space.

This was the first summer in five years that she wouldn't be working in a kitchen. Andie had known when she was in high school what she wanted to do. Her mother, who had never liked cooking, was more than happy to let her daughter take over. Now, at twenty-three, she felt more at home in a kitchen than she did anywhere else.

Once she got a feel for how the kitchen was set up, she began reorganizing it to her preference. A kitchen was magic to her. Whenever she went to work in one, it was like she became a different person. Or like someone else took over her body.

Before she realized what she was doing, she'd barked out orders to Fulton and started making more sandwiches. She nosed around the refrigerators and found some vegetables she knew would be perfect for a veggie sandwich. After all, not everyone liked roast beef or ham.

"Can you peel these?" she asked Fulton, passing him a handful of carrots.

He looked at her like she'd grown two heads. "You're putting carrots on a sandwich?"

"Yes, a veggie sandwich. And I need them cut pretty thin. Can you do it, or do I need to take over?" She issued the last part like a threat, knowing that by doing so, he would have no other choice than to slice the carrots.

"I think I can handle a few carrots. I just don't know of anyone who's going to want them on their sandwich."

"I'm not putting them on the meat one, just the veggie."

He mumbled something under his breath, but picked up a knife.

"Uh, you should probably peel it before you slice it," she said when it became obvious he was going straight for the slicing and dicing. "Peeler's by your right elbow."

"I knew that," he snapped, but put the knife down and picked up the peeler. He went to work, attacking the carrots with such vigor, she wondered if there'd be anything left to slice.

She shook her head and went back to her own pile of vegetables and started cutting the mushrooms. She wanted to have everything else finished so she could start on a vinaigrette to serve with the sandwich.

"What was supposed to be for dinner tonight?" she asked.

He shrugged as he destroyed another carrot. "I don't know. Probably a choice of fish or chicken."

Fulton held the knife in a knowledgeable grasp, so he obviously knew his way around one.

"Where'd you learn your knife skills?" she asked.

He looked up in surprise at her question. She nodded at his hands. "The way you hold it, you're not afraid. You've been around knives before." She smiled. "Just maybe not in the kitchen?"

A quick glance comparing his carrots to her mushrooms was all the evidence needed to verify it wasn't food he had cut.

"I guess my lack of cooking talent is evident," he said, and she thought there might be just a little bit of a smile at the corner of his mouth. "My grandfather was into woodcarving. I spent some summers with him."

She couldn't have been more surprised. "I thought for sure you'd say hunting or something. Woodcarving? Hmm. Do you still do it?"

"Sometimes. Usually, I practice my knife skills in other ways."

"What other ways?"

She knew as soon as the words left her mouth, it was a dumbass stupid question to ask because he got *that* look in his eyes. The look he'd given her seconds before telling her to undress in his office.

The mushrooms needed cutting. She turned her attention back to them. "Forget it. I don't want to know."

"But, Miss Lincoln." His voice was low and seductive. "I want to show you."

He didn't say he wanted to tell her; he'd used the word *show*. She didn't know him all that well, but from what she gathered, he wouldn't have said *show* unless he meant it.

And, god help her, there was a part of her that wanted him to show her. She placed the knife on the countertop, let go of the mushroom she'd been slicing, and dropped her hands to her side.

"You keep surprising me. Do you know that?" he asked in that voice. The one that sent shivers up and down her spine. It was low and gruff, and she imagined that would be how his hands would feel on her body.

"No, Sir," she whispered.

"Every time I think I have you figured out, you do something unexpected."

"You've only just met me."

"So I have, and yet, you're still a puzzle."

She looked at the floor because she couldn't bring herself to look in his eyes, and besides, wasn't that what a submissive did?

But he must have been a mind reader as well as a hot professor and Dom because the next words out of his mouth were "Look at me, Miss Lincoln."

And though she didn't want to, she tipped her head up and met his gaze. Before, in his office, she'd found his eyes to be ice cold. They were the opposite now. The temperature in the kitchen must have gone up; that was the only reason she could think of as to why she felt so hot.

"For most of your time here, you'll only look down in certain instances. Especially with me, the eyes show too much emotion to be hidden away. Understood?" He spoke softer than he had in his office, but the power behind his words was still there.

"Yes, Sir."

"Very nice. Now come step in front of me and close your eyes."

On legs that she couldn't believe held her upright she walked the few steps to stand before him. She knew her body trembled, and she could only hope it wasn't noticeable to him. When she made it to where he wanted her, she stopped and closed her eyes.

Terrence had told her BDSM often involved mind play. She hadn't understood exactly what that meant until she'd stood with her eyes closed, waiting for what seemed like forever. But eventually her heart stopped racing and her legs felt sturdier, even though her mind was still wondering what the hell he was doing.

"You've settled down," he said, and this time he spoke so low, she had to strain her ears to hear him. "That's good. I like for you to be anxious, but not scared out of your mind. Take some deep breaths."

She filled her lungs slowly and exhaled the same way. Then she did it again. By the third time, she was surprised at how much calmer she felt.

Even still, when he lightly stroked her cheek, she jumped.

"Nothing to be afraid of," he murmured. "This is just a little demo."

He continued stroking. She sucked in a breath. His touch was almost the way she'd imagined it would be. His hands weren't soft— she could tell he was man who had done manual labor in his past— but they were gentle. She hadn't been expecting that.

"You see, Miss Lincoln, I've got you here, all nice and soft and pliable. You're enjoying my touch, maybe wanting a bit more." He leaned in close and his breath tickled her ear. "So this would be the perfect time for me to take the knife in my other hand and oh so calmly slice the clothing off your body. You'd be completely naked before you even knew what had happened. I'm that fast."

Her eyes flew open. She was certain he had the knife poised and ready to rip through her shirt. But when she looked, his hands were empty.

"Tsk, tsk, tsk." He shook his head. "I didn't tell you to open your eyes."

"I thought you had a knife and you were . . ."

He continued to shake his head. "Trust me. You haven't even started your training. There is no way, no how, I'd use a knife anywhere near you, even during a demo scene."

As soon as he said it, it made perfect sense, but in the heat of the moment, she hadn't been so sure.

"I see it now," she said.

"What?" He picked the knife up from the counter and resumed his carrot chopping.

"Terrence said a lot of BDSM was mental. I didn't get it until now."

He nodded. "Terrence was right."

"I thought you had the knife and were going to slice the clothes off of me, but you weren't." She spoke it out loud to let the meaning of the words sink into her head as she went back to her station to work on the mushrooms.

"Not yet anyway."

She almost sliced her finger and the knife clattered to the countertop. Fulton, of course, didn't move. He kept right on chopping carrots, though she could see the huge grin he now wore.

"Careful with the knife, Miss Lincoln. I don't think you're ready to see my needle skills any more than you were my knife skills."

AFTER FINISHING THE lunch service and getting a head start on the dinner prep work, Andie left the kitchen, making sure to let Fulton know that all the veggie sandwiches she'd made were gone. He huffed at her, but she could tell he was impressed.

Next, she'd have to see if she could get him to try one. Probably not. He looked like a total meat-and-potatoes kind of guy, but you never knew. Terrence loved her veggie sandwiches.

Terrence!

She needed to call him. Crap. She took her phone from her pocket and saw that he'd sent several texts she'd missed, and there was a missed call. Standing outside of her room, she typed a text back.

Sorry. I volunteered to take over the kitchen after the chef sliced her finger open. Still able to call?

He didn't reply immediately. Not that she expected him to be sitting around, waiting for her to get back in touch with him. He was probably out with the other cast and crew members.

She opened the door, not surprised to find Maggie in the room, on her laptop. Her roommate looked up when she walked in.

"They really put you to work, didn't they?"

Andie shrugged. "It's okay. I like being in the kitchen." She noticed an envelope with her name written on the outside in a flowing script, propped up on a small table next to the door. "What's this?"

"It's probably from your adviser, setting up a meeting."

She'd read that during her time at the academy she'd meet every other week with a submissive on staff to talk and go over how things were going or discuss any questions she had. It sounded like a good idea, but after her first meeting with Fulton, she wondered if she'd be facing the same sort of reception from her adviser.

She opened the letter. It was from a woman named Mariela and she wrote that she'd like to talk with Andie tomorrow before classes started on Monday.

"Who's your adviser?" Maggie asked. "Did you get Mariela, too?"

"Yes. Do you know her?"

"She's the lady who sat down with me at lunch when you left for the kitchen. She's really nice and seems sweet."

"That's good." Hopefully, she was nothing like Fulton. Andie wondered what Fulton would think of Maggie. Would he like her? She was willing to bet he wouldn't have made her strip down in his office.

Maggie sat down on her bed a little bit too enthusiastically and Andie knew what was coming. "Sooooo, Terrence and John?" She raised an eyebrow.

Andie shook her head. "Most people call him Terrence. John is his middle name."

"Got it. For a second I thought maybe you were in a poly relationship and had two Doms." That mischievous look of hers came back. "That would have been something. But, oh no, just a guy who goes by two names."

Andie almost laughed. Here she was thinking Maggie had figured out she was dating Terrence Knight and in reality, she thought Andie belonged to two men. The possibility of her dating a celebrity had probably never even occurred to Maggie. And why would it?

"What can I say?" Andie replied. "I'm boring like that." She looked around her side of the room. She had some unpacking to do before she went down to start dinner. Maybe unpacking would help to clear her mind of this afternoon's kitchen assistant.

CHAPTER

Four

The next morning, about an hour before lunch, Andie stood outside of Mariela's office. Maggie had told her the woman was sweet and polite, but just two doors down was Fulton's office and she couldn't help but remember how he'd treated her yesterday. At least how he'd treated her in his office. In the kitchen he'd turned into someone else.

She took a deep breath and knocked on the door.

"Come in," the woman called out.

She wasn't sure exactly what she'd been expecting, but it wasn't anything near what she found when she opened the door. Along one wall of the office was a long mirror, complete with a wooden bar that reminded her of her ballet classes as a child.

"You must be Andie," the petite, dark-haired woman said, a welcoming smile on her face. "Please, come have a seat."

Andie followed her to a small sitting area in one corner of the room. There were a love seat and a chair. Andie took the smaller of the two.

"You look much better today than you did yesterday," Mariela told her.

"I am. Thank you."

"Master Matthews can come across a bit . . . rough, but underneath it all he's a good guy."

Andie agreed. Mostly. After all, he hadn't been that much of a jerk in the kitchen.

"What do you think so far?" Mariela asked.

"Other than that moment you witnessed yesterday, so far, so good," Andie said. "I get along great with my roommate—I think you're her mentor as well. I'll meet everyone else at the get-together tonight. I didn't have a chance to see them yesterday, since I was working in the kitchen."

"So you're responsible for the veggie sandwiches! They were so good. Nothing against Ms. Claremont, but it was nice to have a little bit more variety for lunch."

"I told Mr. Matthews the same thing yesterday. Well, almost the same thing. He said no one would eat the sandwiches." Andie rolled her eyes.

"That's not surprising," Mariela said with a chuckle. "So do you want to talk about what happened yesterday?" she asked.

"Mr. Matthews questioned my being here." That probably sounded stupid. "I just. . . I don't know. I guess the stress of being here, at finally deciding to explore BDSM, put me on edge, and then he acts like I shouldn't be here?" She shook her head. "I promise I don't cry over every little thing."

"I wouldn't have said anything if you did. I was just concerned about you and wanted to make sure you were okay. It can be a bit intimidating your first few days here."

She remembered the boat ride over. "The environment doesn't help much either."

"Creepy, right? I hear that from a lot of new students. But it'll grow on you. And one night, when the moon is out, you should walk along the water. It's so beautiful, you may never think of the island as creepy again."

"Really?"

"Really." She had a soft and genuine smile. "And don't let Master Matthews get to you. He's a good guy. I promise."

Maybe that's what it was. Maybe she'd caught him at the wrong time yesterday morning. He didn't act as if he disliked her when they were in the kitchen.

She shivered, thinking about the way she'd stood in front of him and that low seductive voice he'd used. Even when he'd told her he wasn't going to come near her with a knife *yet,* her body had reacted like it'd be the hottest thing in the world to do a knife scene with him.

Must be the air in this part of the country, because if I was anywhere else, the words knife scene *would have me looking for the nearest exit.*

"Classes start tomorrow and you'll be spending a lot of time with Master Matthews, and even though you won't be starting on the physical elements of BDSM until later, everyone will be taking my dance class."

Andie wrinkled her nose. "I took ballet as a child. I sucked."

Mariela lightly brushed her fingertips across Andie's arm. "You'll like my class. I promise. We focus on the interaction between partners and the way a couple moves. Very different from the ballet lessons you took as a child."

"Do you dance in here? Is that why you have a barre in your office?"

"I find it beneficial sometimes to dance. It's a stress reliever for me. Plus, it helps me think. When I'm dancing, it's like my feet know how and where and when to move and that allows my mind to think."

"Almost like being a submissive? You're free."

"Yes. Very much like submission." She winked at her. "You're a quick learner. You'll be fine."

"I hope so. That's why I'm here."

She thought once more about Terrence and how wonderful it would be when she could offer him her whole being. Would he want to collar her? She glanced over to Mariela. She didn't have a collar on or a wedding ring. A quick once-over told her there were no pictures out on her desk. Was she single?

"I'm unattached," her adviser said, obviously aware of Andie's not-so-subtle snooping.

"I'm sorry." Andie felt her cheeks heat. "I didn't mean to pry."

"That's okay. I don't mind." She wiggled her eyebrows. "Now, I read your application. Tell me about your man."

Andie smiled, pleased to talk about Terrence.

FULTON COULDN'T WAIT to escape from the get-together thrown for the newly arrived summer class. There were ten of them: five men and five women. Each carefully selected and matched with a play partner to train with for the duration of the program.

48

He stayed through the introductions and said a few hellos to the students. He noticed Andie at the edge of the crowd. She smiled and chatted when spoken to, but he never saw her seek out company.

When he was certain he wouldn't be missed, he took the bag he'd brought with him and walked to the deck of the boathouse. The afternoon sun was buffered by clouds and there was a light breeze blowing. He sighed in pleasure and sat down to work, pulling out a block of wood and a knife from his pocket.

He was making fairly good progress when a shadow fell across the deck. He looked up.

"Sorry," Andie said. "I didn't realize you were out here."

He kept working, but nodded to the empty chair beside him. "You can have a seat if you like."

"Thanks." She sat down, but didn't talk. He appreciated that, someone who didn't mind a bit of silence.

He wasn't sure how long they sat there, but the shadows had grown longer and he felt her eyes on him. Even then, she didn't talk to him immediately. He looked up at her and she flushed slightly at being caught, but didn't look away.

She nodded toward the wood in his hands. "What are you making?"

He held it up. "A dog. You may be able to see if you squint and tilt your head a bit."

He laughed because he didn't think she would do it, but at his word, she squinted her eyes tightly and tilted her head just a bit to the right.

She smiled at his amusement. "Ah yes, there we go. I think I see it. Maybe."

It didn't look that much like a dog, he had to admit. At least not yet. "Give it time," he said. "In a few more days, this will be the best-looking dog you've ever seen."

By the look she gave him, he didn't think she believed him.

"If you say so," she said, confirming his belief.

He grunted.

"What are you going to do with the dog once you finish with it?" she asked.

He hesitated just a minute before answering the question. "There's a children's home in Portland," he said. "I go every few weeks. The kids like toys."

She was silent for a second, and he wondered if he should have told her. It wasn't something he shared with a lot of people. But for some reason, he wanted her to know.

"I think that's very sweet," she said. "To give back to the community, not a lot of people do that. And the world would be a better place if more people did."

"I grew up in that home."

And he really hadn't told a lot of people that.

"Then you know what it's like," she said softly.

"Yes."

Somehow she seemed to understand the enormity of what he had shared with her. She didn't say anything else, but sat by his side until he finished. When it grew too dark for him to work anymore, he put his tools away and held out his hand to her.

"Thank you," he said, helping her out of the chair and then dropping her hand. She simply nodded, and they walked together back to the academy.

Five

Fulton always got up early, but on a new class's first day, he got up even earlier. He didn't have to be in the classroom until eight, but he was up by five, had jogged and showered by six, and at six thirty he carried his coffee and breakfast out to the back patio, off the dining area, overlooking the sea. It was his favorite spot to eat breakfast. Beautiful, serene, peaceful.

He froze the second he made it outside.

Someone was sitting in his spot. Okay, so technically, it wasn't his, but it might as well have been. He always sat there.

Andie.

Of course.

He smiled. He'd enjoyed sitting with her the night before. Surprisingly, he didn't feel self-conscious around her. She calmed him, for lack of a better word. And he was even more surprised to discover he actually liked that she was sitting in his spot.

He'd have to figure that out. Why her? What was it about her that piqued his interest?

After he'd left the boathouse last night, he'd thought about it. It wasn't because of her looks, though she was pretty. And it couldn't be because she was a submissive, or *thought* she was a submissive. He was around submissive women all the time and none of them made him feel the way she did.

He wondered briefly if it was because she was dating a celebrity. Maybe it was that *forbidden fruit always looked sweeter* sort of thing. But honestly, he didn't think it was that either. If that was the case, he'd have been attracted to every submissive woman who came to the academy. A teacher dating a student was strictly forbidden.

Which left him with just little things. The way she volunteered to take over lunch and had stood up to his teasing about the veggie sandwiches. The apprehension mixed with the *oh yes, please, Sir* look in her eyes she probably didn't even know she had when he'd talked about knife play in the kitchen.

Maybe he had some sort of fascination with her because she was a virgin. After all, they didn't get many of those at the academy. Was that it? Was it the potential of seeing her awaken her sexuality?

He wasn't sure. All he knew at the moment was that she was in his spot. Texting. He frowned. She was sitting in his spot, not even enjoying the surroundings, when she could text from anywhere.

He coughed and she looked up. A small frown covered her face when she saw him.

"Good morning, Miss Lincoln."

She put her phone down. "Good morning, Sir."

"Lovely morning, isn't it?"

"Hmm?" She looked around as if only just realizing she was outside. The sun reflected off the water. Her eyes widened. "Yes, it is."

He indicated the spot beside her. "Mind if I join you?"

"No, please. Have a seat."

She scooted over a bit, taking the opportunity for a quick glance at her phone. He wasn't sure why that pissed him off, but it did. People who couldn't be apart from their phone annoyed him.

"Am I disturbing something?" he asked.

"No." She put her phone away. "It's after nine in Pittsburgh. I was talking with Terrence."

Ah, the big-time Hollywood actor. For some reason, hearing her talk about him pissed him off, too. He gritted his teeth. "Do you need to keep talking with him?"

She shook her head. "No, he's got to get back to the set."

He wondered for the first time how Andie managed to not only meet Hollywood's newest heartthrob, but end up dating him as well.

"Mariela told me I should come out here at night. She said it was beautiful."

"She's right."

In fact, he enjoyed being out here right around twilight. When the moon touched the water. At that time of day, there usually were a few like-minded people out around the docks. It was a favorite spot for Lennox as well. The introverted headmaster spent most of his time inside, but he would venture out at night to walk.

"I'll have to make it a point to come out here later." She looked down at the breakfast he hadn't started eating yet. "Your food's getting cold."

Right. He'd been so caught up in her, he'd damn well forgotten his omelet. He took a big bite, once again wishing she didn't affect him the way she did.

"Ready for your first day?" he asked between bites, because he couldn't think of anything else to say. And because he knew she was in for a surprise when it came time for the students to get together with their partner. He was still trying to get over it himself.

"Yes, Sir." But she bit the corner of her lip.

He raised an eyebrow.

"What?" she asked.

"Are you really?"

"It doesn't matter one way or the other, does it? It's happening whether I'm ready or not."

He gave a little snort. "True. Are you going to eat anything? Or did you already have breakfast?"

"I ate already. The kitchen wasn't ready to serve when I came down, but Ms. Claremont said to feel free to help myself to the kitchen anytime I want to."

"She's probably hoping you'll be inspired to cook more."

"She did tell me to let her know if I wanted to look over the menus with her."

"Do you?"

"I don't know. It's not really why I'm here, you know?"

Yes, he did. He knew all too well why she was here, and if she had any doubt, she would probably be gone by noon. "I know exactly, but I'll make you a deal. If you decide to look over the menus and need a spare hand, give me a call. Deal?"

"Deal," she said with a grin, holding her hand out for him to shake.

He took her hand, but instead of giving her a firm shake, he couldn't help but enclose it with both of his hands, stroking her fingers. *What are you doing?* He had no answer. He wanted to touch her. "I look forward to it, Miss Lincoln."

Her cheeks flushed a light pink. A lovely shade. He couldn't help but wonder if the rest of her skin would turn the same hue under his hands. But thoughts of more turned Andie's hand into fire, and he dropped it immediately.

You aren't going to find out.

Yet, he countered. He most certainly would. As soon as the class moved beyond the first part of their lessons, he would have his hands on her and he'd know. He clenched his fist so he wouldn't be tempted to touch her again.

Andie, for her part, looked as out of sorts as he felt. She glanced at her watch.

"I better go. I need to stop by my room before class." She ducked her head and took off.

He found, after she left, that it was almost depressingly lonely. He hadn't thought he wanted any company in the morning, but he rather liked hers. He wasn't sure if she'd be in his spot again the next day, but he knew he would. Just in case.

He finished eating quickly and went inside the dining room, hoping to find Mariela. As expected, she was sitting by a window, drinking coffee and reading. He pulled out the chair across from her and sat down.

She glared at him over the top of her novel. "No, Master Matthews, I'm not expecting anyone. Why don't you have a seat?"

"Who pissed in your cornflakes this morning?"

"No one. It's just that one day, there might be someone who will join me."

He tilted his head. Mariela was never in a bad mood. Someone must have really ticked her off. Her head suddenly ducked down, as if she wanted to appear busy. Fulton glanced over his shoulder.

Lennox.

"Good morning, boss," he said.

The headmaster looked their way, saw Mariela, and grunted something before continuing on his way.

"That was either 'good morning' or 'what the fuck do you want.' Kind of hard to tell. Really, it could go either way. What do you think?"

But across the table, Mariela looked like she was getting ready to burst into tears.

"Hey." He reached out and took her hand. "Are you okay?"

"Yes." She sniffled. "I'm sorry. It's just . . ." She took a deep breath, as if trying to convince herself to go on. "I asked Lennox to do the demo with me."

Fulton couldn't talk for several seconds. At the beginning of every new season, Lennox would ask her and a Dom to come into the classroom for the first day. Always she brought David—always. Lennox didn't even play. Ever.

"I've never known Lennox to play." He finally settled on saying that. It seemed safe enough. Besides, it was the truth. Never, in the few years he'd been at the school, had he ever seen the headmaster play. He'd never even *heard* of him playing.

Of course, it stood to reason he had once. After all, he owned and operated a world-renowned BDSM academy. No one did that by being a bystander.

"He doesn't play now, but he did once," Mariela said. "And he was damn good. I think it'd be good for him to get back into the scene. He has to crave it. He has to. I thought if I asked him to do the scene . . . I mean it's not even a full-fledged scene, you know?"

Yes, he did know. But he was more curious about why Mariela was all of a sudden so interested in getting Lennox to do a scene. Fulton wanted to question her, but he knew if he badgered her too much, she'd shut down. Already, she looked uncomfortable with the little she'd shared. He should change the subject.

"Should I talk to David about the demo?" he asked.

She shook her head. "I did it already. After Lennox rejected me and shut down."

Mariela was taking Lennox's response personally. He knew the headmaster didn't mean it that way and he didn't understand why he hadn't done anything to console Mariela. It didn't fit with the man Matthews thought Lennox was.

He searched his mind for something to say, but before he could settle on anything, she pushed back from the table.

"I have to go get ready," she said. "I'll see you in a few."

ANDIE LOOKED AROUND the classroom, trying to collect her nerves. All the students sat at a large wooden table in the shape of a semicircle. The area in front of the table was empty. She assumed it was for demonstrations and Fulton. The walls were covered in dark wood paneling, but the room was kept from being too dark by light-colored carpet. Ten plush leather office chairs were located around the table. Yet she only counted nine students. One of the guys she'd met yesterday, Sam, wasn't there. Was he running late? Class didn't start until eight o'clock, but she found it hard to believe the twentysomething who'd recently graduated from law school had overslept.

But now that she thought about it, where was Fulton? She knew *he* hadn't hit snooze on his alarm one too many times. Oh no, he'd been up early enough to join her for a just-past-dawn breakfast. And hadn't she been just a little too excited when she discovered it was him and not some other faculty member or student?

The man in question marched into the room at that exact moment and let the door close behind him none too quietly. As she thought, he moved to the front of the room and stood before the table.

"Sam Clark has decided to leave the academy," he said. "It is unfortunate we were so mistaken in his professed desire to further his education as a Dominant. As you are all aware, there were several hundred people who were turned down so he could have this spot."

Six hundred and two to be exact, Andie couldn't help but think sarcastically. But only because she knew if she wasn't sarcastic, she'd be thinking, *Oh my god, if he quit, maybe I should, too.*

"However," Fulton continued, "I do have to credit him in that he didn't waste any more of his time or the academy's on a fruitless quest. You should only be here if you know, without a shadow of a doubt, that you are serious in your desire to further your BDSM journey."

Lord help her, he was staring right at her. And making no secret of it. And just to show him what she thought of his not-so-subtle hint, she lifted her chin.

Bring it, Bad Boy.

He raised an eyebrow as if he'd heard her, and for a minute, she feared she'd actually spoken out loud. But no one else was looking at her, so she must have only thought the sarcastic reply.

He was undeterred. "If anyone decides, after the morning session, that they'd like to leave, I'll be in my office during lunch."

Well, she wouldn't be there, so he could shove it. But he still looked around the room, catching everyone's eyes. Was it her imagination or did his gaze linger longer on her?

He cleared his throat. "As you may be aware, RACK Academy was built by our headmaster, Lennox MacLure, to be the preeminent training school for those looking to further their BDSM journey. It is to be a safe place, an honest place, and a place that will stretch you and make you grow.

"As such, we have several rules and expectations. These have been given to you, but I'm going to go over them again, so there is no excuse if they are broken. First and foremost, the universal safe word here is *red*. All play stops immediately. Anyone who continues to play when their partner has said *red* will be severely disciplined and will have formal abuse charges filed.

"The lower private playrooms are off-limits to summer students. Those rooms are only for staff and students who attend either the fall or spring sessions. Those are more advanced than our summer program. If you're found in one of those rooms, you will be punished.

"Always clean up after your scene. It's common courtesy. If we can't trust you to take care of our equipment, you can be damn sure we won't put a human being in your care.

"Student Doms are not to be addressed as 'Sir' or 'Master'

until after graduation. Staff members will let you know what form of address to use.

"Finally, I shouldn't have to say this, but treat each other with respect. What you're here to learn and discover cannot abide with pettiness, rudeness, or the like. Anyone caught acting like a spoiled child will be asked to leave and not come back." He clapped his hands. "Any questions?"

No one spoke.

"Okay, then," he said. "Let's get to work."

No sooner had he said that than a knock on the door captured his attention and he turned away and walked to answer it.

"Master Nader," he said. "Why don't you and your sub come in? We're ready for you."

"Thank you, Master Matthews." A tall, good-looking gentleman Andie recognized as a staff member entered first, followed by Mariela. But the dance instructor looked very different from their meeting the day before. Her head was down as she followed Master Nader into the room, and she was naked.

When she'd reached the middle of the room, Master Nader lifted his hand and she stopped. At his nod, she dropped to her knees.

Fulton moved to stand beside them both. "Master Nader and Mariela came in today as representatives of the roles you're here to train for."

Everyone's eyes were on the couple at the front of the room.

"There are four of you listed as a Dom, and five subs. I want you to watch as these two do a few very simple demonstrations, and when they finish, you are to write a paragraph on something you realized for the first time. I don't care how many times you've played or observed play, you can always learn something."

Andie gripped her pencil tightly and opened her notebook. She hadn't thought that they would jump right in like this. But they were all adults, so maybe it made sense. She focused on the couple in front of her.

This should be easy. After all, she'd never been in a scene before. She hadn't even had sex. It would be easy as pie to find something she realized for the first time. Already her head was spinning with questions.

Was Mariela only being a submissive for Master Nader or did they have a more serious relationship? From where she sat, there didn't appear to be any deep emotional attachment between the two. But maybe it wouldn't be obvious if the couple were playing. She hoped it wasn't like that with her and Terrence. Surely he would have some emotion in his expression or in his voice when they played?

She bit the corner of her lip. No, Master Nader looked as if he was running through a to-do list, and Mariela didn't look much better. Andie strained her eyes and leaned forward. Had Mariela been crying? She was almost positive she had been. Her eyes were red. Or at least they looked that way when she lifted her head slightly.

Before Andie could tell with any certainty, Mariela looked back down to the floor. Andie tapped her pencil against the notebook she had in her lap. Now that she'd had a few seconds to think about it, she didn't think commenting on the lack of emotion would be a very good idea.

Master Nader gave Mariela a few verbal commands, but they were mostly just changes in position. Mariela flowed through them effortlessly. Andie jotted down a few notes. She noted how quickly the submissive responded. How Master Nader watched her intently. And even though there wasn't any emotion present between the two, there wasn't any animosity either.

After a few minutes, Master Nader stopped speaking, and the two remained still. Fulton came back to the middle of the class.

"I would like for you to write a one-page paper on what you realized, its meaning, and why you hadn't noticed it before." Fulton leaned over and whispered something into David's ear. They both moved out of the way so only Mariela remained in the center of the room.

"I want you to look at Mariela," Fulton said. "As she kneels, write down the adjectives that come to your mind as you see her. There is no wrong or right answer, only your opinion. If you are a submissive, also indicate which of these adjectives you have felt before. If you are a Dominant, write down what seeing this sight does to you."

The only sound in the room was the scratching of pencil over paper. Andie wrote down anything that came to her mind. She would go back later, she thought, and make it look pretty. Neater.

Ten minutes later, Master Nader walked back to Mariela, and tapped her on the shoulder. She stood up and smiled at him, but this time Andie could definitely tell that she had been crying.

"Thank you, Master Nader," Fulton said. "I'll let you get back to your office now. And thank you, Mariela. We'll see you this afternoon for dance."

The two staff members nodded and left the classroom. Everyone looked expectantly to Fulton.

"You are here not just to learn how," he said, "but why, and what if. You are here to expand your knowledge. To expand your thinking and your mind-set. There will be times that you will be pushed. And this is good, because it leads to growth. And that's why you're here. To grow in knowledge and understanding."

Everyone nodded as if they had complete understanding of what he said. But Andie didn't. Yes, she understood that they needed to expand their mind and grow, but she needed the basics. Surely, they would go over that next.

But Fulton had something else planned. He instructed everybody to go around the room and introduce themselves, sharing with the group how they identified and how long they had been in the lifestyle.

Andie took a deep breath and waited for it to be her turn. Her anxiety grew as each person gave their answers. No one else was a newbie. Everyone, every blasted person in the group, had some sort of experience. She actually gave some thought to lying. But of course she couldn't. Not with Master Matthews standing in the middle of the classroom, arms crossed, watching everybody and listening to what they said.

No, it would have been slightly embarrassing to be the only person not to have any BDSM experience, but embarrassment would be better than facing Fulton if she lied.

"Miss Lincoln?" he asked when the person next to her had finished.

"My name is Andie Lincoln and I'm a submissive." She paused, heart thumping, as she tried to work out the best way to say what would come next. "I don't have any experience."

She waited for the gasps and whispers, but there weren't any. A few of her fellow classmates look surprised. One even gave Master Matthews a questioning look. To her great relief, he didn't reply to the unspoken questions. Instead, he called on the girl sitting next to her and Andie sank back in her chair with a sigh.

When everyone had finished, Fulton once more stood before the class. "As you may be aware, we have set you all up as couples. This was done based upon the information you provided in your application. Unfortunately, with Sam's departure, we're down a Dom."

Was he looking at her? He was. Why?

"I'm passing out a sheet with the couple assignments. I want everyone to meet in the dungeon after lunch, around one thirty. Stand with your partner. Miss Lincoln, you were paired with Sam. Now you'll be working with me."

CHAPTER
Six

Andie wasn't able to eat lunch. Her stomach was in a million knots. She picked at her salad while Maggie chatted with one of the other submissives.

A quick glance around the dining hall showed most people eating, but Fulton had finished and he was walking out the door. Andie stood up without even thinking about where she was going.

"Andie?" Maggie asked. "You didn't eat anything. Are you okay?"

"Yes. I'm going to head on down to the dungeon." She didn't wait for a response, but threw out her lunch and followed Fulton out of the dining hall.

"Master Matthews," she called.

He stopped and waited for her to catch up. "Miss Lincoln."

Now that she had his attention, she wasn't sure what she wanted to say first. She looked up at him and remembered his concentration as he carved the wooden block, making it into a dog, and his softly spoken "I grew up in that home." He was a good guy under his gruff exterior, she was certain.

"Why didn't you tell me?" she asked.

"I only found out last night after the party and it didn't seem like an appropriate breakfast topic."

And that was that. She really didn't have a reason to argue with him. "I would have preferred to have known anyway."

"I understand," he said. "But none of the other students knew their partner. I couldn't show you favoritism."

"None of the other students will be the teacher's partner."

He wasn't going to budge—that much was obvious. It was probably for the best she drop the subject.

"I'm thinking," he started, looking at her as if she were his favorite treat and he was trying to decide the best way to unwrap her. "Yes, come with me. We'll go set up."

The meaning of what it meant to be Fulton's partner hit her. Not only was he going to touch her; he'd be using her to teach. Part of her was turned on by it, but another part of her worried that she'd mess up royally.

He was already walking down the hall. Before he got to the door of the back staircase, he looked over his shoulder and crooked a finger at her. "Come on, Miss Lincoln."

She hurried to catch him. He opened the large wooden door and motioned for her to enter first. She stepped past him to make her way down, and as she did so she couldn't help but smell him, a fresh just-out-of-the-shower scent. He must have showered at lunch because she noticed for the first time that his hair was wet.

The staircase was dim. The only light came from faint lamps low on the wall by each step. She took her time going down, Fulton following close behind her. She stopped once she reached the bottom of the staircase and waited for him to tell her where to go next. There were four closed doors that she could make out from where she stood.

"Second door on the left," Fulton said. "Turn on the light."

She walked hesitantly toward the indicated door and opened it slowly. It made a low creaking noise as she pushed it open.

"Looks a bit like a dungeon, doesn't it?" he asked.

"Yes, Sir."

"There are private dungeons downstairs. This is set up as a classroom."

Taking a deep breath, she stepped inside, turned on the light, and stood near the door. Fulton followed. The space was huge and completely empty as far as she could tell. With stone floors and walls, it certainly looked like a dungeon.

"Go stand in the middle of the room," he commanded.

She walked to do as he bid, hyperaware of every move she made since she knew he was watching her intently.

"Now," he said, when she'd made it to where he wanted, "most of the time when you're waiting for a Dom to start a scene, you'll be kneeling. Go ahead and move to your knees. Bow your head and place your hands on your knees, palms up."

Her heart raced. She'd never knelt for anyone before. She slowly dropped to her knees and positioned herself the way he'd asked. It felt odd at first, but only, she thought, because it was new.

"Very nice, Miss Lincoln." He walked to stand in front of her, but stood just far enough away that she couldn't see any part of him. "For a Dom, to see his submissive waiting for him like you are? It's a heady feeling. You're doing more than offering yourself.

You're putting yourself in a vulnerable position. Showing your trust to your Dom. Telling him without words that for whatever time you're together, you are putting yourself in his care."

When she'd researched Terrence's preferred lifestyle, that had been one of the things that appealed to her so much. It was a certain type of freedom to allow someone else to be in complete control. To trust that person enough to grant him the freedom to make all the decisions for her.

"Do you feel it?" he asked. "In the position you're in, you can probably feel the submission you're giving. Would you agree?"

She certainly would. As she knelt, she was acutely aware that she was in a subservient position before him. But for whatever reason, she discovered the longer she stayed, the easier it became. Unfortunately, she couldn't tell if it was because she identified as a submissive or if it was because she enjoyed kneeling for Fulton.

"Yes, Sir," she replied.

"There's only one thing out of place."

She searched her mind, trying to figure out what could possibly be out of place. She'd positioned herself the way he'd asked. Her head was down and her palms were up.

"Normally, you'd be waiting for your Dom naked," he said so matter-of-factly that she almost didn't catch what he was saying.

Oh god, he wasn't going to . . .

"Stand up, strip, and kneel again, Miss Lincoln."

Oh yes, he was.

She only hesitated for a second before moving to her feet and drawing her T-shirt over her head. She reached behind her back and unclasped her bra, letting it fall to the floor. Then, with trembling fingers, she pushed her jeans and thong down and carefully stepped out of them. The entire time, she kept telling herself that he'd already seen her naked. That he would, no doubt, see her naked again before her time at the academy was finished.

As soon as she realized that, she wondered if Fulton was single. Did he have a girlfriend? A wife? A collared submissive? Andie wondered how his significant other felt about his work. If she cared that he worked with submissives all day.

"You'll find with practice that this becomes easier and easier." He walked behind her. "I'd like for you stay in that position while everyone comes in. You're doing such a great job. I can show you off as an example."

His words washed over her in a way she had not expected. Yes, she felt a tiny bit nervous about being naked in front of everyone, but she knew to expect that. What caught her off guard was the pull she felt toward Fulton.

"I'm good like this," she told him. More than good. With him beside her, she was great.

AFTER CLASS WAS over, Fulton led everyone to the ballroom for Mariela's dance class. Mariela's smile was easy when they arrived and he couldn't help but mirror her. Mariela just had that effect on people. Sweet, bubbly, and bright, she made him forget for a few seconds that he hated dancing. Though that hadn't always been the case.

"Welcome, everyone." She waved them into the classroom. "Take any chair you want."

She made sure everyone was settled in the large half circle she'd arranged the chairs into before heading to the front of the room. She walked the way dancers did, with toes pointed slightly out, back pin straight.

"Okay," she started. "For those of you I haven't had the chance to meet individually, I'm Mariela, and this is your dance class."

Her statement was met with several moans and groans. Undeterred, she laughed and looked toward the back of the room. "Master Matthews," she said. "Why do you think it is that the subject of dance causes so much distress?"

"I don't know," he relied. "But I do know that I agree with them."

She faked a heavy sigh. "You're completely impossible."

"No, not completely. Just mostly."

"Anyway," she said, reining the crowd back in. "Dance is part of your lessons for several reasons. For one, you learn nonverbal ways to communicate. Second, while there is touching involved, it's nonsexual. Or at least it is in my classroom. And third, the night of your graduation, the academy will host a formal ball. You are all invited." She didn't add that it was expected all the students would attend. They all knew it.

The graduation ball was a tradition at the academy. Though he didn't like to dance, Fulton didn't mind the ball. In fact, it was usually one of the highlights of each term. He enjoyed watching the new graduates take to the dance floor in a subtle form of BDSM play no one who wasn't in the know would pick up on.

"BDSM is a dance," Mariela said. "With each participant moving in sync with the other. A Dom can only lead if the sub follows. Apart they are nothing, but together, they create a being of grace, beauty, and movement."

Fulton had heard her say the same thing before, and though he wanted to believe it, he wasn't sure there was a partner for him.

* * *

I⊤ WAS FRIDAY night and though the rest of her classmates were heading to the beach on the far side of the island to celebrate finishing the first week, Andie stayed back. She didn't think a bonfire would be good for her asthma. Though it hadn't acted up on the island, she didn't want to tempt fate.

She thought she'd spend the time writing an assigned essay on her goals for the summer, but she didn't get far. It was too hard to concentrate, knowing her classmates were partying. After about thirty minutes, she gave up and decided to explore the castle.

Andie walked down the stairs, deciding to check out the class dungeon rooms, and took a second to look out the huge picture window. It was dark, so she could see the bonfire in the distance and, if she squinted, she could make out shadows moving around in what looked like a dance.

She bounced down the remaining stairs and almost knocked Mariela over.

"Oh goodness," Andie said, stepping back before she trampled on top of the dance instructor. "I'm so sorry. I really need to watch where I'm going."

"I'm fine. I think my head was in the clouds, too." Mariela glanced down the hall to where the administrative offices were and then snapped her attention back to Andie. "Heading out to the beach?"

Andie glimpsed the bonfire outside one of the hall windows. "No, I better not. I have asthma and the smoke isn't good for me."

"I understand." Mariela patted her shoulder. "I'll let you finish your walk. Have a good night. Just remember, the private dungeon rooms are off limits."

"No problem, thanks," Andie said, watching as Mariela knocked on Lennox's door. *Was he still working?*

She walked down the opposite hall. There was a library she hadn't been in yet, but it was dark, so she decided she'd come back to it during the day. Other than restrooms and the classroom, there wasn't much else in that particular wing.

At the end of the hall was a door, leading to the stairs they took to get to the class dungeon. Dim lights illuminated the steps, so she didn't have any trouble walking down.

She stopped at the first landing. The private dungeons were down the next flight of stairs and she was horribly curious. Everyone—well, almost everyone—was at the bonfire. She could run downstairs and peek inside one and be back up in her room before anyone even thought about coming back from the party.

Looking over her shoulder and feeling satisfied no one was nearby, she crept down the stairs to the lower level. The hallway appeared to be the same as the one upstairs that held the classroom dungeons.

She counted three open doors on each side of the hallway. She peeked inside the first one and found it smaller than the classroom dungeon upstairs. Not only that, it was filled with all sorts of equipment. She didn't even know names for some of it.

There was an odd bench in the middle of the room. If she moved just a little bit closer, she could take a quick peek before heading upstairs. She stepped into the room, studying the bench. It appeared to be leather, and looked so soft she could practically feel herself lying on top of it, the contact with her skin.

"Miss Lincoln."

She jumped and yelled. Damn. She was caught. By Fulton.

She turned around slowly. He stood in the hallway watching her with his arms crossed over his chest. His eyes narrowed in displeasure.

"What are you doing?" he asked.

She knew she couldn't lie and say she wasn't aware this was an off-limits area. And she really doubted she could claim to be lost. There was nothing to do but tell the truth.

"I was curious." It was simple. To the point. And the truth.

"You are aware this is a restricted area?"

"Yes."

He lifted an eyebrow.

"Yes, Sir."

"Go wait for me in the dungeon we use for class, kneeling."

That didn't sound good at all. Heart pounding, she walked by him and up the stairs. Damn it. What was he going to do?

When she got to the classroom, she undressed as fast as she could with her fingers trembling the way they were. She looked around the dimly lit room once she was naked. Where did she put her clothes? Putting them on the floor was messy and there wasn't a chair or anything in the room. She finally decided on the wooden countertop and folded them into a neat pile to set on the edge.

There.

She knelt in the middle of the room and got into the position he'd shown her. Then she closed her eyes, took a few deep breaths, and waited.

And waited.

And waited.

She opened one eye to make sure she hadn't missed him coming into the room. Seeing nothing, she opened the other. Where was he?

How long should she wait? How long had it been? There wasn't a clock in the room and she'd put her phone on top of her clothes.

Better to wait, though. When he walked through that door, she wanted him to see her doing exactly what he'd commanded.

But when what felt like another five minutes passed and he still wasn't anywhere to be seen or heard, she rose to her feet. Maybe he'd sent her a text and she'd already undressed when it arrived. She'd just check quickly. It would only take a second. Maybe two.

She stood, muscles aching from being in the same position for so long. She didn't even make it to the countertop before Fulton walked into the room. She froze where she was and her body turned cold as his expression changed from chilly to arctic.

He closed the door and crossed his arms. "What are you doing?"

Damn. Damn. Damn. Fucking damn. "I was worried you weren't coming, so I thought I'd see if you sent me a text." *And I wanted to check the time*, but she thought it best not to say that part.

"What are you supposed to be doing?" His voice held that rough edge again, like the first time he saw her.

"Kneeling and waiting for you, and I was. I just—"

He held up his hand. "It doesn't matter if you were kneeling for an entire hour before I got here. When I walk through that door, you're to be naked and on your knees." His eyes roamed over her body. "At least you got the naked right. I half thought I'd come in to find you in a bra and thong."

She lifted her chin a touch. "That never even occurred to me."

He walked the few steps needed in order to stand directly in front of her. "Need I remind you, yet again, you will address me as *Sir* or *Master Matthews*. Understood?"

"Yes, Sir," she said in a whisper.

"Now, I believe that was not the first time I've had to correct your form of address. I don't even think it was the second. Add on top of that the way you were standing when I arrived, not to mention the real reason you're in here, and I'll say we have ourselves a little problem. What do you think?"

What she thought was anything she said would be taken the wrong way. Either that or it'd be used against her. "I'm not inclined to answer that question, Sir. For fear that my thoughts would only make the situation worse."

He hadn't expected that and he laughed at what had to be shock at her answer. "You're probably correct, Miss Lincoln. You're probably correct."

She knew she was.

"Unfortunately," he said. "The fact remains you were in a restricted area and I'm going to have to discipline you."

Those seven words echoed in her mind *I'm going to have to discipline you*. Suddenly, her dry mouth became even drier. She licked her lips in an attempt to get some moisture somewhere.

"You mean . . . ?" She couldn't finish.

"Yes, Miss Lincoln, I'm going to spank you."

She almost protested. In fact, she opened her mouth to do that very thing, but before she could get a word out, it dawned on her. This was why she was here. She wanted to live this lifestyle with Terrence and this was part of it.

Besides, she *knew* she shouldn't have gone downstairs and she knew she should have stayed kneeling on the floor. That was why it took her so long to actually get up. She'd been trying to convince herself that she could get up and be back in her spot before he came into the room. It was a calculated risk to move and she took it. As such, she should have been prepared to handle the fallout.

"Yes, Sir," she said. "I understand."

He'd been expecting her to argue. She could tell by the way his mouth opened but closed before he could get any words out.

"You do?" he finally asked, confirming her thoughts. "I expected you to try and get out of it."

She shrugged, but inside she was secretly pleased she'd caught him off guard. "It's a matter of black and white, really. I went where I wasn't supposed to. You told me what to do and I disobeyed. The reasons why I disobeyed don't have anything to do with it."

"Very perceptive, Miss Lincoln." He walked to the counter where her clothes were still in a pile. "Tell me, have you been spanked before?"

Her cheeks grew hot. "No, Sir."

"Never?"

"Never, Sir."

He opened the drawer and took something out. Then he walked to the back of the room and pulled out a long padded bench that had been hidden in the dark corner.

"Since this will be your first spanking, I'll go a little easy on you," he said, situating the bench just so.

"Thank you, Sir." She didn't want to tell him that she was so nervous she felt like she could vomit. And yet, at the same time, she was insanely curious.

"I said a little easy." She could hear the smirk in his voice. "You'll still feel it."

"I would expect nothing less, Sir," she added.

He gave a grunt, whether in agreement or surprise or something else altogether, she wasn't sure. She dropped her head and waited for him to give her further instructions.

"Why didn't you go to the party?" he asked.

"The last bonfire I went to triggered an asthma attack."

"Of course," he said, and mumbled something under his breath. "Did you bring your inhaler to the playroom?"

"No, Sir."

"I need you to bring it next time and keep it with you at all times. If something were to happen, I want it within reach so I don't have to go search your room for it."

That was going to be a huge pain, but she could tell he wasn't going to back down.

"It's a safety issue, Miss Lincoln. I won't risk your health."

She nodded.

"When you're ready, lean over the bench," he said.

That surprised her. She'd anticipated being told what to do. That he would wait until she was ready told her that he recognized how new and strange this current situation was for her.

Part of her wondered why he would have her over a bench instead of taking her over his knee. In her fantasies, she was always bent over her Dom's lap when he spanked her.

But Fulton isn't your Dom. He's your teacher and being put over someone's lap is probably more intimate than he wants to get.

"That's an awful lot of thinking going on, Miss Lincoln. It's really not that difficult. You bend over the bench to give me access to your ass, and then I correct your behavior by spanking it long and hard."

Why did his words make her shiver with need?

"Are you cold, Miss Lincoln?"

"No, Sir." She stood.

"That was a shiver I saw."

She sighed. He was going to make her say it. "Your words turned me on."

There. Maybe the truth would satisfy him.

She risked a glance at him. He was smiling. But it wasn't a happy-go-lucky kind of smile. It was a smile she'd picture a lion having right before he took off after a zebra. Calculating. Captivating. And altogether seductive.

"Did they?" he asked. "In that case, you should enjoy the lesson in class next week. We'll be discussing and practicing erotic spankings."

Oh yes, please. She bit the inside of her cheek to keep from saying it out loud. Maybe then he'd take her over his lap.

"There you go with the thinking again," he said. And he didn't say anything else, but she could easily read his body language.

Time to get on with it.

She told herself she could handle this and that if she did, the next time she was in this room, maybe one of her fantasies would come true.

She made her way quickly to the bench and leaned over it. Holy hell. Why didn't any of the BDSM novels she'd read talk about how exposed it was to be in this position? Or if they did, why hadn't she paid closer attention?

She sucked in a breath as Fulton came up behind her and ran a large hand over her butt.

"Spread your legs. Such beautiful pale skin," he murmured when she'd obeyed. "It will be a joy to punish it."

His inquisitive fingers didn't stop there, but gently teased the upper inside of her thigh. Close but not touching where she longed to be filled.

"You were right about the effect my words had on your body. Your arousal is obvious."

Fuck. That was embarrassing. She moved her legs back together, earning a hard swat from Fulton.

"I didn't say to close your legs. Spread them. Wider." This time he made her spread them even more than they were before. "When you're receiving a spanking and you're bent over, you keep your legs spread, offering all your parts to your Dom. It shows you're accepting whatever correction he feels necessary to give you."

Oh lord, she hadn't expected a lecture. But it made sense: she was at an academy and he was a teacher.

"Tonight," he continued, "I'm only going to spank your ass and I'll use my hand, since it's your first time."

As he talked, he started slapping her backside with short and quick slaps. They weren't painful and she had the feeling it was only a precursor for what was yet to come.

"Sometimes, though, your Dom might choose to spank your pussy." Once more his fingers teased her. So close, but not quite what she longed for. "Sometimes, he may decide to fuck your ass. Ride you hard for his own use and not let you come. Can you picture it, Miss Lincoln? You bent over a bed, your Dom behind you, thrusting his cock in and out of your ass and all you can do is be still and take it? Would you take your punishment like an obedient submissive? Maybe with the hope that he'll have pity on you and let you come? Or will you be bratty? Grinding yourself against his cock? Hungry for more and desperate in your need?"

Speaking of need and being desperate, his words were a strange sort of punishment by themselves. At first they shocked her. Granted, he'd used them in class, but that was different, almost clinical. It certainly wasn't like now, when they were directed at her and her mind pictured every scenario he whispered. The more he talked, the more aroused she became. She could feel her sex growing wet, longing to be filled with something. And there was nothing she could do about it. She couldn't even get herself off when she was alone in bed later tonight.

It was so unfair.

And he kept on talking, working her backside with his hand and working her mind with his words. It really should have been illegal to make her feel so hot and bothered during a punishment.

"Fuck," he said at one point. "You are soaked. Look at how turned on you are. Tell me, Miss Lincoln, do you think it's possible you can come from dirty talk alone?"

"I don't know, Sir." She was shocked at how gritty and throaty her voice was.

"Too bad we can't find out tonight. I'll put it down on the list of things to explore later."

He was silent for a few more minutes and the only noise in the room was from his hand slapping her ass.

"Okay," he finally said. "I think that has you warmed up. Before I spank you, tell me why you've earned a punishment."

Her mind was still trying to comprehend that he hadn't really started yet, but she rushed out, "I went to a restricted area, I didn't stay in position, and I failed, repeatedly, to use proper terms of address, Sir."

"Very good. And what is your punishment?"

"You're going to spank me, Sir."

"Yes, I am, and it's an honor to be the first one to spank this virgin ass." He rubbed the flesh on her backside. "Sometimes you'll be asked to count or thank the Dom punishing you. Since this is your first spanking, I'm not going to have you do either. I just want you to be still and quiet. Understood?"

"Yes, Sir."

"And your safe words?"

Her body went rigid. Was he going to spank her that hard? That she would have to use her safe word?

His hands immediately went to her shoulders and began a soothing massage. "Relax. I'm not saying you're going to need them. I'm simply reminding you that you have them. You're brand-new to this and I don't want you to forget."

"Green. Yellow. Red." How could she feel so close to him and how could he be so in touch with her feelings? They hadn't known each other that long.

"Are you okay for me to continue?" he asked, and she knew she'd have to think on those questions later.

"Yes, Sir."

Without waiting for further confirmation, he started spanking, and after his hand struck once, she knew the difference immediately between the light taps she'd felt moments earlier and the real spanking. Now it felt hard and ruthless and, damn it all, it hurt like hell.

She reached out to cover her backside as tears started to fall.

"Back on the bench. Now. Or I double what you have coming."

That was probably the only threat that would work and she put her hands back in place and clenched her fists. Fuck. *This* was him going easy?

"Yes, Miss Lincoln," he said, and she realized she'd spoken out loud. "Believe it or not, I usually spank much harder."

She made a vow to herself then and there that she would never do anything to warrant another spanking from Master Matthews.

"Relax and allow your body to accept it," he said when she tensed up again.

She forced her body to relax as much as possible and she was surprised when she discovered that doing so made it easier.

"Last six," he said, and she was under no impression that they would be lighter. They were just as hard, if not harder, than the ones before.

"There we go," he said as the last one fell. "All over."

She didn't know if she should stand up or stay where she was, so she decided not to do anything other than sniffle. Within seconds, though, he settled a blanket over her and pulled her into his arms and sat on the floor with her in his lap.

"Damn stupid of me not to bring a chair in here," he said, stroking her hair. "I'm sorry, Andie."

The fact that he'd used her name instead of Miss Lincoln barely registered because she was thinking about how comfortable she was in his arms. She nestled in deeper, loving the feel of his strong arms around her and marveling that she could feel that way even after he'd spanked her until she cried.

How was it possible she felt closer to him now than she had twenty minutes ago? It didn't make any sense. Nor did the thought that she'd like to stay in his arms for as long as he allowed. How messed up was that?

She didn't care at the moment though. She simply wanted to enjoy the here and now of being in his arms. Their time together tonight would be over soon and since she'd already decided she'd never give him a reason to spank her again, she might never be in this position—with him anyway.

CHAPTER
Seven

Andie knelt in the classroom dungeon two days later, right after lunch. Fulton had pulled her aside after the morning session and requested her to be in place five minutes early. Not long after she'd gotten into position, she'd heard him enter, but so far, he hadn't said anything.

Her classmates filed in silently, and quickly got into their places. Only then did Fulton move to stand by her side.

"As you can see, Miss Lincoln has been kneeling here, waiting." He put a gentle hand on the top of her head. "Tell me, Miss Lincoln, have you been a good submissive today?"

"Yes, Sir."

"Hmm." He walked closer. "You have been a good submissive. I think you deserve a reward."

Yes! She wanted to pump her fist in the air, but decided that was not something a good submissive would do.

She could hear him move past her. Then she heard the sound of furniture being dragged across the floor, followed by a still silence. She closed her eyes and told herself this wasn't a punishment; it was a reward and she would like it. That is, she hoped she'd like it. What if it was a reward and she hated it?

"Seems to be an awful lot of thinking going on inside that head of yours." He didn't sound angry or irritated, but more amused than anything. "Am I right?"

That was a direct question and she was supposed to answer those. "Yes, Sir." Her mouth was so dry. She licked her lips, but that didn't help. "I find it hard not to overanalyze everything."

"Is that what you were doing just now?"

"Yes, Sir." She hesitated telling him what it was she was overthinking; he'd probably think it was stupid.

"I know I've said it repeatedly," Fulton addressed the class. "But good communication is key."

She should tell him.

"Tell me," he insisted, taking the decision away from her.

Since it was a command, it was easier to obey than try to decide what to do on her own. "I was telling myself you had a reward for me and I was thinking, what if I don't like it?"

"You were worried that you weren't going to like your reward?"

It sounded even more stupid once she said it out loud. "Yes, and I know it's stupid. I just—"

"Stop."

She stopped and stared at the rug she was kneeling on until the colors blurred together.

"This type of thinking is toxic," he said to the class. "A good Dom will stop it immediately."

She sighed. She didn't care what he said. Stupid was stupid.

"Don't ever belittle what you're thinking," he finally said to her. "If you were worried you weren't going to like a reward, you were worried. I can see why you might think that."

He could? She began to feel a little better.

"This is all new to you and you have no idea what I have planned for a reward. And since it's so new and unknown, it's not unheard of that you may worry it's something you won't enjoy."

The way he explained it made it sound not so stupid.

"Now," he said. "I will tell you that I've never had anyone complain about not liking a reward I gave them. But I guess there's always a first time."

She wasn't sure if he was teasing or not. He was so hard to read sometimes.

"I'll tell you what. If we start and you don't like what I'm doing, use your *yellow* safe word, okay?"

That made her feel better. "Yes, Sir."

"I'd like for you to stand up. Take my hand—you've been kneeling far longer than I had planned."

She looked up and took the hand he offered, wincing as her bones creaked from finally moving.

"Are you okay?" he asked.

She almost said yes, but decided to tell him the truth. "I'm sure I will be in a second, Sir."

"Shake your legs. Move around a little."

Her legs started to feel better within seconds of her stretching. As she moved around, she couldn't help but notice he'd moved what looked like a love seat nearby. The sight of it did nothing to calm her nerves. Neither did the nine pairs of eyes watching.

Though it wasn't as uncomfortable to be naked around people as she'd feared.

It'll be fine, she tried to reassure herself. And if she didn't like what he was doing, all she had to do was tell him.

He let go of her hand and sat down on the love seat. Once again she reminded herself she could stop everything with the word *yellow.*

He patted his lap. "Over my knees."

Holy shit, his reward was going to be an over-the-knee spanking. Not only was it part of one of her fantasies but it was Fulton who'd be giving it to her. Why did that make it even hotter?

She draped herself across his lap and tried to take mental notes of everything. There were the obvious things, like how scratchy his jeans were against her naked flesh. Being so close to him, she caught the faint, spicy scent of his soap.

Then there were the less obvious details: the stillness of the room and the subtle movement of his breathing.

If she focused on those things, maybe she'd forget she was going to be spanked in front of people.

"This will be an erotic spanking." He stroked her backside while he talked to the class. "Watch first and then we'll have discussion."

His hands felt good and it was all she could do not to grind herself against his leg.

"Widen your stance," he insisted in a low voice. "Remember what I said last time." To the class he said, "When a Dom uses this position, he wants easy access to whichever part of you he desires."

As he talked, his hands were busy showing her what he meant.

They gently squeezed her backside, lightly brushed her inner thighs, and teased by stroking so close to where she wanted him.

"Maybe he has you like this and it's a punishment. Maybe he'll make you count each time he strikes your ass." He gave her right butt cheek a hard spank. "Or maybe he has you in this position because he wants to punish your pussy."

Punish her what? She almost leaped off his lap, but his hand was quicker and he landed a swat right between her legs in explanation. A hot pleasure she'd never experienced radiated from the spot he'd struck to every last cell in her body, and she let out a moan.

"Liked that, did you?" he teased, giving her another.

"Holy shit. Yes, Sir."

"I think I've given enough explanation for now. How about we get started on that reward?"

She no longer worried about not liking it. Now she worried about liking it too much. She pushed away the guilt that tried to swallow her, the embarrassment that danced around the edges of her mind. "If you would like, Sir."

"So polite," he mused. "Yes, I would like."

He started with light swats that slowly built the ball of want and need growing low in her belly. She'd never thought a spanking could feel this good. She reached blindly for something to hold on to and madly clutched the denim covering his legs.

The swats grew stronger, but he alternated between fast and slow motions. Then every once in a while, he'd stop altogether and massage her with sensual touches that brought her right to the edge, but kept her from falling over.

"Please, Sir." She didn't care that she was begging. She needed to come so badly, but even so, she felt she couldn't. Not in front of the class.

"How much can you take?" he asked, landing another swat against her pussy. He chuckled. "I'd ask you if you liked your reward, but there's no need. I can feel how much you're enjoying it."

She was, so much so that it was almost embarrassing. How could something like what he was doing turn her on so much?

"Miss Lincoln doesn't want to come in front of you," Fulton said to the class. "What are some things I can do to change her mind?"

Several people called out ideas and she was glad her face was down so she didn't have to look anyone in the eye. Fulton agreed with a few before apparently settling on one. "Finger her. Excellent."

His fingers inched closer to that spot that needed him the most, and all her thoughts of embarrassment disappeared. He was going to touch her there. Finally. Before, he'd stopped, but this time, she didn't think he was going to.

"Remember, you are never to be ashamed of what you want. Show me how much you enjoyed your reward," he commanded in a rough voice. "Come for me, Andie."

One finger swept her clit while two more pushed deep inside her. It was too much, the pleasure was too much. His fingers pumped twice and she gasped as the climax washed over her. Her body shook and pleasure consumed her entirely.

TERRENCE KNIGHT WAS a fucking idiot.

Fulton could barely stand to think his name without cursing. There was no way any man with a lick of sense in his head would turn over someone like Andie to an academy instead of watching and cultivating her sexual awareness himself. No, the only explanation was that Terrence was a fucking idiot who didn't deserve her.

He told the class to remain silent and then he pulled Andie up into his arms and covered her with a blanket after her climax. She was soft and sexy and she snuggled into his embrace like she belonged there. He searched his mind for some feeling of regret, some thread of remorse at what he'd just done. But the only thing he'd have done differently is that he'd have her positioned so he could watch her face as she came.

"Are you okay?" he asked after her body stopped its tremors and she was still silent.

"Yes, Sir," she said. "That was amazing."

"I'm glad you no longer have to worry about not liking one of my rewards."

"Not if they're all like that."

He laughed softly, stroking her hair. Usually by this time with a submissive, especially a submissive student, he'd be ready for her to get off his lap. Anyone else he'd most likely be helping to her feet and waiting for her to dress. He wasn't ready to let Andie go. He wanted to hold her longer. And, from the way she held on to him, she was in no hurry to leave either.

"I didn't know," she said.

"Didn't know what?" he asked.

"That it could be like that. That it would feel that good." She sighed. "I feel like there's so much I don't know."

"You're not supposed to know everything. That's why you're here."

Master Nader entered the classroom and nodded to Fulton. He'd arranged for the instructor to take over so he could give Andie proper aftercare. It was her first public scene and he wanted to make sure she was okay.

"Thank you, Master Nader," Fulton said, picking Andie up. "I'm going to take her next door."

"Where are we going?" she asked, peeking out of his arms.

"Aftercare."

He walked the short distance to the next room, sat down in a big plush chair, and pulled her into his lap.

"How are you feeling?" he asked.

"Good. It wasn't as awkward as I'd feared."

He hid his smile. Maybe Andie had a bit of an exhibitionist streak in her. He bet Mr. Hollywood hadn't planned on that.

He paused for a minute, unsure if now was the right time to ask the question he wanted to. Yes, he finally decided, now was the perfect time. "If you don't mind me asking, why are you here? At the academy, that is, instead of Terrence training you himself?"

He hoped the question came across the right way and not like he didn't want her at the academy. He truly wanted to know what would make someone send Andie to strangers to be trained. The irony that he only had a job because people did so wasn't lost on him.

"Him training me never came up." She pulled back slightly so she could look at Fulton while they talked.

"I don't mean to be rude or act as if there's anything wrong with it. I simply wondered." He debated asking the other question he had. Fuck it, he decided. In for a penny . . . "And you're both okay with physical contact here?"

She shifted off his lap and drew her knees up to her chest, wrapping her arms around them. She didn't look at him while she talked.

"We had several long discussions before I left." She looked out over the room at the back wall. He wondered what she was thinking. "We decided it would be for the best if I had what you might call a free pass for the summer."

"A free pass?" he asked.

"Right. It's okay for other people to touch me. He didn't want me to feel guilty about that."

Fulton had to admit, it was a good idea.

"And you're okay with that?" he asked.

"I was shocked the first time he brought it up, but now that I'm here, I see it was a good idea."

"I did wonder if you were okay with the way I touched you."

He didn't miss the way her cheeks flushed slightly at his words. She was really very lovely.

"No," she said softly. "I didn't mind."

He decided it would be best to change the subject to something a little less personal. Or at least not as personal as him touching her. "Did it come as a shock when he told you he was a Dom?"

"The night he told me he was a Dom, I kind of went crazy researching on the Internet."

He smiled. Yes, he could certainly see her doing that.

"The academy kept coming up, over and over, as *the* place to be trained. The next time Terrence and I talked, I told him I wanted to enroll. That was when he told me he knew Master MacLure."

"How do they know each other?" Fulton asked, more to himself than anything.

"Terrence called him years ago to act as a consultant on a movie set. He'd only heard of him then, but they became good friends. Terrence told me about the school and said if I really felt serious about trying out the lifestyle, he'd see if there was space." Her eyes grew sad. "I didn't know there would be so many other people wanting in. I mean, I should have known, because the academy is so well-known, but it never occurred to me. I still feel bad. Like I took someone else's spot. Someone who was more deserving." She tried to get out of his embrace. "I should get dressed and go."

He'd be damned if she would leave the room thinking that. "Andie, it was wrong for me to say what I did on that first day. You have just as much right as anyone to be here."

She didn't look convinced.

"If anyone should feel bad for taking someone's spot, it's Sam. He didn't even make it through the first day."

"That could easily have been me." She wasn't trying to get out of his arms anymore.

"I'm so glad it wasn't," he said before he even thought about what he was saying.

"You are?"

"Yes." He tried to think of something to say that wouldn't make him sound like a sleazebag who was after another man's girl. "You've done really well so far. You've embraced your training and you're doing a great job."

She had finally settled back into his arms, fully. "I told myself I was going to kneel on that floor until you told me to move and if I had to stay there all day, I'd stay there all day."

"I could tell. And I had no intention of making you stay like that all day." Of course not; he'd been looking forward to getting his hands on her ass too much.

"How did you know the other night? Where I was?" she asked, and then looked around. "I know. I bet there are cameras in the rooms."

Fulton looked over to the wall where the camera was mounted.

"Something like that," he said. "Would you like some water?"

"Yes, now that you mention it, I am rather thirsty."

He passed her the bottle he'd chilled before the session started and made sure she drank enough. Once she finished, Andie asked if she could get dressed, and he watched while she got herself back together.

Fulton was too wound up to even think about going to his room, and since David had taken over the class, he didn't want to interrupt. A walk sounded like a good idea. Maybe Andie would like to go with him.

But just as he was getting ready to ask, he remembered the other students would see them when they finished and she might not want to be seen outside of class with him. On second thought, maybe a walk wasn't the best thing to do, at least not together.

Andie hid a yawn.

No, no walk today. She needed to rest.

But damn it all, he wasn't ready for the day to end.

"Let me walk you back to your room," he said.

"Okay." She tied her hair back. "Ready?"

He wanted to take her hand, but he knew how it'd look if someone saw them, so he shoved his hands into his pocket. "Ready."

They walked out of the room and into the hallway. With most

everyone in class, the normally bustling hallways were eerily quiet. As they walked up to the main floor, he noticed Andie glance outside and he wondered if he'd made the right choice in not asking her to walk.

They made it to her door and stood for an awkward second.

"This is strange, isn't it?" she asked, addressing the elephant in the room. "I keep feeling like I should say '*Thank you for a wonderful time,*' but then I remember it wasn't a date and you spanked me." She wrinkled her nose. "And even though it felt good, I can't bring myself to say '*Thank you for the awesome spanking.*'"

He laughed. Her easygoing humor was delightful and made him smile. "Perhaps I'll just say good-bye and see you soon?"

She unlocked her door. "Would you like to come in?"

It was tempting. It would be so easy to say yes. To step inside her room and spend more time with her. And why shouldn't he? They were both adults and he could respect that she had a boyfriend. But the look on her face after she offered the invitation looked as if she couldn't believe she'd just asked that.

"No," he said. "I better not. I'd hate to be in here when your roommate comes back."

She nodded absentmindedly. "Okay. That's probably better for me anyway. I'm expecting a phone call."

Right. Mr. Hollywood would want to call his girlfriend and make sure her week went well. He couldn't blame the guy for wanting to touch base. It was the least he could do to make up for not being here with her.

He should actually thank the boyfriend. If Mr. Hollywood had been here, Fulton wouldn't have had the chance to teach Andie. Though he was probably enjoying it more than he should have been.

"Good-bye then," he said. "I'll see you tomorrow, if I don't see you at dinner."

She smiled her good-bye, then ducked her head and opened the door. He didn't head to his own room until he heard the door before him lock.

He thought about going for a jog or taking a sailboat out for a few hours alone. But as he unlocked his own door, he knew that neither activity would make him forget how hard he'd grown while spanking her. Even now just thinking about it had his cock straining against his zipper. He'd spanked plenty of students, but none of them affected him the way Andie did.

He stepped inside his room, knowing there was only one thing that would give him relief. He gathered what he needed and headed into the bathroom. He wanted the shower hot and he turned the knob as far as it would go. Andie was never far from his mind as he waited and the small room filled with steam.

He undressed and, finally, stepped into the shower. His hands immediately dropped to his erection and he let his thoughts about Andie run wild.

He would allow her access to the lower-level dungeons. One floor below where they'd been today. She'd be waiting for him in the same position. Almost everything would be the same, except this time, before they started, he'd tell her to make him hard. She'd take his pants down and they'd both laugh because she wouldn't have to do anything.

He would tell her of course he was already hard—wasn't she already wet for him? She'd agree, but he wouldn't take her word; he'd make her show him.

Fulton's hand flew over his cock as he imagined her dipping

her fingers into her pussy and showing him how turned on she was. He couldn't decide if he'd lick her fingers clean or if he'd make her do it. Fuck, it drove him crazy just thinking about it.

He wouldn't be able to do anything other than take her and they both knew it. He'd push her to her hands and knees, position himself behind her, and, holding her ponytail so her back arched, he'd thrust into her. She'd be so tight, and she'd tell him he felt bigger in that position. He'd slap her ass and tell her to be quiet and take it like the good slut she was.

Fulton came with a moan all over his hands and he leaned his forehead against the shower wall to catch his breath. He shouldn't have been having such fantasies about a student. It was wrong, but at the moment, he really didn't care.

He dried off and when he reentered his bedroom, the halls were filled with the sounds of the students returning to their rooms. Was Andie still on the phone with Mr. Hollywood? Would she tell her future Dom that Fulton spanked her?

THE FOLLOWING WEEK, on Monday afternoon, Andie knelt in the classroom dungeon fifteen minutes before class started, waiting for Fulton and trying unsuccessfully to keep her mind off the large padded table that had been placed in the middle of the room. There were so many things a table like that could be used for. It'd be silly of her to try to guess what Fulton was going to do.

Then she realized he probably put the table in middle of the room because he knew she'd think of nothing else until he entered. And really, the joke was on him because she was still thinking of the table even after she heard him enter the room.

"You look a bit out of sorts, Miss Lincoln," he said, from what sounded like the doorway. "What's wrong?"

"My mind hasn't had a second's rest since I stepped inside the room, Sir." She wanted to add *as was per your plan, I'm sure,* but decided she'd rather see what he had planned for her instead of getting another spanking.

"Now why would that be?" he asked.

She couldn't help the snark. "I'm fairly certain it has to do with that big-ass table in the middle of the room, Sir."

He laughed and it occurred to her that he did that often in the playroom. She liked it and couldn't help but wonder if Terrence would be as lighthearted or if he'd be one of those stern Doms that never cracked a smile during a scene.

"Sometimes mental games are obvious and sometimes they're very subtle," Fulton said, dragging her away from thoughts of Terrence. "This one was on the in-your-face-obvious side."

"The table is just there to mess with my mind?" She actually felt disappointed. It wasn't until she realized it was only a mind game that she understood how much she'd wanted him to use it.

She told herself not to pout like a petulant child.

"Oh no," he said. "I very much plan to use the table today. A little mind play was just a nice extra."

"Then let me applaud you, Sir, because you're brilliant at it."

He chuckled. "Flattery won't get you bonus points, Miss Lincoln."

"I wouldn't even try to do that, Sir. You're way too smart to fall for it."

She pictured him standing in the doorway with his arms crossed, looking at her with one eyebrow raised.

"You're doing it again."

"Maybe a little, Sir."

"I can honestly say I've never taught anyone quite like you before," he said. "You're like a breath of fresh air."

Why did the word *taught* make her sad? She didn't want Fulton for anything other than teaching her. She had her own Dom waiting for her. Yet, no matter how many times she thought it, it never seemed to take her sadness away.

"Let's put your mind at rest." He walked toward her. "I think I've mindfucked you enough for one day. Hop up on top of the table. On your back, please."

She scurried up to her feet and over to the table. She rolled over onto her back, and the cool air of the playroom swept across her body and she had to refrain from covering herself with her hands. She felt more exposed in this position than she did standing or kneeling before him naked. Which, again, was no doubt his intent.

"Our last session was fun," he said, acting like it was nothing that she was spread out before him like a Thanksgiving feast. "But I can't help but think your boyfriend wouldn't like too many sessions with my hands on you. I know if the roles were reversed, I'd be hesitant to let anyone touch too often what was mine."

She'd told him Terrence didn't mind after their last session. Why did Fulton keep bringing it up?

"Andie," Fulton whispered.

She looked up and caught Fulton's eyes. They were so intense and focused, they made her shiver. Was she really going to let thoughts of Terrence overshadow her session with Fulton? Hell, no. She shoved all thoughts of Terrence out of her mind and turned her attention to Fulton.

Damn, he looked hot in his jeans and faded T-shirt, which accentuated every muscle he had. He was especially hot with the hint of worry in his eyes that ever so slowly faded.

"I'm not sure what just happened or what you were thinking," he said. "But whatever it was made you more relaxed."

She could say it was nothing, but she didn't want to do that. She decided to be honest. He deserved her honesty. She couldn't give him her body or her heart, but she could give that. "I decided to block everything out of my mind except you and this moment."

Pure, unadulterated joy covered his expression. "It pleases me greatly to hear you say that."

She found she couldn't put into words exactly what it did to her when he said that. She'd listened to a lecture days ago that gave several explanations for why it pleased submissives to make their Doms happy. But to hear about it from the other submissives in her class was no match for actually experiencing it firsthand.

Seeing Fulton's response to her made her want to please him again and again. She'd never had an addiction problem, but she surely hoped there was a ten-step program for getting over Fulton Matthews when the summer was up, because she was suddenly fearful she'd just experienced her first high and she wasn't about to give it up.

The rest of the class started to come in. Fulton motioned for them to stand around the table, but didn't let them get too close.

"Today I'm going to run a little scene with Miss Lincoln. You are to watch, but not say anything. When I finish, you may begin your own scene as we discussed this morning. Some of the other staff members will be joining us soon to offer assistance."

He took a step closer to her and gave a reassuring grin.

"You'll see I haven't bound her to the table. She'll need free range of motion for this exercise."

She noticed he was fully clothed, so unless he started stripping down, it didn't appear that he was going to be very active in whatever it was he had planned. She considered the possibility that he'd want her to undress him, but dismissed it. Surely if he wanted her to do that, he wouldn't have had her get on the table.

"You're thinking about something very hard again," he said to her with a smile.

"But this time it's about you, Sir," she assured him, not wanting him to think she'd already taken her mind off him and the moment. Especially when he'd just finished praising her.

"In that case, think away," he said, and she laughed. There were a few muffled chuckles from the class. "But not for long, because I have something I want you to do."

Maybe he wanted her to undress him after all. But after a few seconds, she once more decided that wasn't it. He hadn't moved at all and undressing him wouldn't happen with her on the table.

Finally, he spoke. "As a submissive, you have to be able to communicate to your Dominant what you like and enjoy. Also, you have to be completely uninhibited with him. As a Dom, you have to help your sub get to that point. Today's session will help you accomplish both."

She suddenly had a feeling she would rather have a spanking. Because as hard as she tried, there was only one thing that would both help her pinpoint what she liked and further break down her inhibitions.

She took a deep breath and waited for him to give the order she knew would be coming.

He was still standing beside her when he spoke. "For the next twenty minutes or so, I want you to masturbate, but not orgasm, while I watch."

Since she'd figured out that's what he'd probably want her to do, she wasn't all that shocked. But still, hearing it out loud. . . . ugh.

"You're frowning," he said.

"I know, Sir. It's just a bit outside of my comfort zone to do something like that."

"One of my jobs is to push against the walls of your comfort zone."

She snorted. "Easy for you to say, Sir. You're not the one masturbating in front of a classroom."

"Is that a dare, Miss Lincoln?"

"No, Sir. Just a statement."

"Rest assured, I would never ask of you anything I wouldn't do myself." A look that could only be described as wicked covered his face and she knew she was in for it then. "In fact." He unbuttoned his jeans.

Wait. What was he doing? He wasn't going to do what she thought he was going to do, was he? With the class watching?

He kept his focus on her as he pushed both his jeans and boxer briefs down, revealing a massive erection to the gasps of several of her classmates.

Holy. Fucking. Shit.

She felt like she should look somewhere else, but she couldn't bring herself to turn away.

"That's it," he said, taking hold of himself with one hand. "Watch me."

She had fooled around with old boyfriends before. The sight of a cock wasn't completely new. But Fulton's? His was long and thick and set off damn near every one of her *fuck me now* receptors. She tried to imagine what it would be like to touch it, how it would taste, and what it would feel like inside her.

Could her body even handle something that large? It didn't seem possible.

She told herself to stop it. Fulton's cock would never come anywhere near her. It didn't matter how big it was and there was no reason to worry about whether or not it would fit inside her. She should have been thinking about Terrence's cock. But now she knew that as soon as she saw Terrence naked, she'd compare him to Fulton.

"I know what you're thinking," Fulton said, stroking himself slowly. "You're wondering what it would feel like inside you. Whether it's too big."

Though it seemed impossible, as she watched he grew harder and bigger.

"If you were mine," he continued, "when I took you the first time, it wouldn't matter one way or the other. I'd line myself up and push into that virgin body of yours."

She watched as his hand tightened around his cock. It was as if the class members disappeared one by one with each dirty word Fulton uttered.

He let out a groan. "Oh, hell, yes. You'd be so tight and feel so good. Hot and wet and wanting me inside you so badly. You'd whimper a little as I pushed farther."

Talk about hot and wet and wanting. With his words, she was quickly becoming all three.

His hand was still stroking, slow and purposeful. "I'd tell you to watch as I made my way inside you. When your eyes hit the spot where we were joined, I'd give one hard thrust and where would I be, Miss Lincoln?"

She was desperate for something, anything, to touch her. Never had she been so turned on before, and he'd only been talking. What would she do if he were to touch her? She wiggled, trying to get some relief.

"Tell me and I'll let you touch yourself," he said. "You know you want to. Where would I be Miss Lincoln?"

"Inside me, Sir."

"What part of me is inside you?"

"Your cock, Sir."

"That's it. Touch that pussy. Tell me how wet it is for me."

This time, at his command, she didn't hesitate, but dropped her hand and felt how wet she was.

"You're very wet, aren't you?" he asked.

"Yes, Sir." There was no use denying it.

"You're imagining me inside you. How good I feel as I thrust inside you completely." He nodded toward her. "Do it. Use at least three fingers."

She whimpered as she obeyed, having no trouble substituting his cock for her fingers in her mind.

"You feel so good, I can't hold still. I thrust in and out slowly a few times, and mmmm, you feel so good." His hand increased its speed. It was fascinating to observe. He began to pump his hips in time with his hand. Almost without thought to what she was doing, she mimicked his movements.

"That's it." His voice was rough. "I'm fucking you now. You wrap your legs around my waist because even though it's a little sore, you can't get enough of it. You beg me to go faster, harder, and deeper."

She would, too. She could picture it in her mind. He'd feel so good. She'd thrust her hips up to meet him, wanting to help him in his quest.

"You like dirty talk, don't you?" he asked, his hand never stopping. "You don't even have to answer. I can tell from where I am that you like it. It's so hot to see you fuck yourself with your fingers, knowing you're picturing me."

She closed her legs, feeling slightly embarrassed to have reacted so strongly to his words. Well, not just his words—the sight of him pleasuring himself was damn near the most erotic thing she'd ever seen.

"Absolutely not," he said. "You keep those legs open so I can see. Close them again and I'll tie you to that table."

She parted her legs.

"Wider."

She obeyed, even though they were now farther apart than they were before.

"That's it. I can't fuck that pussy, but you better be damn sure I'm going to watch as it responds to my words." He threw his head back and worked his hips, thrusting harder and faster into his hand. "I decide to comply with your wishes and I'm pounding into you. Pushing deeper inside with each pass of my hips. You feel it? Can you?"

She moved her fingers faster. "Yes, Sir. So good."

"I'll always make it good for you." He slowed his movements, becoming more intentional, and rocking his hips at the end of each thrust. She didn't know if she'd survive a night in his bed. Just watching him was enough to almost do her in.

"I tell you to come." His voice was strained. "And when you do, you clamp down on my cock so hard. I try to hold off, but it's impossible. The only question is: do I come inside you, on your belly, or in your mouth so you can suck me dry?"

Images of all three popped up in her mind, and they all sounded fine to her.

"Tell me, Miss Lincoln. Where do I come?"

She arched her back as her orgasm threatened to undo her and answered with the first one that came to her mind. "My mouth, Sir."

"Excellent choice. Keep going." He reached to the end of the table and took a cloth. Once it was wrapped around his cock, he continued. "I jerk out of you and tell you to open wide. That today you get the privilege of my come in your mouth and you're to swallow it all. And I whisper that you can't come until you do."

Jesus, what the idea of him in her mouth did to her. And fucking hell, she needed to come.

Fulton continued on, his voice straining more and more with each word. "You open that pretty little mouth I'm getting ready to fill up and I'm barely past your lips when I spill myself down your throat. You swallow quickly, not wanting to miss a drop, and I tell you that you're a good girl. A good little cocksucker. You're so good, by the time I finish, I'm still in your mouth and growing hard again. Not waiting to recover, I tell you to get on your hands and knees because it's time for me to fuck that ass."

Andie shook her head as he came into the cloth. There was no way that cock would fit back there.

"Trust me." He was breathing heavily as he wiped his cock and set about to getting his clothing back in order. "It'd fit. I'm sure your Dom will have no problems showing you exactly how it's done."

Her fingers kept moving. Terrence. Damn it all. She kept forgetting him. Or maybe forgetting wasn't the right word. More like Fulton was overshadowing him. Pushing him out of the way. It fit with Fulton's personality, she thought. To crowd out everyone else. He would never be so uncouth as to try to take someone's place. She didn't even think it was deliberate on his part. It just happened naturally. And to be honest, it scared her a little that she could forget Terrence so easily.

"I bet you're ready to come now, aren't you?" He threw the soiled cloth into a nearby basket. "Close your eyes and make yourself come."

She closed her eyes and pictured Terrence, letting her hands move across her body. There. That was good. This felt good. She could do it.

In her mind, Terrence lowered his head and nibbled on her skin. Ahhh, yes. Just a bit of his teeth. Enough to feel. He'd command her to hold still and she'd do the best she could. It was so hard not to move when everything he did felt so good.

He mumbled that she was doing great, but he didn't lift his head when he spoke. Instead he kept it down and when he talked his lips brushed her skin and made her squirm. That earned a hard slap on her inner thigh and another command to be still.

She braced herself for the onslaught of pleasure she knew was coming her way as he worked his way down her body. Lower and lower. She sucked in a breath because he was blowing warm air across her clit and she knew there was no way she would be able to continue to be still. When he shifted and teased her slit, she jerked against him.

He sighed heavily with displeasure and she cursed herself in her head, afraid he'd stop, upset at herself for disobeying.

But instead of smacking her thigh again he looked up. "I'm very displeased with your inability to follow simple instructions, Miss Lincoln. I told you not to move."

"No!" she shouted, because it wasn't Terrence driving her crazy in her fantasy. It was Fulton.

THE NEXT DAY at lunch, Andie ate quickly so she could spend some time by herself, thinking. The class with Fulton the day before had left her confused and she didn't know what to do. It bothered her that Fulton was now playing a role in her fantasies. Always before it had been Terrence.

The entire reason for her being at the academy was to prepare her for service to Terrence, not to spark teacher fantasies. She needed to do something to stop the current path she was taking. Nothing good would come from getting closer and more involved with Fulton.

She couldn't do anything about her classes. He was the instructor and that was that. But she could do something about them being paired up. She had learned so much in such a short time, but working only with Fulton needed to come to an end. Maybe she should suggest that he rotate student submissives. To continue on would be foolhardy and risk the relationship most important to her. Terrence.

As if he knew she was thinking about him, her phone buzzed, and she smiled at his text.

Can't stop thinking about you today. Wish I was there.

She typed back quickly, **I was just thinking about you and how I missed you.**

His answer surprised her. **I have next weekend off. They're shooting some retakes I'm not in. Guess where I'm going.**

Yes, yes, yes. This was what she needed. She needed to spend time with Terrence so she could remember why she had come here in the first place.

She typed back, **I'm hoping you're coming here.**

Yes, he replied. **It's not common for students to get visitors, but I cleared it with Lennox.**

Thank goodness the headmaster had said yes. Even if he only allowed a short visit, she was sure seeing Terrence again would further solidify their relationship and she'd know without a doubt that Terrence was the only man for her.

But until then, she had to deal with Fulton. One way or another, she had to stop being his partner in class. He'd be disappointed, but that couldn't be helped. She didn't need thoughts of another man coming between her and Terrence.

Maybe she could text Fulton. That way she wouldn't have to see him or his disapproving frown. But that would be taking the easy way out and she was better than that. She needed to do it in person.

You still there? Terrence sent.

Yes, just thinking. So happy to see you soon. Can't wait.

XOXOXOXO I'll do it in person soon.

She ran a thumb over his words. And if her heart didn't react to his promise of hugs and kisses like it'd done in the past, she told herself that was because she'd been busy with school.

Which was exactly what she was worried about.

The free pass Terrence had given her wasn't making her better. It was making her feel worse. It would be exactly what ended up tearing them apart.

FULTON WATCHED FROM the window in his office as Andie hurried out of the main building to walk the grounds of the academy. She hadn't been her normal easygoing self today. Something had been off and he had a feeling he knew what it was. He'd gone too far in the class session.

Spanking her had been fine, but that was where he probably needed to have kept the line drawn. Even if he'd stuck with his original plan and had her masturbate for him. Even *that* would have been acceptable. But when he'd joined in—granted, he hadn't touched her—he'd changed the dynamic between them, making it more intimate, and she hadn't liked it. That much was obvious the way she looked at him after.

He was an idiot. What had he been thinking in the first place? This is why teachers shouldn't have been paired up with their students.

The blurred lines weren't good for anyone. He'd thought he'd been helping Andie, but in the end, he was doing the opposite.

He turned away from the window and sat down at his desk, but he wasn't able to get any work done. He ran through his motives in his head. Was that why he'd jumped at the chance to be her partner? Did he really think he'd been putting her needs first when he'd suggested that? He knew how it worked. Deep inside had he wanted her to grow attached to him? Hadn't he known what would happen?

He didn't like the answers he discovered.

He hadn't purposely tried to sabotage the relationship between Terrence and Andie. He'd never bad-mouthed Terrence, out loud at least. He worked very hard to keep all communication about him with her very neutral. If he wanted to vent about Doms who left their submissives in the hands of others, he vented to other staff members. That was safe and acceptable.

He even tried to keep anything negative he had to say about the actor outside of Lennox's earshot. Heaven alone knew why the headmaster liked the twerp so much. And he couldn't begin to guess what Andie saw in him.

Part of him knew he was being unfair to the man. It really wasn't acceptable to have an opinion about someone you'd never met. Andie seemed to a good judge of character and if she saw something in the actor, that should be all he needed to know.

He still didn't like him.

He jumped at the knock on his door. "Come in."

Andie cracked the door open and poked her head in. "Have a minute?"

He hid his smile. Was this perfect or what? Now he could properly apologize and assure her nothing like what had happened in the last session would ever happen again. Judging from her current expression, she needed that assurance.

"I always have a moment for you, Miss Lincoln," he said, and hoped his words didn't sound as creepy to her as they did to him. "What can I do for you today?" Where were his manners? His grandmother would've beat him over the head. He waved at the chair across from him. "Here. Have a seat."

"That's okay. I'll stand."

Nothing good would come from her not sitting down, not when her refusal to do so was paired with the determined look on her face. He had a feeling he was not going to like what she said next.

"The thing is," she started, and shifted her weight from one foot to the other. She cleared her throat and tried again. "The thing is, I don't think it's such a good idea for us to continue partnering together."

He struggled to keep his expression neutral. "I need to apologize for the last session. I took it further than I should have and I'm sorry. It won't happen again."

"I know it won't. Because I'm requesting you rotate subs so we're not going to do sessions anymore."

He recognized the look of determination she had. Mariela often had the same look in her eyes. He was fighting a losing battle, but he intended to go down swinging.

"I understand your concern, but I don't think that will be in the best interest of the class. So much of BDSM is about trust and in creating pairs, and that's what we're doing." He shook his head. "To change that now would be to risk the trust that's been cultivated."

She sighed and dropped into the chair. "I get that. Truly, I do. It's just being near you has me so confused. It's like I don't know what I feel, and what I do feel, I don't know if it's real or just a reaction to what we're doing."

"It was never my intention to make you more confused." He said the words, but his head shouted at him, *Yes, you did. You know you did.*

She shook her head. "It really doesn't matter what your intent was—the damage is done."

"I'm sorry." But he knew he really wasn't.

"It's better this way." Now she was trying soothe him.

"Fulton."

He looked up to find Lennox standing in his doorway. The headmaster glanced down and saw Andie.

"I'm sorry," Lennox said. "I didn't know you had someone in your office."

Andie jumped up. "That's okay. We're finished. I was just leaving."

"No." Lennox put his hand on her shoulder. "You should stay. This actually concerns you."

She sat down and gave Fulton an *oh shit* look. He shrugged. He didn't know what Lennox wanted.

"Terrence called me today," his boss said.

Andie didn't appear surprised, but when she saw him watching her, she dropped her gaze to her lap. Fulton raised an eyebrow. Was this why she came to his office demanding he rotate students?

"What did Mr. Knight have to say?" Fulton asked.

"There's a production break next weekend and he asked if he could come see Miss Lincoln."

114

And Lennox told him no, Fulton assumed. Students didn't get visitors.

"I told him of course he was welcome," Lennox finished.

Fulton sat up in his chair. "You did what?"

Lennox held up a hand. "He wasn't able to travel with her and get her settled in. It's a bit unorthodox, but I see no reason not to let him come and see that she's adjusted."

So that probably was why she wanted to stop being his partner. Why couldn't she have told him that?

But then a more pressing question came to mind. "How does this concern me? Why are you telling me?"

"You're her primary instructor and we all know she's relatively new to the lifestyle."

Fulton nodded. He noticed Andie's cheeks were flushed, and she squirmed in her seat.

Lennox didn't seem to pick up on her discomfort. "I thought it might be a good idea for the two of you to work together privately some. A bit like tutoring. Just to ensure she has the basics down."

"That's okay, Sir," Andie addressed Lennox, but she was looking at Fulton. "No need to trouble Master Matthews. I'll be fine."

"I assure you, Miss Lincoln." Fulton smiled. "It's no trouble. I'd be happy to do it."

You're unbelievable, she mouthed at him. He winked at her and looked back up to Lennox. "When do you want us to start?"

"I'll let you two work that out." Lennox turned to walk out. "Keep me updated on what you decide."

"I can't believe you." She was practically seething. He was surprised she'd waited until Lennox left before she ripped into him.

"What?"

"'It's no trouble. I'd be happy to do it'?" She repeated his words back to him.

"You're acting like this is my fault. Like I'm the one who suggested it. Need I remind you, it is your boyfriend who's showing up. He is the reason Lennox wants us working together. If you want to get angry with somebody, I suggest you pick him."

She glared at him. He would never tell her, but she was damn hot when she was pissed off.

"I don't suppose there's a way around this?" she asked.

"Not that I can think of." He pulled up his calendar on the computer. "What time works best for you?"

"I don't think I have any free time. I guess I'll have to do without the extra training sessions."

"Not an option, Miss Lincoln." But of course she knew that. "Listen, I get that you don't want to do this with me. Unfortunately, we don't have a choice. Unless you want to quit the academy."

He stopped talking for a few minutes, hoping she would move past her anger and into acceptance. Finally, she nodded.

"I understand." She ran her hand through her hair and sighed. "Let's make this as painless as possible. What do you suggest?"

"You have most of the basics down," he said. "I think we can get away with only two sessions."

"I was thinking one."

"One would not seem sufficient to anybody. Two is pushing it, but I can handle it."

"Can we do this during the day?" she asked.

He looked for an opening in his calendar. "How does Saturday sound for the first one and Wednesday evening for the second?"

With a resigned nod of her head, she replied, "Yes, Sir."

Silently, he promised not to fuck up this time.

WEDNESDAY EVENING, ANDIE prepared a bag of sandwiches for her session with Fulton. Because everything had gone so well on Saturday, he said the Wednesday session would be fine for them just to talk. She'd thought he might cancel it altogether, but secretly she was glad he wanted to keep appearances up for Lennox.

She said good-bye to the kitchen staff, happy they'd welcomed her into the space whenever she wanted to visit and had time. Of course, she supposed the fact that she either cooked something for them or made a special treat for the entire school helped.

They weren't meeting in a playroom this time, but rather in his office. She knocked on his door, surprised it was closed. Normally, he kept it open.

"Just a minute," he called and then spoke something else that was too mumbled for her to hear. His voice rose just a touch, but as much as she strained her ear, she couldn't make out what he was saying. She didn't hear anyone else's voice, so she assumed he was on the phone.

"Come on in," he finally said, and she couldn't help but notice his voice didn't sound too happy.

She tentatively opened the door. He sat at his desk, staring at his computer with a blank look on his face. She frowned. That wasn't like him at all.

"Is this a good time, Sir?" she asked. "If not, we can reschedule. Terrence doesn't arrive until Friday night."

"No, now is fine. Just an unpleasant phone call." He sighed, but lifted his head and smiled at her. "How are you tonight? Have a seat."

"I'm well." She set the bag on his desk. "I brought sandwiches."

He raised an eyebrow. "Sandwiches for carnivores or tree huggers?"

"Just because someone eats a veggie sandwich doesn't make them a tree hugger."

"Somehow I knew they'd be tree hugger sandwiches." He opened the bag and peeked inside. "Yup, nothing but greens and veggies. I probably don't even know what half of this stuff is."

"You should at least try one and if you don't like it, I'll make you a carnivore one."

"I did say I'd try one of these, didn't I?"

She nodded, pretty sure he was teasing her. His eyes finally had their normal hint of playfulness. "I put the dressing in a different container, just in case you don't like it."

"Hmm," he said, but he didn't seem to paying her any attention. He was taking a wrapped sandwich out of the bag and putting it on his desk. "Are you going to have one?"

"No, Sir. I snacked in the kitchen."

He didn't even taste the dressing first, but lifted the top slice of bread and poured it all over the sandwich. He picked up something that fell out. "What is this?"

"That's quinoa, Sir."

"Say that one more time."

"Quinoa. It's a grain, but with protein."

He ate it. "Not bad." He took a bite out of the sandwich and his eyes widened in surprise.

Score one for the tree huggers.

"Not bad, Miss Lincoln. In fact, this is rather delicious."

She thought she might burst with pride. "Thank you. I'm glad you like it."

"I never thought a meatless sandwich would taste good, but I'd actually eat this again."

And that was pretty much the highest praise he could give her. Her mind raced, trying to think up other things she could cook for him.

"What time does Terrence arrive?" Fulton asked.

Terrence. Damn it. Why was he always the last thing on her mind when she was around Fulton?

"Did I say something wrong?" he asked. "Is he not coming after all?"

Was it her imagination or had he sounded hopeful when he asked that? Probably her imagination.

"No, he's still coming. Friday at four."

"I was thinking you should wait for him in the ballroom. Kneeling. Maybe in a dress." He spoke matter-of-factly, like it didn't bother him.

And why should it? They were nothing to each other, besides teacher and student. Hell, he probably wanted her to be with Terrence, in the hopes that she'd see she wasn't submissive after all.

"I could do that," she said, determined that wouldn't be the case. She would spend time with Terrence, graduate, and then get a job somewhere close to Terrence. She'd never have to see Fulton again.

Why did the thought of that make her heart hurt?

"Can I ask you a question?" Fulton had finished his first sandwich and pointed to the second. "Make that two questions: do you want the other sandwich?"

She shook her head.

"Okay, my real question. You're an awesome cook."

"Chef."

"Right. Chef. Sorry. Anyway. When you first arrived, you said you'd be looking for a job after graduation."

"Yes."

"Why?"

She frowned. "Why? Because what else would I do?"

"You're going to be the submissive of an A-list celebrity." He shrugged. "I wouldn't think he'd like you working."

"I'm not just going to sit around his house all day. I mean, we aren't getting married or anything. We're only dating." Though she had to admit, coming to the academy for him put the relationship on a different level.

He nodded around a bite of food. "I didn't mean any disrespect by my question. I was just wondering."

"No, that's okay. No need to apologize." But now he'd added something new for her to worry about. What if Terrence didn't want her working? Then what? There was no way she would sit around and do nothing. Plus, Terrence traveled a lot and she sure as hell wasn't going to spend her life following him from location to location. They had made plans to take a long weekend away, no phones, no Internet, after her graduation. One of the things they were going to do was sort out the logistics of their relationship.

At the time, it'd made sense, but now, it sounded a lot like a business deal.

"I lied," Fulton said. "One more question. It's personal, but again, I mean no disrespect. I just want to make sure you've thought of it."

Oh, dear. This didn't sound good. "What?"

"Now that you've had a little training, do you think Terrence is going to want to get physical this weekend and, if so, are you protected?"

"Are you actually questioning me about my sex life?"

"I'm your BDSM instructor, Miss Lincoln. Your sex life is my job."

Well, when he put it that way.

She took a deep breath. "We had talked previously and agreed we'd wait until after graduation. He's not one to spring things on me, so I don't see him moving that timeline up."

She could have sworn he smiled at that. She must be imagining things.

"How are you still a virgin anyway?" he asked. "Not that there's anything wrong with it. Just isn't typical, you know?"

"I pride myself on being atypical," she said, and flipped her hair for good measure.

He raised an eyebrow.

She started putting the sandwich wrapper away. "It's not anything major, really. It just sort of happened. My parents didn't let me date much, just group things. And then, when I went to college, I was focused on grades and didn't have time for anything serious."

He'd finished eating and was watching her with careful eyes. Not *I don't believe you—there must be more to it* eyes, but careful and studious all the same.

She threw the bag away. "I don't get what the big deal is anyway.

It's sort of like you wake up at twenty and people look at you like you're a freak if you haven't had sex. Seriously, worry about global warming, the national deficit, why the government allows genetically modified food to be sold. My virginity shouldn't be a topic of conversation. It's not contagious."

"Sounds like you're taking it a bit personally, if you ask me."

"I didn't ask you." She stopped. Her fight wasn't with him. But on second thought, maybe it was. "I think my problem is I'm sexually frustrated."

"What do you mean?"

"I mean I'm here, surrounded by sex constantly, and I can't have it."

He grinned, damn him.

"It's not funny."

"I didn't mean to imply it was. I haven't seen this side of you."

She snorted. "I'm not going to say anything else because you'll probably make me masturbate in front of you again and that's not what I want."

"What do you want, Andie?"

Andie. So much better than Miss Lincoln. It was the use of her first name that made her tell him. "What do I want? I want a man to take me in his arms and kiss me. Really kiss me. And I want him to want me so bad, he thinks he'll die if he doesn't have me. I want raw, dirty sex, Master Matthews. The kind that shocks old ladies and that grown men fantasize about. I want to stay up all night with the man I love because we can't keep our hands off each other and we fall asleep at dawn exhausted and sore, but totally blissed out. That is what I want, Sir."

He didn't move for several long seconds. He simply stared at her.

"What?" she finally asked.

He shook himself. "Nothing. It's only I didn't realize so much sexual frustration could fit inside such a tiny body."

She sighed. "And Terrence isn't going to do anything about it."

There was no doubt about it—there was definitely relief in Fulton's expression. She didn't want to think about why that was or why it made her so happy.

UNTIL TODAY, FULTON had never known himself to be a masochist, but he decided he must be. What other reason was there for him to be hiding in the alcove so he could watch Terrence reunite with Andie?

She knelt in the middle of the ballroom. Her thin white cotton dress gave her a vulnerable look that belied how strong he knew she was. Her posture was perfect. From where he stood, he could just make out the faint flush covering her cheeks and he was glad she never quite lost the ability to blush.

A movement from the door caught his attention. Terrence *damn him to hell* Knight stepped inside the ballroom, his attention completely focused on the beautiful submissive waiting for him. He crossed the floor swiftly, and came to a stop before her.

"Andie? Baby?" He reached a hand out to brush the top of her head. "Fuck, you look so beautiful waiting for me like this. I can hardly believe my eyes." His fingers stroked her cheek. "Look at me, sweetheart."

Fulton was glad he couldn't see Andie's expression as she tipped her head up and looked at her Dom. But he wasn't able to stop himself from hearing her throaty, "Hello, Sir."

Terrence let out a growl, pulled her to her feet, and claimed her with a passionate kiss that left no doubt in Fulton's mind that the actor was indeed in love. He should have been happy. For so long he'd worried the man was playing with Andie and she'd be hurt when she found out.

And now he knew the truth, not only about Terrence, but about himself. He'd been hoping Terrence was playing with her so he could sweep in like a white knight and rescue her. Hold her close and comfort her. Tell her it was okay, that she had him and he'd protect her and treasure her submission like the precious gift it was.

But what was a white knight to do when the damsel wasn't in distress?

He hides in an alcove, watching the woman he wants kiss another man.

He closed his eyes. It hurt too much to watch and he was a fool to have come here. Unfortunately, closing his eyes didn't help. He still saw the couple. It was as if their image was imprinted behind his eyelids.

"Can you leave?" he heard Terrence ask.

He cracked one eye open. Terrence still had her in his arms.

"I have a hotel room in Portland," the other man said. "I'd very much like for you to stay with me tonight."

Fulton tried to be happy for Andie. This was what she wanted. Terrence would take her and finally make her his. The Dom in him recognized it was better this way. This way she wasn't hurt.

She would become the submissive of a well-known actor who, from all evidence he'd seen, was deserving of such a gift.

Fuck. He had no idea being a Dom could hurt so much.

And yet even that pain paled in comparison to what he felt when he heard Andie's seductively whispered, "Yes."

Eight

Andie didn't know what her problem was. Terrence stood in front of her, opening the door to his hotel room. She should have been thrilled he was here. She should have been jumping up and down. And she was happy. She was.

She just wasn't as happy as she thought she would be.

When he'd bid her to stand while she'd been kneeling in the ballroom, she'd looked into his eyes and found all the love and desire she'd ever wanted waiting for her. So why wasn't she beside herself?

She feared the answer to that question.

Besides, she didn't want to think about Fulton tonight.

She told herself what she felt toward Fulton was simply a result of spending so much time with him, combined with the fact that he was the first man she'd submitted to.

Holy hell, she hoped it wasn't a mistake to have enrolled at the academy. Surely once she submitted to Terrence, she'd experience everything she felt for Fulton and more. The fact that it didn't seem the same to kneel before Terrence was due to the fact that they'd been separated for so long.

Terrence held the door open for her and she walked in. It was the same room she'd been in weeks before. The day before she traveled to the academy.

"Hey, come here." Terrence grabbed her around the waist and sat down on the nearby couch with her in his lap. "You're so quiet. Is everything okay?"

He was so sweet; tears filled her eyes. But she couldn't tell him the truth. She couldn't explain how conflicted she was. How could she when she didn't understand it herself?

"I'm . . ." She stopped. She couldn't very well say she was fine when it was blatantly obvious that she was anything but fine. She finally decided on "Filled with so many different feelings."

His grin turned mischievous. "Would you like for me to try to make you forget some of them?"

God, yes. She wanted someone else to take control so she could simply feel and not have to think so much. She wanted to be so consumed with her Dom that there wasn't room for anything or anyone else. To reach subspace, where the only thing she had to do was simply be.

"Yes, Sir. I'd like that, I think."

Terrence gave her a quick kiss. "You can go freshen up if you want while I get ready. You can leave the dress on." His voice was all husky. "You won't be in it long."

She stood on shaky legs. It was finally going to happen. He was going to claim her once and for all. She was glad. Once he took her, she knew she'd free herself from thoughts of *him*.

She took her time in the bathroom. Brushed her hair until it snapped with electricity. Brushed her teeth. Checked her reflection in the mirror. She noticed a nail was chipped, so she fixed it.

It wasn't until she brushed her teeth for the second time that she realized she had a problem.

She didn't want to leave the bathroom.

In one crystal clear moment of self-discovery, she knew the horrible truth: she'd rather stay in this hotel bathroom than head out into the bedroom, where Terrence waited for her. *Stupid.* What woman wouldn't want to go to the bedroom of Terrence Knight?

Before she could convince herself to do otherwise, she opened the door and stepped into the bedroom. That she no longer recognized.

In the time she'd been in the bathroom, Terrace had pulled down the room's shades and lit a dozen candles. He'd been sitting on the couch, but stood when she came out. He looked deliciously yummy wearing only his jeans and no shirt.

"I was getting worried," he said. "Thought maybe you had changed your mind and were looking for a way to let me down easily."

She smiled, but didn't say anything for fear he'd find out how close he was to the truth.

He held out his hand. "Come here. Let me hold you."

She went readily into his arms, anxious to be held and hopeful that this time, thoughts of Fulton wouldn't find a way to get in between them. But she knew the moment Terrence's arms closed around her it wasn't to be.

Terrence's body stiffened and she knew he was aware something was off.

"Your body's here with me, but I believe your mind is somewhere else entirely," he finally said.

The tears she'd been desperately trying to hold back escaped with a giant sob.

"Andie?" Terrence asked and, heaven help her, he sounded terrified. "What's wrong? Please tell me. Please." His arms tightened around her as if he knew how close she was to running out of the room.

That only made her cry even more. They weren't even delicate, ladylike sobs, but rather ugly, snotty tears that shook her entire body. And poor Terrence. He just sat still and held her, gently stroking her hair while she cried herself into exhaustion.

Finally, she wore herself out and for a long while stayed in his arms with only little hiccup sobs remaining from her breakdown. She leaned her head against his chest and felt like the world's biggest traitor. How could she be sitting in his lap, with his arms around her, when all she wanted to do was be in Fulton's embrace?

She could have kicked herself. Here she was with Terrence Knight of all people and her mind was on an instructor she'd known for less than a month. She should have herself committed. Why would she even want Fulton? He could be brash and borderline rude.

He probably was used to all the submissive females falling all over him. She doubted there was a class that went through the academy that didn't have at least one of its members develop a schoolgirl crush on him. Because he wasn't always brash and borderline rude; he was kind and gentle and funny.

But the facts were the facts. Fulton was her teacher. He didn't want her. On the other hand, Terrence was right here and he most certainly did want her. Terrence was kind, and generous, and protective.

Hell, she was messed up if she was trying to convince herself she should be with Terrence. What woman alive wouldn't want him? She decided in that second that was that. No more thinking about Fulton. Not when everything she'd ever wanted was here in the room with her.

She took a deep breath and looked up at Terrence. By his expression, he feared another sob-fest would start any second.

"I'm sorry," she whispered. "You came all this way. Made a special trip and I ruined it."

"No, Andie." He pushed a wayward strand of hair behind her ear. "Don't apologize. You're obviously upset. Would you like to talk about it?"

She gave him a weak smile. "Do we have to?"

"Just tell me this: is it the school? Is it too much? Has someone mistreated you?" His eyes searched hers, almost as if he thought he could find the answers there if he looked hard enough. "You don't have to go back."

"It's not the school." *Not really.* "Everyone's been very nice."

"I don't like being separated like we are."

"I have less than two months."

"I know, but even after that, you'll be in Seattle and I'll be filming." He shook his head. "I want you with me, Andie."

He shifted her off his lap and when he knelt on the floor and reached into his pocket, her heart caught in her throat. Not because she knew what he was going to do. But because she knew what her answer would be.

Nine

D avid, the director of admissions, stood outside of Fulton's office when he returned from his morning jog on Monday morning. David wasn't one for idle chitchat, so the facts that he was, one, not in his office and, two, waiting in the hallway meant something was up.

"David." He nodded to the man as he entered his office.

"I need a few minutes of your time."

"Figured as much. I didn't think you were standing in the hallway because you were bored. Come on in. Have a seat." He waved toward the chair across from his desk.

David sat down with a sigh. "I had a visitor this morning."

David probably had people stop by all the time. He was the director of admissions, after all. Fulton lifted an eyebrow. *And this concerns me, how?*

"Terrence Knight stopped by after dropping off Andie," David said.

Andie was back? For some reason, he'd thought she might not return. But she had. She'd come back. He tried his best to school his features.

"What did Knight want?" he asked.

"A few things. First, he indicated that Andie was upset and crying when they arrived in Portland. He wanted to know if something had happened. I assured him you would have told us if there was an issue with Miss Lincoln, and you haven't mentioned anything. Is there a problem with Andie?"

Andie had been crying? What had happened? The couple looked so happy when they left the grounds.

"Master Matthews?"

"What?" He shook his head. "No, there's no issue with her. She's doing great. A natural submissive."

David watched him with eyes that missed nothing. "Good. That's what I told Mr. Knight."

Fulton stood up. "You know, you could have asked me before the staff meeting today. It's not like you to stop by out of the blue."

"There was another reason Mr. Knight stopped by."

Andie was back. She was obviously okay and wanted to be at school, even with her meltdown in Portland. Whatever Mr. Hollywood's other reason for stopping by was, he doubted it had anything to do with him.

"While they were in Portland, Mr. Knight proposed."

All the air left his body and he fell back into the chair. *Andie engaged?*

He stared, dumbfounded, at David.

"Judging by your reaction," David said, "I think we've just un-covered the cause of her emotional distress."

It should have bothered him that his feelings for Andie were so transparent. And maybe when he thought on it later, it would. But at the moment, all he could think about was an engagement ring on Andie's finger.

He had to pull himself together before he lost it. "I don't know what you mean," he told David. She was engaged, after all. Fuck-ing engaged. "If you'll excuse me."

Fulton turned and walked out of the office. David called for him to come back, but he ignored him and continued outside. He wasn't sure where he was going; he actually didn't care. As long as it wasn't here.

Hours later, he returned to the main building. He'd missed the staff meeting, but whatever. He knew there was no way he could have sat in a room with his peers and acted like everything was okay.

He grumbled a reply at the students who spoke to him in the hall-way. Hell, why was everyone inside? It was one of the rare beautiful days without a cloud in the sky; people needed to be outside. Or at least away from him.

He'd also missed lunch. He went into the kitchen, hoping Ms. Claremont would take pity on him and fix him something to eat. Instead, when he walked through the wooden doors into the main cooking area, he found himself face-to-face with Andie.

"Hello, Master Matthews," she said, with a smile that told him exactly how happy she was. No doubt the sexual frustration was a thing of the past.

He glanced down at her left hand. Nothing there, but she was kneading some sort of dough, so obviously she'd taken her ring off. Figured. The rock probably cost more than he made in five years.

"Miss Lincoln." He nodded, pleased his voice sounded somewhat normal. He could do this. Pretend the thought of her marrying *that guy* wasn't tearing him apart. "I hear congratulations are in order."

Her smile vanished. "What?"

Why was she trying to hide it? It wasn't like he was going to blab everything he knew to reporters.

"Drop the coy act," he said. "I know. Master Nader told me Terrence proposed. I assume this means you're no longer the planet's most sexually frustrated individual?"

She shook her head. "I don't know what he heard. Yes, Terrence proposed. But I said no."

"You what?" Andie turned down her Dom? The one she was here for? The one she longed to kneel for and give that beautiful submission to?

"I told him I wasn't ready for that, that I needed more time. Wanted to see other people." She punched the dough extra hard. "Everything's so confusing in my head. I have to sort it out before I agree to anything permanent." She flipped the dough and pushed it down with the heel of her hand. "Is Master Nader really going around saying I'm engaged?"

Belatedly, Fulton remembered David saying Terrence had proposed. Fulton had been the one to assume she'd said yes. Which was probably why David had called after him.

"No, he's not." Fulton ran a hand through his hair. "He, uh, said Terrence proposed. I may have assumed the rest." She wasn't engaged. He felt like punching the air, but refrained.

"You assumed, huh?"

"Yes." But it didn't matter because she wasn't engaged.

"You know what they say about assuming?"

"Are you calling me an ass, Miss Lincoln?" He could tease her now that he knew she wasn't wearing another man's ring.

"I don't recall ever speaking those words."

"You implied it."

"Now, *that* I do recall." Somehow turning Terrence down had brought her playful side back. He was so happy to see it again.

"You're playing a dangerous game," he said, not sure if he was talking to her or himself. "Make sure you don't get burned."

"I'm not even close to the flame," she replied. "Try your best."

"Is that a challenge, Miss Lincoln?" He moved to where she stood, her hands still buried in dough. "Do you think you can handle my best?"

"I'd like to try."

This new side of her was alluring and tempting. He'd have been lying if he said he wasn't interested in seeing where this would go, despite the fact that they'd been down this road before. "Saturday night. The playroom we normally use. Midnight."

"Midnight?"

"Yes. For what I'm planning to do, you don't want the potential for witnesses."

SHE'D ASKED FOR this, she told herself Saturday night when she found herself bound to the table he'd had her masturbate on earlier. But this time was different. Tonight Fulton looked different. It wasn't his clothing. That was the same. It was more like his entire demeanor was different. More intense, somehow. But even more so, this time there was no class or directive from the headmaster. Tonight it was only the two of them, in a scene because they wanted to be.

She was equal parts turned on and scared.

He rubbed her bare shoulder. "Relax. I know your limits. And I know my own. You're going to be fine."

She was glad he thought so, because she wasn't so sure.

"Remind me of your safe words," he said, which was a joke because he didn't need to be reminded of her safe words. He wanted her to be reminded.

"Green. Yellow. Red, Sir."

"Very good." He lifted a blindfold. "You have this listed as okay on your checklist. Is that still the case?"

Oh, yes. If she couldn't see what he was getting ready to do, maybe it would be better. "Yes, Sir."

He tied it over her eyes and she realized it was actually worse not being able to see. She couldn't see anything, but she could hear everything. Newbie assumption, she thought, and then bit back her laugh because assumptions were what had led to this scene.

Not that she minded. She'd told Terrence she needed time, and though he didn't like it when she brought up wanting to see other people, he really didn't have a choice. He'd put the ring back in his pocket and told her it'd be ready when she was. She almost corrected him. She didn't need time to decide if she wanted to marry him. She needed time to decide if she wanted him, period. Or if she wanted someone else. Someone who might be a master professor who currently had her blindfolded and tied to a table.

She didn't think that would go over all that well with Terrence.

Once Fulton had the blindfold in place, she felt him take a step back. "Tonight I'm going to let you experience a different type of feeling. This isn't a paddle or a flogger or anything like that. It's something totally new."

Was he going to use his hands then? She liked that. His hands felt good.

"Open your mouth," he commanded. "So you can taste what it is."

She obeyed, expecting to taste his skin and felt slightly off balance when she tasted cold metal instead. Her eyes flew open under the blindfold. Holy fuck. It was a knife.

"Do you know what that is?" he asked. "Make a fist with your right hand for yes. With your left for no."

She made a fist with her right hand.

"Good," he said. "Now you know why I had to bind you to the table. It's very important that you remain as still as possible. I'm going to remove the knife from your mouth and I want you to answer."

She shivered as he took the knife away, but answered yes, she understood.

"Now that you know what I have planned, do you want to continue or go back to your room? I'm fine either way. It's your choice."

She wanted this. Wanted this experience and wanted him. "Yes, Sir. I'd like to continue."

There was a smile in his voice when he answered.

"Knife play is considered edge play," he started, and part of her almost sighed because she hadn't anticipated a lecture tonight. "It has the potential to be extremely dangerous if the person holding the knife doesn't know what they're doing. Before we start, do you trust me?"

"Yes, Sir," she replied without hesitation, though she noted that was the second time he'd asked her for confirmation to continue.

"Thank you," he simply said. "I like to begin with this."

Something sharp moved down her arm and she waited for pain to follow, but it didn't. Even so, she sucked in her breath as it made its way up her other arm. It was odd, but not painful. Did it leave marks? Was she bleeding and didn't know? Yes, the blindfold was a rotten idea.

"Interesting sensation, isn't it?" he asked.

"Yes, Sir." Freakishly so.

"But there are other ways to incorporate knives into play." She heard a scraping sound and the room was filled with the smell of sulfur. "I could dribble a bit of wax. Let's see. Where do I want it?"

Her body tensed as her mind realized he was getting ready to drop hot wax somewhere on her flesh.

"Relax, Miss Lincoln. I promise you'll like this. It's similar to my reward. Remember?"

Before she could get the words out to assure him that, yes, she remembered, but even so doubted that she would feel the same about hot candle wax, something hot splashed on her belly and she yelped.

"Was it bad?" he asked.

Surprisingly, she found it was not. The initial burn had subsided into something rather pleasant. "No, Sir."

When the second splash landed, she was better prepared and didn't call out. And when the third hit, it was followed by his fingers sweeping across her breasts. That caused her to shiver, but in a good way.

"Feeling more and more like a reward, isn't it?" he asked in a rough whisper.

The fourth drop landed on her nipple, right where his hands had been, seconds before. "Yes, Sir."

"Good," he said. "Because you've been good and deserve a reward."

She wondered vaguely what he meant by that. But she couldn't dwell on it at the moment because he poured more wax on the opposite nipple. It was sharp and hot and one of the most arousing things she'd ever felt.

He continued, following a similar pattern. First, he'd caress part of her body. Then he'd dribble wax where he'd touched. She soon found herself looking forward to the falling wax. The way it would initially sting and then diffuse into pleasure as the warmth spread throughout her body. Then he'd ignite a new spark of yearning on her skin and the routine would start all over.

"I think that has you decorated nicely," he said, after what could have been either minutes or hours. "Would you like to see?"

"Yes, Sir," she whispered.

He untied the blindfold and her eyes were drawn to the blue wax that coated her body. It ran down her limbs, looking like a bizarre winding road, with peaks and valleys. Then she realized he'd made her into a work of art. "I thought it matched your eyes," he said and, for whatever reason, it seemed completely normal that someone would pick what color of wax to dribble all over her body based on her eyes. "Though now we have to remove it." He nodded toward a nearby table where a wicked-looking knife waited.

She swallowed. She'd actually forgotten this was primarily a knife scene.

"Let's get this blindfold back on you," he said.

She was torn between saying no, that she wanted to watch, and yes, because there was no way in hell she wanted to watch. So she said nothing as he returned her to the darkness of her mind.

"Reward, remember?" he asked.

Sure it was, she thought, but she said, "Yes, Sir" because he'd asked for her trust and she'd given it.

"Reminder that you need to be still." His voice was heavy with concentration and she could all too easily picture him holding that big knife.

She wasn't sure what she was expecting, but it wasn't what she felt. It wasn't painful; it was more strange than anything. If he was using the big knife, he was using it in such a way that she couldn't really tell.

If she had to liken it to anything, it would almost be shaving. But that brought to mind shaving with that big-ass knife she'd seen and she remembered his command to be still. She tried not to think about it scraping or shaving her skin.

But then he moved it near her breasts and she hoped he had steady hands.

Of course, he did. He was a smart man, an experienced Dom, and he'd been working with knives since he was a child.

So then why did her heart pound and why was it so very hard to remain still?

Fulton put a hand on her stomach. "Steady," he said, and she wondered if she'd flinched when he approached her nipple.

Her mind battled within itself. The part of her that trusted Fulton completely and the side that whispered, *Sure, but everyone messes up sometimes.*

She squeezed her eyes shut while he finished, relaxing only when he said, "I think that does it."

He didn't take the blindfold off, but he did take the restraints off.

"Stay here," he commanded.

In the short time he was gone, she wiggled her limbs and took several deep breaths. She only knew he'd returned when he draped soft warm towels over her. She sighed at how good it felt.

Then he was whispering in her ear about how well she'd done, how proud he was, and how much she'd grown as a submissive. For a long time he was at her side, simply being there, and she found it hard to believe she'd once thought him brash and rude.

"Are you ready for me to remove the blindfold?" he asked.

"Yes, Sir."

He helped her to sit up and when the dark material fell away, his blue eyes were the first things she saw. He stroked her cheekbone. "Are you okay?"

"Yes, Sir." She looked around for the scary-looking knife, but all she saw was a credit card. That couldn't possibly be? There was no way . . . ? No.

He placed his fingers over her lips. "Shhh." He shook his head. "It's late. Let me get you some water and then I'll walk you to your room. Tomorrow you can sleep in. But I want you to find me in the afternoon. You may need to talk about tonight."

She yawned. She hadn't realized how tired she was until he'd mentioned bed. Suddenly she was exhausted. "I'm not thirsty." If she could just go to sleep, she'd be fine.

"Doesn't matter," he said, like she knew he would. "You need to drink some water before you turn in."

She finally nodded. Arguing with him would only waste time that she could spend sleeping. And she knew he'd get his way eventually anyway.

CHAPTER
Ten

Fulton was on his way to go sailing the following Saturday, when he turned a corner and nearly ran into Andie.

"Whoa!" He held out both hands to catch her, barely getting her back on her feet before she fell. "Where's the fire?"

She looked up at him and her expression caught him off guard. Her eyes were wide with worry and her smile was fake. "It's nothing, Sir."

He tightened his grip on her shoulder. "Now, Miss Lincoln, you know better than that."

"I'm being honest, Sir. It has nothing do with the academy."

"That wasn't my question."

She took a deep breath. "I got an e-mail saying I'm missing teaching hours for my cooking certificate, and if I don't get them in within the next two weeks, I'll have to take a remedial course."

He let go of her and placed his hand on her lower back, steering her to Lennox's office. "We can't have that. Let's go talk to Master MacLure and see what we can work out."

The headmaster listened as Andie explained what had happened and what she needed to do. When she finished, he simply nodded and said he'd see what he could do and would she come back to his office in two hours?

Fulton didn't follow her out of the office, and he waited until Andie had cleared out of the hall before he spoke.

"I was thinking, boss."

"Yes?" Lennox said, one eyebrow arched as if he wasn't completely sure he wanted to know what Fulton was thinking.

"I had planned to visit the children's home this weekend." He stuck his hands in his pocket, trying to act indifferent. "If she needs to go somewhere on the mainland, I can take her."

Lennox tapped his pen on the desk. Fulton stood as straight as he could, knowing he was being studied. "I was thinking I'd send Mariela with her."

"Mariela hates the mainland, sir." And he was almost certain Lennox knew that. He wanted to launch into all the various reasons why sending him was the best idea. But he kept silent, not wanting to appear too anxious.

Lennox nodded, and though he kept his expression neutral, Fulton saw his jaw clench. "Yes, she does. Very well, Master Matthews, let me see what I can arrange and I'll let you and Miss Lincoln know."

A week later, Fulton and Andie took a boat to the mainland, and stopped by the garage Fulton kept his car at when he was on the island. The day was overcast, with the sun trying to peek through the clouds. He hoped this meant the afternoon weather would be nice, but he wasn't holding his breath.

He glanced to his side. Although she'd seemed pleased he'd be her escort, so far today she'd been withdrawn. He wondered if she was nervous about teaching or if she was having second thoughts.

"You're awfully quiet today," he said when he could no longer stand the silence.

She played with the hem of her skirt and then turned to look out the window. "Sorry, Sir. I just have a lot on my mind."

And whatever it was wasn't good. It was a rare opportunity they had to be away for the day and he wanted her to enjoy it.

"Let's shake things up today. How about you call me Fulton and we drop the *Sir*. We're not at the academy."

"Is that allowed?" she asked. "I was under the impression lightning would strike me dead if I even thought of doing such at thing."

"That's not lightning—it's the wrath of Lennox. But he's not here, so let's be a little less formal, why don't we?"

He thought he might have seen the hint of a smile on her face. "Okay."

"We have a bit of a drive ahead of us. Why don't you tell me what's got your mind so tangled?" The road ahead was long, with nothing to see but massive trees on either side. Andie seemed content to watch them pass by. He supposed she wasn't used to the surroundings and he should have just left her in peace. But he really wanted to talk. "Did you and Terrence have a fight?"

"No, not really," she said, and then sighed as if finally deciding to break her silence. "Everything I thought I wanted is mine for the taking. Terrence. Seattle. It's all coming together and I feel like the world's most selfish person because I'm not sure I want it anymore." She didn't look at him, but continued to study the passing trees. "I spend a few weeks on a private island, learning about submission, and all of a sudden I don't know who I am or what I want."

"It's not wrong for you to take time to decide what you want. Anything and anyone worth having will understand and wait." He placed a hand on her knee and gave it a quick squeeze in what he hoped was a comforting touch. "I don't think you're being selfish at all."

"Thanks," she whispered, still looking outside.

Two hours later, Fulton helped Andie prepare the classroom at the local community college. After their talk in the morning, she had been in a much better mood. Fulton was surprised how much he enjoyed both watching her shop in the little organic market she found and talking about nothing in particular. He took her to one of his favorite downtown burger joints and laughed at her for discovering they had a vegetarian menu.

When the cooking students started coming in, Fulton stood in the back. He didn't have to stay; he could easily have gone for a walk or hit one of the many food carts in the nearby park, but he didn't want to leave. He was enjoying watching this unseen side of Andie. He knew she was a good cook, but she was also a good instructor. She was patient and kind, and didn't make anybody feel silly for their questions.

In some ways, it was like she was an entirely different person. He liked island Andie, but he could tell he liked Portland Andie also.

There was about another hour left in Andie's class when Fulton's phone rang. He pulled it out of his pocket and frowned at the display. Lennox?

He motioned to Andie to let her know he was stepping outside.

"Hello, boss," he said. "What's up?"

"How's the weather in Portland?" Lennox said by way of response.

The weather? What the hell?

Fulton looked up at the sky. "It's not doing anything here, but the sky looks ominous."

"That's what I was afraid of. It's storming here. There's no way the boat can go out tonight."

"Are you serious? It's that bad already?"

"Looks like you and Miss Lincoln will have to spend the night in Portland."

Fulton looked over his shoulder and watched through the window as Andie helped a student with some dough. Since their earlier talk, she had been in such a good mood today. He hated to share Lennox's bad news.

By the time she finished teaching and cleaning up after the students had left, the rain was coming down in droves. From the way it beat on the roof, there was some hail mixed in as well.

He was staring out the window when Andie came up beside him. "This looks beyond cats and dogs. More like horses and cows."

"Not only that, but it's put a wrench in our plans."

Andie gave a resigned sigh. "We're stuck here tonight, aren't we?"

"Yes. And we won't be able to make the children's home." He hated that. He'd actually looked forward to taking her there and showing her parts of his past.

She brushed his shoulder. "I'm sorry. Makes sense, though. If it's this bad here, I can't imagine what it's like out on the water."

She sounded very calm, but he'd been watching her and cataloging her responses for weeks now. She licked her lips multiple times and bit that one inside corner. Fulton wondered if it was because she'd be staying overnight in the city with him. He didn't think she'd mind so much had it been Mariela or her roommate, Maggie.

"We don't have clean clothes, toothbrushes, or anything to sleep in," she said, half to herself.

"The hotel we stay at will have toiletries for us, but I can't do anything about clean clothes, unless you want to go shopping. As for something to sleep in? No problem. I sleep nude."

She turned and looked him straight in the eyes. "Why does that not surprise me?"

"You don't sleep naked?"

She crossed her arms over her chest as if covering herself up. "No, I do not sleep naked."

"You might tonight," he said, and he couldn't help the little wink he threw in.

ANDIE SIGHED AND pretended not to notice the king-size bed in the hotel room. Unfortunately, if she looked in the other direction, she found herself staring at Fulton. She finally decided on Fulton. He was on the phone with Lennox, who was apparently giving him an earful.

"Boss, honestly. You're acting like it's my fault Portland has three major conferences and a dance expo this weekend. We were fortunate to get the one room."

He was silent as he listened to Lennox. Andie couldn't make out what the headmaster was saying, but she could hear him.

"Yes, I know." Fulton said, and she could tell he was trying to keep his temper in check. Probably because she was in the room. Not to mention he was on the phone with his boss. "She still would have been a bad choice and she hates the mainland so much, she'd probably have tried to swim back."

More words from Lennox and this time, Fulton actually held the phone away from his ear. When Lennox took a breath, Fulton spoke again. "Why don't I let you talk to her?" He held the phone out to her. "Here."

Andie really didn't want to speak to the headmaster. Especially if he was going to have a piss-poor attitude. Seriously, being stuck in a hotel with Fulton was not a good idea, no matter how you looked at it. But she took the phone anyway.

"Hello?"

"Miss Lincoln," Lennox said smoothly and calmly. "I apologize for not being more careful. It was not my intention to have you stay overnight in Portland."

"It's not a problem, Sir. No one holds the weather against you."

"Did you get your time in for your credits?"

"Yes, Sir. I did. Thank you for arranging everything so I could get that taken care of."

"Don't even think about it. I was happy to do it for you. I'm going to call Terrence and let him know what's happening."

It was on the tip of her tongue to tell him not to worry about telling Terrence. Did he really have to know? But deep down, she knew one of them needed to tell him.

It made her sad when she thought about it. Her being trained

151

at the academy was supposed to bring them together. So why did it feel like it was tearing them apart?

"Thank you, Sir," she said, secretly glad Lennox was the one telling Terrence and not her.

Coward, she told herself.

After she'd not only turned his proposal down, but also told him that she wanted to see other people, she didn't want him to guess how she really felt about Fulton. She bit her lip. On the other hand, maybe it'd be better if she called him. If she didn't, would he think she was hiding something?

Damn.

Fulton had taken the phone back and was wrapping his conversation up. Head nodding, he spoke into the phone. "I promise to sleep on the couch and I won't touch a hair on her body. I have to say, boss, I don't like this insinuation that she's not safe with me."

Lennox said something else and Fulton ended the conversation. He threw the phone on the bed and looked at her. "How can such a tiny little thing like you cause so many problems?"

Feeling cheeky, she replied, "It's a gift."

He laughed softly and she smiled. Smiled and tried to stomp down on the part of her that really wanted to spend the night in the room with Fulton.

Lord help her, she was bat-shit crazy.

He stood up and walked to the large bay window. "I didn't bring my ark, so unless you did, I suggest we eat at the hotel restaurant tonight."

She'd noticed it when they checked in. Italian. And if she remembered correctly, the chef had won several awards for his signature salmon dish. "That sounds good," she told Fulton. "Want to go now? I'm starved."

That got a smile out of him. "We can't have that, can we?" He held out his arm. "Let's go eat."

She took his arm to walk to dinner and told herself it meant nothing. He probably offered his arm to anyone he took to dinner. It didn't mean anything because he didn't have a choice. He had to take her to dinner.

She couldn't stop herself from looking up at him as they walked down the hall to the elevators. He was smiling and appeared more relaxed than he did when he was at school. That seemed rather strange, but maybe it was because he'd just gotten off the phone with Lennox and he didn't have to worry about seeing his boss until the next day.

They stepped off the elevator and into a mass of people in the lobby. Fulton gave a low whistle. "Damn, I should take a picture. That way there would be no doubt in Lennox's head that we scored the last hotel room in the city."

"I'm sorry if I caused you problems with him."

He brushed the top of her hand, where it still rested near his elbow. "Don't apologize. You did nothing wrong. Lennox is just being paranoid."

"Does he really think something would happen between the two of us?" She wanted to know if it was the same for him. Did he feel the chemistry between them? She knew that's what it was because she didn't feel it when she was in the presence of Master Nader or any of the other Doms. Just Fulton.

Then she wished she hadn't asked because his smile was gone.

"No," he said. "I think he was just reminding me—not so subtly, I'd say—about what my job is and is not."

They made their way through the crowd and, fortunately, all the groups seemed to be congregating at the bar and not in the restaurant. The hostess was able to seat them immediately.

Andie saw the salmon and closed her menu, decided.

Fulton looked up. "Do you know what you want already?"

"The chef's known for his salmon."

"Is he?" At her nod, he closed his menu. "I'll get that, too. Would you like some wine?"

"That would be wonderful." And it just might steady her nerves. Because as it was, she had a hard time keeping her mind off the fact that this was exactly what a date with Fulton would have been like.

He leaned back in his chair once the waiter had taken their order. "Tell me," he started. "How did you meet *the* Terrence Knight?"

And just like that, she was reminded that this was not a date. "You mean, how did a small-town nobody like me meet and capture the attention of a Hollywood golden boy?"

One look at his expression, and she knew that was the wrong question to have asked.

"Look at me," he said, and she recognized his voice from the classroom. "Terrence Knight is damn lucky to have you and I don't think he would appreciate the way you put yourself down. I know *I* don't appreciate it. I'm trying to make conversation, but we'll sit in silence before I allow that line of thinking."

"I'm sorry." She was slightly taken aback by his forceful reaction. "The few times we've been out in public together, I've seen the way people look at me. It's not always nice."

He looked at her strangely. "Is that why you turned down his proposal?"

She sucked in a breath, not expecting the conversation to go there. But it had and she had to be honest. With everyone. "No, that's not why I turned him down." And she hastened to add, "I wouldn't say I turned him down either. I just told him not right now."

"Sounds like a turndown to me."

The waiter arrived with their wine and Andie waited until he'd poured it and left before continuing. "I told Terrence that I wasn't in the right place to make a decision like that. There's too much stuff going on now. I'm not thinking clearly. I told him I needed a break."

"You broke up with him?" His eyes widened.

"No, not really. I wouldn't say that."

"Is he free to see other people?"

She bit the inside of her cheek while she thought about the conversation they'd had. "I told him I wanted to see other people and I told him if he wanted or needed to see someone else, I wouldn't stop him. It didn't seem right to hold him to me since I asked for time."

Fulton seemed to be thinking on her words. "How very noble of you."

Anger rose in her belly. "What the fuck does that mean?"

"Did he take you up on your offer? Do you think he went straight to a kink club?"

"I don't know."

"Why are you with him, Andie?"

His questions were making her head spin. He was hot and

cold. Sweet one minute and sour the next. What the hell was wrong with him?

The possible answer, when it came to her, felt like someone had punched her in the gut.

What if he's struggling with his feelings for me, just like I'm struggling over my feelings for him?

Was it possible? Did he have feelings for her? And maybe Lennox knew and that's why he got all bent out of shape over them sharing a room.

Holy fuck. Could that be it?

"Frankly, I think it's a bad sign if you have to think that hard about it," he said with a frown.

"Think about what?" Had he asked a question? All she could think about was the possibility that he had feelings for her.

"I asked why you were with him."

"Oh." She searched her head for an answer, but it was filled completely by Fulton. "We've been friends forever."

He tilted his head and whispered, "And that's a reason to spend three months of your summer learning about kneeling, being spanked, and sucking cock?"

She felt her face flush. "What do you want me to say?"

He leaned across the table and his eyes were very serious. "I want you to tell me you love him madly and deeply and can't imagine life without him. I want you to tell me that you long to serve him and only him and I'm just a path to get you to that point. I want you to look me in the eye and tell me that I can go straight to hell for even thinking about—"

Her cell phone rang loudly, but she was so transfixed by his words, she didn't move.

"Answer your phone," he finally said, and was it her imagination or did he seem somewhat relieved that he hadn't been able to finish what he was saying?

Her fingers fumbled as she turned it over. *Terrence.*

"Hey there," she said.

"Hey, Andie," Terrence started. "I got a call from Lennox. You're in Portland with a teacher?"

"Yes, he brought me to the class I had to lead and we got stuck here because of the weather."

"Are you okay sharing a room? Lennox said there wasn't any other option, but tell me, Andie, if you don't want to and I'll make it happen."

"I'm fine. I promise."

"If you're sure," he said, but didn't sound convinced or happy. She'd learned over the last few weeks that Doms were good at reading their subs and she couldn't help but wonder if he somehow knew she was struggling to sort out her feelings about Fulton.

"I'm sure," she said, right as the waiter brought their salmon. And though moments ago she'd been excited to try it, she knew it'd taste like cardboard now.

She said her good-byes and hung up. Fulton was watching her again with those eyes of his, which missed nothing. She lifted up her fork and took a bite. Yup, cardboard. With a sigh, she put her fork down.

Fulton put his down as well. "That's it."

She looked up. Great, he was still upset. Seriously, Terrence, Fulton, and Lennox were all out of sorts. Maybe she'd spill her wine and upset the restaurant staff, too.

"What?" she asked, not even trying to keep the irritation out of her voice. She swore, if he brought up why she was with Terrence again, she was going to fillet him with the butter knife.

He eyed the butter knife in her hand as if he knew what she was thinking of doing. "You're pissy. I'm pissy. And we're stuck here tonight, right?"

She tightened her grip on the knife. "Is this supposed to be a pick-me-up speech? Because if it is, you suck at it. Like bad."

"I was going to suggest we go have some fun."

Around them, well-dressed people chatted politely with their tablemates, interrupted only by the waitstaff. The rain pounded on the windows and night had fallen. Yet for all that, something inside her whispered, "Yes."

"I'm glad you agree," he said, and she realized she'd spoken out loud. "Let's get this wrapped to go and we'll hang out at the bar."

"And we'll have drinks?"

"Of course."

She was starting to like the idea. Much better than going back to the room, sitting around, wondering which man she'd pissed off more and if she really cared.

"Only if we promise there'll be no talk of the academy, Terrence, or what we're going to do tomorrow," she said and was pleased at the excitement that filled his eyes.

"Agreed. For tonight, we're just Fulton and Andie. It's what we said this morning, but we seem to have forgotten with the rain and everything."

"Just Fulton and Andie," she repeated. "I like it. Let's do it."

He lifted a hand to capture the attention of their waiter and as they sat while he wrapped up their meals, she couldn't help but think this night was either going to be a really good idea or the worst mistake she'd ever made.

FULTON KNEW AS soon as they took their seats at the bar that he'd made the right decision. After one step out of the restaurant, he'd sensed Andie relaxing. He'd thought he knew her before, but it seemed as if each day brought more new discoveries about her.

Like tonight, it was as if he could see the burden she carried at knowing Lennox and Terrence weren't pleased with the sleeping arrangements. And it had only been made worse by the fact that she couldn't do anything about it. It tore her up inside. He sat across from her at the table and watched while it happened.

He'd be damned if it was going to happen any more tonight. That's why he'd brought her to the bar. He'd noticed earlier it was packed with people, and Andie loved to be around people. He had a feeling that was part of why she'd decided to become a chef. So she could share her gifts and talents with others.

She wiggled at his side. "Who are all these people?"

He pointed to a sign on the wall. "Looks like the Pacific Northwest Swing Dancers."

"Really?"

"Really," he replied and though he shouldn't because once he did, he could never take it back, he asked, "Do you swing-dance?"

"Oh yes," she said, still looking at the laughing couples around them, like she was trying to guess which ones were the dancers and which ones were just regular hotel guests. "I learned when I was a teenager. My mom taught me." She bit her lip. "I'd love to one day dance with Terrence, but he hates swing dancing."

The night just got ten thousand times better.

"Does he now?" he asked as he waved the bartender over. If this was leading where he thought it might, he was going to need something stronger than wine.

Fortunately, Andie didn't seem to notice what he was or was not drinking. She'd struck up a conversation with the couple sitting next to her. He half listened as he sipped his whiskey. He'd much rather watch her than discuss the pros and cons of shoes to dance in.

He signaled the bartender to refill her martini glass. Andie took it with a smile and a whispered "Thank you." She must have told the couple she was a chef because the conversation had switched to recipes and they were asking about some French dish he couldn't spell if his life depended on it.

Fulton was fully enjoying his whiskey when he heard: "And what does your boyfriend do?"

"He's not my—"

"I'm a teacher." He offered his hand for her to shake. "Fulton Matthews."

"Nice to meet you, Mr. Matthews," the lady said. "What do you teach?"

"A little bit of everything." It was his standard reply when someone from the vanilla world asked him about his job. Most of the time it was enough to satisfy people. He'd learned most of them were only asking to be nice.

His reply seemed to satisfy her and she went back to talking food with Andie. Who didn't, he couldn't help but notice, try to correct the assumption that he was her boyfriend a second time.

He took another long sip from his glass and thought back to his last girlfriend, Phoebe. She'd been the picture-perfect submissive. Perfect posture. Perfect responses. Perfect in all areas except one: he'd found her playing without his permission with another Dom at a local Portland club. Two years later and thoughts of her still made him angry.

He considered himself a reasonable man. If she'd told him she wanted to play with someone new, he'd have arranged it. Or at least that's what he told himself. But for her to have not even asked him, much less have a discussion about it, smacked of deceit.

Yup, two years and the pain of her betrayal still stung. Hell, a shrink would have a field day with him. It was that feeling of betrayal and deceit that made him keep his hands off Andie as much as he possibly could. He didn't want to be *That Guy.* No, he wouldn't do that to his worst enemy.

But since Andie had turned down Terrence's proposal, did that mean she was free? He told himself he was only looking for a way to justify his actions. *Potential actions,* he corrected. He hadn't done anything.

Yet.

It was as if the word hung suspended between them. *Yet* meant the potential existed. *Yet* was *maybe's* naughty kid sister who always got in trouble. Ripe for the picking and begging to become a *yes.*

He threw back what was left of his drink and signaled for another.

What would it take to get Andie to say yes to him? Was that even a path he wanted to explore? He shouldn't. He was her teacher and that alone should have been enough to have him turn and run in the opposite direction. He typically did everything he was supposed to do. Why was she tempting him to do differently?

No, he wouldn't do anything. He'd be patient and bide his time. He'd let Andie graduate and search for what she wanted. That way, if by some slim chance she wanted him, there wouldn't be any reason for them not to be together.

He felt better, having made that decision. Now he could simply relax and enjoy the evening and Andie's company. He picked up his glass and noticed it was empty. How many drinks had he had? Beside him, Andie was giggling and finishing what was left in her glass. Fuck, how many had she had?

He stood up. They needed to get back to the room and away from the alcohol. Maybe they'd turn in a bit early. That way they could start back to the island first thing in the morning. He was about to tap Andie's shoulder and tell her the plan when a new couple walked up toward them.

"Dancing at the club on the top floor," they announced. "Everyone's welcome."

He didn't miss the brief flash of excitement in Andie's eyes before she schooled her expression. The look of sadness that followed twisted his insides and he knew he'd do anything to bring the excitement back.

Even revisiting his past.

"Let's go see," he said to Andie.

"But what? You don't dance. You always tell Mariela—"

He couldn't stop himself from bringing his finger up to her lips to quiet her. "Shhh. I said I don't much like dancing, not that I don't dance. I actually used to swing-dance a few lifetimes ago.

Besides"—he grinned at her still stunned expression—"sometimes I just say things to annoy Mariela."

"You swing-dance?"

"Yes, ma'am. And if you'll come with me, maybe I can show you a thing or two."

"How?"

"An old girlfriend taught me."

She didn't need any further convincing, but hopped off the barstool and took his hand. "I'm in."

Her speech was clear, but she wobbled a bit. He tried to convince himself that he only put his arm around her to steady her. As they joined the other couples heading to the elevators, he realized his *wait until she graduates* plan was going straight to hell.

ANDIE STOOD IN the elevator with Fulton's arm around her, still trying to make sense of where the night was going. Fulton danced? She still wondered if she'd heard correctly. How could it be possible when he only ever complained about their dance lessons?

Unless . . . He'd said it was an old girlfriend who'd taught him. Maybe she'd broken his heart and he could no longer stand to do an activity that reminded him of her.

It wasn't funny. It wasn't. But even though she told herself that, the very idea of a man as tough and gruff as Fulton letting the memory of a woman keep him from dancing made her giggle.

She felt bad about it, but that only made her giggle more.

"What's so funny?" He leaned close to whisper the question in her ear.

"I can't say—it's awful. Just awful." She prayed he didn't push her to answer.

"How many drinks did you have?" he asked instead.

How many drinks? She tried to think, but couldn't come up with a number. "Oh, shit. I'm drunk."

"Not yet. I think you're just tipsy, but you're well on your way to drunk, so we probably need to stick to water."

She nodded and tried to remember the last time she'd gotten drunk, but it made her head hurt so she stopped. "That's right," she said as it came to her. The elevator reached the top floor and everyone got out. She didn't miss the fact that Fulton's hand rested low on her waist.

"What's right?" The big band was so loud he had to bend low to whisper in her ear, and in doing so his lips brushed her earlobe.

"I remembered the last time I got drunk."

"When was that?"

"The night I learned Terrence was a Dom." It'd come as a surprise to her and she'd discovered that the more she drank, the more sense it made. "That sounds bad, doesn't it?"

"Yes." There was a strange look on his face.

"We'll talk about it later," she said, wanting to strip the strange look off his face. "I shouldn't have even said anything. We promised it was just Fulton and Andie tonight."

He looked like he wanted to say something, but he nodded. "Want to watch for a bit?"

"Sure."

The upstairs club was almost completely made of windows, and even with the storm raging outside they had an incredible view of the city. When she was finally able to tear her gaze away from the twinkling lights outside, she noticed the large dance floor that took up the majority of the space and how it was already crowded with people dancing.

Fulton stood by her side, his hand still on her waist. She could feel the electricity radiate throughout her body just from his touch.

She shook her head. Damn, she was drunk.

A new song started and the couples on the dance floor broke out into various swing moves. Some of them really impressed her, but the majority of them . . .

"I can do better than that," she said as one couple twirled past them.

Fulton chuckled. "I was just thinking the same thing." He took his hand from around her waist and held it out. "Ready?"

His eyes were dark and his expression heated her just as much as his touch had. She had the craziest feeling she was saying yes to more than a turn around the dance floor. But she placed her hand in his anyway and replied, "Yes."

It's just a dance. Just a dance.

She kept repeating it to herself, certain if she thought it enough, maybe she'd believe it. But as they stood facing each other, waiting for the music to start, she saw something in his eyes and she knew she was trying to convince herself with a lie. It wasn't just a dance for him either.

She wasn't able to look too closely into his eyes to try to decipher what she saw because the music started, he took her in his arms, and just like that, her world tilted.

She said she'd danced before and she had, but until Fulton held her she'd never *danced*. How was it possible a man of his size could move the way he did? Part of her wanted to sit back and watch him, because the way he moved his body was artwork in motion.

But sitting back and watching would have been barely brushing the tip of an iceberg, because watching him while he led her through the dance was heady. The world slipped away and she saw no one other than Fulton. It was as if they'd been dancing together for years. How else could it be that she instinctively knew what he was going to do next?

How was it possible that his hand was always, *always* right where she needed it to be, when she needed it there? It seemed improbable that his feet stepped exactly where she thought they should. It was like he read her mind. Or she read his.

She'd been with him in several training sessions, but it wasn't until that moment, that dance, that she knew beyond a shadow of a doubt his true self. He was a combination of sultry fun and seductive sexy, all mixed together with a strong sense of control. And yet that strength was tempered by hands that could carve details into wood or silently lead her through a dance.

How could such a man exist? There were too many parts that didn't seem to fit together, but that somehow did. The resulting combination created a man who was as quirky as he was seductive and as steadfast as he was bewildering. And then to top it off, he had a body that was made for sex. Raw and hard and rough. She knew that's how it would be with him.

Sure, he could probably be gentle, but the gentleness was only a thin layer, covering the man underneath. What surprised her more was the fact that she wanted that. She wanted hot and messy and real. And she realized as they stood surrounded by strangers, in a hotel they were only in because of a freak storm, that she wanted him. Only him. When she was with him, she couldn't think of anyone else. No, with Fulton, there was just him, and somehow that's all she needed.

She didn't have to worry about whether she was enough. Or if she'd always be second to a career. Or, she finally admitted to herself, that she was just comfortable and common.

The next song was slow and even though she wouldn't have thought he'd want to dance to a slow song, Fulton pulled her close. She raised an eyebrow in question at him.

"You don't think we can dance to this?" he asked.

It really should have been a rhetorical question; he was already guiding her through the steps.

"Stop thinking so hard," he whispered into her ear.

If she thought their first dance was heady, that was only because she'd yet to dance slow with him. Once again, he moved with a certainty and fluidity that amazed her. But more than that was the way he'd pull her in close before she'd spin back out. His arms were warm and protective and every time they came together, his intense gaze hit her with a look of pure lust.

She spun out, trying to catch her breath, but within seconds she was back pressed against his chest. He pulled her close and she took in his scent: cedar and pine. He ran a finger down her cheek before letting her go.

Over and over, they spun. The dance became a game. A sultry and sexy game where they teased each other, neither wanting to admit anything, but unable to deny it anymore. She saw the truth reflected in his eyes,

The song came to an end and he brought them to a stop near the edge of the dance floor. Another song, a faster one, came on, but they didn't start dancing. He brushed her upper arm with his fingertips and let them travel down to the crook of her elbow. She shivered when he stroked her there.

"I don't want to dance anymore," he said, his fingers still teasing her skin and his eyes searching.

Her heart pounded. And when did her mouth get so dry? "Me either," she finally managed to get out.

He nodded and captured her hand in his. Her head was fuzzy, but she knew this was what she wanted. This was the man she wanted. And she wanted it right now.

There were people in the elevator, but that didn't stop Fulton from touching her. He put his arm around her and pulled her close to his side. She sensed the hard muscles of his chest and she wondered what they would feel like pressed against her.

It seemed as if they stopped on every floor before finally reaching theirs. Fulton opened the door for her. As soon as she stepped inside, he closed the door and pushed her up against it, his hands on either side of her head.

"I'm going to kiss you." His voice was rougher than she'd ever heard. "Tell me now if you don't want me to. Tell me and I'll go sleep on the couch."

She couldn't tell him no. She'd been fantasizing about those lips and she wanted them on her. She wanted to taste them.

By way of response, she looped her arms around his neck. "Kiss me. Kiss me like I've never been kissed and kiss me so I forget every kiss except yours."

No sooner had the words left her mouth than Fulton covered her lips with his. He was demanding and ruthless in the way he claimed her mouth. She tightened her fists, grabbing part of his shirt in the process.

His kiss mirrored the way she envisioned him: strong, sexy, and unyielding. His hips pushed into hers, and the touch of his erection made her gasp. More than that, it made her *want*. She gyrated her hips, desperate for friction.

He pulled back. "So needy."

There was too much space between them and she could almost whine for the lack of his touch. She felt flushed and she didn't know if it was from him or the drinks or something else entirely.

"You liked it when my cock rubbed against you, didn't you?" he whispered into her ear.

"Yes." There was no reason to lie. "So much."

He closed in on her again, this time alternating between words and kisses. "My cock liked feeling you, too." He ran a line of nibbles down her neck while his fingers fondled her breasts. "In fact, my cock is so hard and so ready for you, I don't think there's a drop of blood in my body that's not in my dick."

She wanted to feel him, needed to feel him. While his lips tasted her collarbone, she slid her hand down between them to cup him.

He sucked in a breath as if he was in pain. "Andie . . ."

She jerked away. "Sorry. Should I not?"

He took her hand and guided it back to his cock. "Don't stop. You didn't do anything wrong. What you did felt good. Too good. I'd hate to come too soon for you."

His confession filled her with feminine pride. She had made him hard, made him desire her so much he almost lost control.

She thought she knew quite a bit about him and she knew he very rarely lost control. It was that knowledge that gave her the courage to say what she wanted.

"Let me touch you." She worked the button on his jeans, her fingers trembling with nerves. Hell, she'd never touched Terrence's cock. She froze at the thought of his name and somewhere in the back of her head, she heard herself asking, *What the hell are you doing?*

But she chose not to listen to that voice. She looked up, wanting to focus on Fulton's expression, and gave him a teasing smile. "Please."

He didn't speak; it was as if he was afraid he'd totally lose control if he did so. He simply nodded and closed his eyes.

Excitement flooded her body, sweeping away the nerves she'd experienced only moments ago. *Yes!* She couldn't wait to get her hands on him. *Might as well get up close and personal,* she decided, and she dropped to her knees. It was a bit like a classroom session, except this time, she was free to move and explore his body as she wished.

What she'd really like to do was to have him completely naked. She almost stood up and had him remove his shirt, but at that second, he dropped his hands and unzipped his pants.

"Take it out," he said through clenched teeth. "If you want to touch it, take it out."

She jerked his pants down, not able to take them off completely since he still had his shoes on, but enough to give her room to work with.

He wore boxer briefs underneath.

"I always envisioned you as a commando man," she mused, stroking him slightly through the cotton. He twitched and jerked and she swore he grew even bigger.

He chuckled. "You were teaching a cooking class. I thought the situation called for boxers."

She couldn't help but smile at his logic. "Does that mean you typically don't wear them?"

"Are we really going to have this conversation right now? Because I don't mind discussing underwear, but if you're not planning to . . ."

She didn't let him finish his sentence. Instead she pulled the garment in question down, freeing his cock.

"Fuck!" he said as she wrapped her hand around him.

She let go. "Sorry. Did that hurt?"

"No, your hands just feel damn good."

What she really wanted to do was take him in her mouth, run her tongue along the length of his flesh, taste him, to see if she could fit all of him in her mouth.

She was getting ready to ask him if she could when someone knocked on the door. She jumped to her feet, face flushing, like she'd been caught stealing.

"What the hell?" Fulton asked.

"Delivery for Ms. Andie Lincoln," a voice on the other side of the door said.

A delivery? Who would be delivering her anything at the hotel? And at this time of the night?

"Just a second." Fulton swore under his breath as he pulled up his pants and straightened his clothes.

When they were both more presentable, he opened the door. Andie looked around him and saw a hotel bellhop holding a bouquet of roses. Fulton turned and walked away.

"Andie Lincoln?" he asked.

She moved forward. "Yes, that's me."

"These are for you." He thrust the flowers into her hands. He waited a few seconds as she looked for a card. "So, do you really know Terrence Knight?"

The bathroom door from inside the room slammed behind her, and she sighed as she threw her head back in frustration.

"Yes," she said. "But let's keep that our little secret."

"Sure." He nodded. "Cool."

She fumbled in her pockets for tip money and he went on his way. She took a deep breath and turned around. Time to face Fulton.

Except he was still in the bathroom. And she knew without anything being said that they would not be picking right back up where they left off. With a sigh, she put the flowers on the bed and read the card.

> *Hate that you're stuck in Portland with an academy instructor. Hope these cheer you up.*
>
> *Terrence*

It was ironic in a way. His thoughtful gift had put a stop to what would have cheered her up.

"Or if you had to send something, why couldn't it be something useful like pajamas?" she asked the empty room. "What the hell can I do with roses?"

As soon as she spoke it, an image of her in bed surrounded by rose petals came to mind. She was waiting for a man. And it wasn't the one who'd sent her the flowers.

The bathroom door opened and Fulton came out. He was perfectly presentable once again. Not a piece of clothing or a strand of hair out of place. And the seductive expression he'd had earlier was gone, too. In its place was a mask of indifference.

"What happened between us was entirely my fault," he said. "I take full responsibility and it won't happen again."

And just like that, any part of her previous easygoing attitude flew out the window. "What the hell does that mean?"

"Exactly what I said. I screwed up and I take the blame and it won't happen again."

He spoke it so calmly, like he hadn't been mad with lust just ten minutes earlier.

"Excuse me? I think there were two people here, Mr. High and Mighty. I'm a grown-ass woman who is perfectly capable of making her own decisions." And her decision tonight was him. She'd wanted him. Hell, part of her still did.

"That decision is enough to get me fired."

She'd been ready to argue, but that shut her up. She'd only ever thought of him as off limits because of Terrence. Now, she realized, it was still complicated because he was her teacher. But still . . .

"It still would have been my choice," she said.

"It would have been a damn stupid choice." His eyes were no longer warm. In fact, they were so cold, she shivered. "I'm not the man for you, Andie. You have Terrence. Just think about it. If that delivery hadn't stopped us, I'd probably be balls deep in you right now, without even a thought to your virginity."

"This is all because I'm a virgin?" She couldn't believe it. That he was throwing that into the mix. "What the fuck does that matter?"

"You came to the academy with two requirements: train you in submission and keep your virginity intact."

"It's *my* damn virginity. I should be the one who decides when to lose it."

"Should you?" he asked. He walked closer and his smell reminded her of how just moments ago she'd been on her knees, stroking him. If they could only go back and redo that moment, not give a thought to the knock on that door. "I think the moment you decided you wanted to be a sub for Terrence, you gave up that right."

Had she given up that right? She'd never thought about it like that, but maybe he was right. If she intended her future to involve submitting to Terrence in the bedroom, didn't it stand to reason that he should be the one to dictate when and how she lost her virginity? Not to mention to whom.

"But when I'm with you . . ." she started and then stopped, trying to decide if she wanted to be completely honest. She took a deep breath. Yes. Yes, she did. She owed it to herself. "When I'm with you, I feel different. And it's even different than what I feel with Terrence. I feel more connected with you. Or something."

She waited, heart pounding, to see how he responded. Very rarely had she ever put herself out there like that.

"Miss Lincoln," he stated, and she knew that was that. No good would come from him calling her *Miss Lincoln*.

"Back to that, are we? I thought we were Fulton and Andie today?"

"That was a bad call on my account. It confuses things. Blurs lines." He took a deep breath. "Even if you want to see other people, it can't be me. I'm employed at the academy you pay."

She couldn't believe he was doing this. How could he after the night they'd shared? She clenched her fist so tightly, her nails dug into her palms. "You don't feel anything between us?"

"I was the first man you knelt for. The first one to spank you. And I'm willing to bet that I'm the first one you've stripped in front of as well." He shook his head, but he didn't look at her. "I could have been anybody and you would have felt the same."

She didn't believe him. Not for one minute. It wasn't that he was the first she'd done those things with. It was more. It was all of him. From his voice to his touch to the way he looked after her. It was two hundred different things. And she knew he felt something toward her. That dance . . .

"Look me in the eyes and tell me I'm no different from anyone else," she challenged him.

At first she didn't think he'd do it, but he turned to face her and his voice was edged with steel when he spoke. "You are my student and I'm your instructor. That is all there is between us. That is all there is ever going to be between us."

Her eyes prickled with the tears she knew she wouldn't be able to hold back for very long. "I would have picked you," she whispered. Without looking back, she walked to the bathroom and slammed the door. Luck was on her side and she was able to get the shower running before the tears fell.

Not long after that, she heard the door to their room close and she knew he'd left. He didn't come back before she went to bed.

For a long time, she stared up at the ceiling, thinking about all the things he'd said. When she finally decided what to do, she rolled over and looked at the clock on the nightstand. One in the morning. Wondering when he'd make it back to the room, she fell into a restless sleep.

CHAPTER

Eleven

She woke with a jerk and sat straight up in bed, trying to figure out what had startled her. She heard it again and realized it was the coffeemaker. Fulton stood with his back to her, fully dressed and ready to go, getting out cups for their coffee.

Damn, she wasn't ready to face him yet. But with her decision fresh in her mind, she focused on that and what she had to do in the coming hours.

Fulton turned around. "Good, you're up." His voice was just as cold as it'd been the night before. "We need to head out in twenty minutes. We'll pick up something to eat on the way."

"I'm not hungry."

She expected him to argue with her. To tell her that she needed to eat. But he simply said, "Fine. We'll stop and pick up something for me to eat on the way."

Men.

She'd slept in her underwear, knowing she'd have to wear the clothes she'd had on the day before. She tossed aside the blankets and her gaze fell to the foot of the bed. Which was covered by a new pair of jeans, a T-shirt, and undergarments.

"Picked you up something to wear" was all he said. He handed her a bag with a top-end store printed on it. "You can put your dirty clothes in here."

She wanted to ask him how he managed to buy new clothes in the few short hours since he'd walked out the door. Stores hadn't even been open. But that would involve talking with him and she wasn't ready for that.

She scooped up the new clothes, mumbled a "thank you," and headed to the bathroom.

Andie managed not to say more than ten words to Fulton on the long ride back to the coast. Thankfully, he was silent as well. Probably, she decided, because he didn't want to talk to her either.

She watched out the windows aimlessly, not even able to work up enough energy to comment on how green everything looked after the previous day's rain. The roads were still damp and a low fog hovered just above the pavement. It was really quite beautiful.

Out of the corner of her eye, she caught Fulton glance at her. He wasn't as unaffected by the last twenty-four hours as he'd try to portray. And though it hurt her chest, there was a small comfort in that. And besides, it only reinforced her determination to carry through with the plan she'd made the night before.

She closed her eyes and pretended to sleep, all the while telling herself she was doing the right thing.

*　*　*

THE SUN WAS actually trying to break out of the clouds as they pulled the boat up to the dock, but in the distance they were ominous. Andie squinted as she stepped out, balancing on her own so she didn't have to reach for Fulton's help. Mariela stood at the top of the deck and pulled her into a hug.

"I was so worried when I heard you two were stuck on the mainland."

Andie relaxed for what seemed like the first time in hours, thankful for the secure arms of her kind adviser.

"Here, let me take your bag," Mariela said, taking it effortlessly from her hand. "Did you eat? Are you hungry?"

It had to happen now, or else she'd lose her determination. It would take nothing to fall back into her old routine. And she couldn't risk it.

"Actually," she said in a voice low enough that Fulton couldn't hear. "I need to speak with Master MacLure. I know it's Sunday, but is he around?"

"He's always around. Doesn't matter what day of the week it is." Mariela looked back to where Fulton was tying up the boat. "Is everything okay? With you and Master Matthews?"

"Just fine." It was amazing how easily the lie fell from her lips.

The look Mariela gave her suggested she knew the answer was less than truthful. But Andie stood her ground and the other woman eventually sighed. "Okay, come with me. I'll take you to his office and then I'll take your stuff to your room."

Andie followed her, telling herself she was doing the right thing

179

and she had no other choice. She tried to think only about the conversation she was going to have with Master MacLure. The rest of it would take care of itself.

She hoped.

Just as Mariela said, Lennox was in his office. She knocked on the frame of the open door. "Excuse us, Master MacLure. Miss Lincoln needs to speak with you."

The headmaster looked up with a smile. "Thank you, Mariela." He stood up and indicated the empty chair in front of his desk. "Have a seat, Miss Lincoln."

She sat down in the comfortable leather chair and folded her hands in her lap. Her knees were trembling and she couldn't get them to stop.

"I see you and Master Matthews made it back safely."

She nodded. There was a large picture window along one wall of his office. She could see the dock in the distance. She almost said something about the pretty view, but decided she wasn't in the mood for small talk.

"And I take it this not a social call," he said.

"No, Sir. It's not." She took a breath. *Just say it.* "I want to withdraw from the academy."

His forehead wrinkled. "You do? Why? Did something happen with you and Matthews?"

"No. He wasn't even in the room when I went to bed and when I got up, he was already dressed," she hastened to answer. Whatever happened, she didn't want Fulton to get in trouble. Even if she did want to cut off a certain part of his anatomy and use it as fish bait. "You heard Terrence proposed?"

"Yes, and he said you needed more time."

"Right. The thing is, I turned him down because I'm not sure he's the one for me."

"I see."

"Being here has awakened me to so many things. Not only my submissive side, but other stuff. I'm not even sure I want a restaurant in the city anymore." She shook her head, knowing she wasn't making sense. "The bottom line is, I can't continue to let Terrence pay for me to be here, when I might not be with him after it's over. And I can't afford tuition on my own." It was the one thing Fulton had said the night before that made sense. Except he'd been wrong. She wasn't paying; Terrence was.

"Let me summarize: you wish to drop out, not because you've realized you aren't submissive, or because something's going on with you and Matthews. Rather you don't feel comfortable letting Terrence pay your tuition since you're not sure you're going to be with him."

"Yes, Sir."

He looked at her with those knowing eyes that missed nothing and she wondered if he could see right through her.

He tapped his pen on the desk. "The summer session doesn't have much longer. It would be a pity for you to leave now, but I understand and respect the fact that you don't wish to mislead Terrence."

Her cheeks felt hot at his words, because she already *had* misled Terrence.

"May I ask a favor of you?" he asked.

"Yes, of course."

"Give me a day or so to think about how to work this out. Don't do anything hasty. I believe I can come up with something that will work for all parties involved."

He did? She wished he'd tell her now what it was. "You do?" she couldn't help but ask.

His smile was kind. "Yes, Miss Lincoln, I believe I do."

It felt like a huge weight had been lifted off of her. Master MacLure was a very nice man, not anywhere near as scary as people said he was. It was only because he was so reclusive that people thought the worst of him. And because no one had watched him play.

She thanked him and grabbed her purse, practically floating out of his office. Lennox would help her, she was certain. Finally she could breathe again without feeling as if she had to be and do everything perfectly while trying her best to keep everyone around her civil.

She peeked her head into Mariela's office, but didn't see her. Maybe she was in her classroom. She turned down the hallway that led to the classrooms when she heard footsteps from the hall she'd just left.

"David!" It was Master MacLure. "Find Matthews and tell him to get his ass to my office. Now. We have an issue to take care of."

CHAPTER
Twelve

Fulton had expected to be called to Lennox's office. As soon as he saw Andie walk inside with Mariela he had a hunch that was where they were going. At David's call, he wiped his wet hands on his jeans and prepared for the worst.

Lennox sat at his desk, silently waiting for him. Fulton couldn't tell anything from his expression. The man should have been a professional poker player. He couldn't be sure what Andie had told him, so to play it safe and not bring any heat on her, he'd answer the questions as truthfully as possible, without giving any details. If Lennox wanted a pound of flesh, he would have to settle for Fulton's because he refused to let Andie take any blame.

"Have a seat," Lennox said. Fulton had a feeling he now knew exactly how submissives felt when they'd done something wrong. It just might be the most uncomfortable position in the world to be in.

"Would you like to tell me why Andie Lincoln's first order of business after arriving back here was to come to my office and announce that she's leaving?"

Leaving?

The thought hurt him, but he knew he couldn't show any emotion to Lennox. "Probably not, boss. I make it a point to never try to understand why women do the things they do. It's a lesson in futility."

"Be that as it may, she was perfectly well-adjusted when she left here yesterday and twenty-four hours later, after a night out with you, she comes in ready to quit."

"I'm not so certain she was as well-adjusted as you think. Remember my misgivings the day before she came?"

"Yes. And I've watched her overcome them. As a result, in part, of your extra attention."

Fulton tried to cover the surprise he felt at the fact that Lennox had picked up on that, but he didn't think he did a very good job of doing so. Across the desk, Lennox gave a half smirk, just like the sly bastard he was.

"You think I don't know everything that happens at my academy?" Lennox asked.

"Of course you do," Fulton admitted.

"It was not a mistake for me to allow for it to happen. The mistake was letting you continue to instruct her once I realized feelings were involved. And not only that, but encouraging it before Terrence came."

He hadn't realized he was that transparent. "I don't know what you're talking about. I'm her instructor. There are no feelings beyond that. I slept for two hours last night and they were spent on a couch."

"It's not just your feelings, though heaven knows that's enough. It's what she feels toward you."

Fulton shook his head, but in his mind he recalled Andie's pained whisper. *I would have picked you.*

"It's nothing. What she feels toward me is just because I'm her first Dom. That's all." It would have to be.

"That's a lie and you know it. You can't be that blind."

"Yeah, well," Fulton said, without thinking. "You're a fine one to talk."

That gave the headmaster pause. "What do you mean by that?"

"I mean it's pretty damn clear to everyone, except apparently you, that Mariela is completely in love with you, has been for years, and you treat her like shit."

He regretted the words as soon as he spoke them, but it was too late to do anything about it now. Fuck. His ass was probably going to get fired.

Lennox turned a deathly shade of pale and closed his eyes tightly. For a minute, Fulton thought he was going to pass out. He'd started to stand up in order to catch him, when Lennox replied in a voice strangely devoid of any emotion, "Mariela and I lost someone who was very dear to both of us. Time has not healed those wounds, Master Matthews. I suggest you leave her out of this discussion."

It was the most he'd ever heard about the headmaster's past and he was curious for more information. But, at the moment, he had other problems to deal with. Curiosity would have to be swept to the side for now.

The color had returned to Lennox's face. "All that aside, there is still the matter of you, an instructor, and—"

"MacLure!" the gentleman who maintained the dock, burst into the room. He was an older man, and running had obviously taken its toll on him because now he was bent over, wheezing.

"Jeffery!" Lennox shot up from his desk as Fulton helped him into a chair.

"I tried to stop her," Jeffery panted. "I tried. But she wouldn't listen."

Fulton had a sick feeling in his stomach.

"The young lady. She said it was urgent she get to the mainland." The older gentleman looked positively petrified.

"Someone took a boat to the mainland without putting a request in." Lennox kept his voice calm. "That's not so much of an issue, is it? It's happened before."

"Yes, but look." Fulton and Lennox followed Jeffery's finger as he pointed out the window. "Storm's back."

"Fuck," Lennox said.

"What young lady was it?" Fulton asked, dread filling his body as he looked at the approaching storm. "What did she look like?"

Fulton was already on his way to the door as Jeffery replied, "Long, dark hair. About this tall. Looked like she'd been crying."

At that, he took off running toward the dock with Lennox a step behind him.

"She'll be okay," Fulton said, mostly to convince himself and because he couldn't imagine any other possible outcome. He waited for Lennox to agree, but the wind lashed at them, drowning out any sound other than its own ominous howl.

* * *

SHE SHOULDN'T HAVE taken the boat. She knew that now but it was too late to go back. At the time, she hadn't known what else to do. From the sound of the headmaster's voice as he called for Fulton, things were not going to go well for him. And she couldn't have that. She'd thought Lennox was going to work out a way for her to stay at the academy. And he probably was, but from his tone of voice, there was no doubt in her mind, Fulton would be fired.

The most logical thing seemed to be for her to leave. It was what she'd planned on doing anyway. Who cared if she moved the timeline up? If she wasn't there, Fulton could stay. Besides, the academy had several boats. She'd taken one of the smaller ones that reminded her of the ones she grew up driving on the Georgia lakes her family vacationed at. Her father had taught her at an early age how to operate his boat.

Unfortunately, there was an approaching thunderstorm and she was stuck. She was closer to the mainland than she was to the academy. If the storm held off for fifteen minutes she could make it. Surely, she could make it. She pushed the boat forward.

The first huge wave that crashed over the boat took her by surprise. She'd been focusing so intently on the dot of mainland growing bigger in front of her that she'd paid no mind to the port side.

"Damn it."

It was raining hard now and even though the island had been farther away, she should have turned back before. Now the storm was all around her and she was afraid to go anywhere but straight ahead.

At least, she hoped she was going straight ahead. The boat

rocked, dipping dangerously low, and her stomach turned in response. She wiped the water away from her face as her chest tightened in panic and another wave sent set water rushing into the boat.

You will not have an asthma attack.

You will not have an asthma attack.

But her body wasn't listening to her and she couldn't get her lungs to work. She reached for her pocket even though she knew her inhaler wouldn't be there. It was shoved to the bottom of her purse. The air in this part of the country didn't affect her the way it did back home, and she hadn't used her rescue inhaler since she'd been at the academy.

Deep breaths.

She tried to calm down, but her body knew it was in trouble and panic threatened to seize her. When her chest and neck tightened, she barely had enough time to turn the boat off before her legs collapsed under her. Darkness crept in from beside her. She saw it approaching. She tried to get away, but her legs weren't listening.

She crawled to the side of the boat, grabbing on in a desperate attempt to stand up. She managed to get to her knees, but before she could push herself up, another wave struck the boat, this one washing over her. It might as well have been ice it was so cold. Her body hit the deck hard, knocking what little breath she had out.

Breathe.

Breathe.

Breathe.

But her body wasn't listening. As it crept closer, the darkness didn't look so scary. It appeared almost peaceful, so instead of fighting it, she let it embrace her.

Thirteen

There were twenty steps from one wall of the hospital waiting room to the other. Fulton knew because he'd counted them fifty-six times. One step at a time, back and forth across the thin carpet the ugliest color of green imaginable. He kept track of all the numbers in his head because if he didn't, he was going to beat the shit out of somebody in order to get some information about Andie.

"I'm sure they'll let us know something soon," Lennox said from his spot on the couch.

"You said that forty-five minutes ago." Fulton cursed under his breath. They wouldn't let him back to see her because he wasn't family. They didn't seem to care that she was the single most important person in his life. That didn't seem to carry any weight at all.

He kept waiting for Lennox to say something. After rescuing Andie and getting her to the hospital, he was reasonably certain his boss no longer believed the "I'm just her instructor" line. Though he was almost positive he'd never believed it in the first place.

Fulton still shivered when he remembered the sight of Andie's motionless body on the deck of the boat. She was so cold and wet. But the worst was her unresponsiveness and the pale blue hue of her skin. He was thankful Lennox had been with him. One thing he could say about his boss: the man had a cool head.

Lennox's phone buzzed and he looked down to read the text. "Terrence says he'll be landing in about an hour."

Fulton bet they'd let *him* go back to see her.

"Good thing they were filming in Chicago this week," Lennox said, as he typed back his reply. "If he'd still been on the East Coast, it would have taken a lot longer for him to get here."

"Right." Fulton snorted. "And what a travesty *that* would have been."

"I'm thinking of Andie. She'll be glad to see him."

"I don't know; she turned down the opportunity to marry him."

"That doesn't mean he's not important to her."

Fulton stopped pacing. "Why won't they tell us anything?"

No sooner had the words left his mouth than the waiting room door swung open and a lady dressed in scrubs and a white jacket asked, "Andie Lincoln?"

"Yes, here." Fulton hurried over to the woman. "How is she?"

"She's stable, but it was a serious asthma attack in combination with a panic attack. Oftentimes in cases such as this, there can be heart and/or lung damage. She's very fortunate she was found when she was."

They might have lost her. Fulton couldn't breathe at the thought.

It was as if some force suddenly drew all the air out of the room. Lennox came over and placed a hand on his shoulder.

"Thank you," Lennox said, not removing his hand. "Will we be able to see her soon?"

"They're taking her to her room now. You can go see her when she's settled; it shouldn't be that much longer."

"And how long do you think she'll be here?" Lennox asked. Once again, Fulton was thankful for his presence. At least he was able to formulate coherent questions. Fulton couldn't get past how close they'd been to losing her.

"We're going to keep her at least overnight. We'll look at the test results tomorrow, see how she's doing, and go from there."

"Sounds good." Lennox shook her hand. "Thank you so much."

"I'm glad we were able to help her. I'll make sure someone lets you know when you can go see her."

"We could have lost her," Fulton said, once the woman had left. "If only—"

"No. Stop right there." The commanding tone of Lennox's voice caught Fulton off guard. "We didn't and she's going to be fine. Don't beat yourself up with what-ifs. It'll only drive you crazy. It isn't good for anything."

There was a grief in his expression that spoke more than words could. Fulton wasn't sure what had happened, but he knew the man was speaking from experience.

"Do you want to talk about it?" Fulton asked.

"God, no. Do you know how many years I've been in therapy? I don't even want to think about it. I want to forget about it. Have it surgically removed from my brain. I most certainly do not want to talk about it."

Fulton wasn't going to push him. And he was glad in a way that Lennox had declined. Though he wanted to know more about his boss, at the moment all he could think about was Andie.

"I wonder how *it shouldn't be much longer* translates to real-people time?" Fulton asked instead.

"We probably don't want to know." Lennox said. He sat down again, but Fulton didn't resume his pacing. He stood by a window, looking out into the city, looking for answers he wasn't sure he wanted.

When they were finally told it was okay to see her, Lennox waved Fulton on. "You go. I'll stay here for a few."

Fulton wasn't sure why his boss was giving him alone time with Andie, but he wasn't going to argue. He forced himself not to run, but to remain calm. He just needed to see her. Needed to see her breathing. Needed to touch her.

A nurse stopped him outside Andie's door and he bit back the frustration of being so close and yet still unable to lay eyes on her.

"Miss Lincoln is sleeping. You can go in; just don't disturb her."

"Of course." He'd agree with anything as long as she moved out of the way and let him see Andie.

She smiled sweetly and stepped aside. Fulton pushed the door open and stopped in his tracks. She lay in the bed with her eyes closed, but she was breathing. He sagged against the doorway in relief. She was okay. She was going to be fine.

But he couldn't get out of his mind how close he'd come to losing her. What if she'd died, still thinking that she was just a student to him? He wouldn't have been able to stand the guilt.

I'd have picked you. She'd said that yesterday. Did she still mean it?

With tentative footsteps he crossed the floor, not wanting to disturb her rest, but needing to touch her. She smiled in her sleep as he approached the bed and he told himself it was because she felt his presence, even in sleep.

His phone buzzed in his pocket, but he ignored it. Nothing was more important than the woman in the hospital bed. Everyone else could wait.

Her right hand rested on top of the blanket and he gently picked it up, careful of the IV infusion site. He ran his hand over her skin. Warm. She radiated warmth. She'd been so cold when he'd found her on the boat. He shook his head, not ready to relive those terrifying moments.

"I'm sorry," he whispered. "I'm so sorry. If I could go back and redo it, I'd do it differently. I lied. You're not just a student to me. And I hope you'll forgive me."

He whispered it to her in her sleep, determined he'd tell her again when she woke up. God, he hoped she'd wake up soon. He needed to see her eyes. Wanted the reassurance that she was okay.

"Come back to me," he whispered. "Let me show you how much I love you."

He would tell her that when she woke up, too. He loved her and it was that simple. He didn't care who knew.

"Come back to me, Andie," he whispered once more.

A cough sounded from the doorway. He looked over his shoulder to find a very pissed-off-looking Terrence Knight.

Fourteen

F uck. How long had he been standing there and how much had he heard? Fulton stood and tried to make his face devoid of any emotion.

"She's sleeping," he said.

"Yes. I see that," Terrence said tersely. "Who are you?"

"Fulton Matthews." He didn't offer his hand, but then again, Terrence didn't offer his either. "I'm an instructor at the academy. I'm also the one who found her this afternoon."

"I see," he said.

Terrence was trying to keep his emotions veiled. Fulton observed so many people every day, it was clear to him when someone was trying to appear unaffected. He found it strange that Andie would be drawn to a man who seemed to be able to mask how he felt. She was the complete opposite. Everything she felt was reflected in her face.

She stirred in her sleep and mumbled something. Fulton spun away from Terrence and looked down at Andie. Her eyelids fluttered and then opened. The smile she'd had while sleeping was back and it was all for him. It was the most breathtaking sight he'd ever seen.

"Andie?" Fulton asked.

"Fulton," she said, her voice scratchy. "You're here."

"Shh." He placed a finger over her lips. "Don't strain your voice."

She nodded and instead lifted up a weak hand to stroke his cheek, and her touch made everything feel better.

"Andie," Terrence said from behind him.

Andie's hand froze and her eyes filled with shock. "Terrence?" she choked out.

"Yeah. And it's suddenly very clear to me why you turned down my proposal." He turned to leave.

"Terrence. Don't," Andie said. The strength Andie needed to force the words out seemed to tax her body.

Terrence stopped. What man wouldn't? The sound of his name, painfully spoken with a raspy voice. It was enough to make anyone want to comfort the speaker, especially if the speaker was the woman he loved.

But Terrence didn't return to her side. He stayed where he was. "I can't stay here right now, Andie. I'll be in the waiting room and I'll come back and see you in a bit. I can tell you're busy."

He walked through the door, past a startled Lennox, pausing only to say, "I hope you plan on firing that instructor of yours," before continuing his way out.

Andie's eyes closed, but not before Fulton saw the tears form.

One leaked out the side and ran down her cheek. Fulton wiped it away with his thumb.

"I'm sorry," he said.

"It's okay," she said in a soft voice that broke his heart.

But it wasn't okay. He'd hurt her. Repeatedly. And not always unintentionally. He made a vow to himself to never do it again and to do everything in his power to make her feel safe, protected, and loved.

A large hand came to rest on his shoulder. "Fulton," Lennox said. "Go get us some coffee. The real kind, not the swill they serve at the nursing station. I want to speak to Miss Lincoln alone."

That sounded like a preposterous idea. "With all due respect, sir. The nurse said—"

"I'm well aware of the nurse's request, as well as Andie's current state. Now, go get us some coffee."

Fulton looked down at Andie. Her eyes were open again and when she caught him staring, she gave him a slight nod.

"Fine," he said, only giving in because Andie was okay with it. He lowered his head and brushed her cheek with his lips. "I won't be gone long."

"Come back any sooner than twenty minutes and your ass is mine," Lennox said as he passed him.

ANDIE WATCHED AS Fulton walked out of the room, leaving her all alone with the cold and aloof headmaster. He currently stood off to the right side of her bed, watching to make sure everyone did exactly as he instructed. Which they did.

When Fulton had left, Lennox turned back to Andie. She assumed he was going to ask about Fulton. What other reason could he have for needing to see her privately? Hopefully her voice would hold out.

But when she struggled to sit up so she could talk better, he shook his head. "No need to get up. I'm the one who's going to talk—you just listen."

He was going to lecture her, then. Just as well, she deserved it. She'd been stupid in taking the boat out. It was only fair. Besides, her stomach still churned whenever she thought of what Terrence must have thought and felt when he walked in on her waking up and smiling at Fulton like he'd given her the moon.

Yes, compared to the pain he must have felt and must still be feeling, this was nothing.

"Relax, Miss Lincoln." Lennox actually smiled. "How are you feeling?"

That was a difficult question to answer. "I don't honestly know. I feel like I've been in a fight and lost, both mentally and physically."

"I understand," he said, and she could tell he did. "I'm not getting ready to give you a tongue-lashing or anything of that sort, I'm simply going to tell you part of my story."

That got her attention. There were rumors all over the academy about what had happened in his past. No one seemed to know, except Mariela, and she wouldn't talk about it.

He pulled a chair up to her bed. "Mind if I sit down?"

"No, Sir," she whispered.

"Very well then." He sat down and took a deep breath, and she had the overwhelming urge to hug him. But of course, she didn't.

She couldn't have even if she tried; she was still hooked up to all of the machines.

"Fifteen years ago, I was working my way up the corporate ladder as a businessman in L.A."

She swallowed around the lump in her throat because she knew, deep in her soul, that this story would not end well.

"One night, at a stuffy dinner party, I was introduced to the most beautiful woman in the world. Her name was Winifred, and she was breathtaking. She happened to be a local artist of some renown, but nothing so major that you would have ever heard of her."

She doubted she would have heard of her either way. She wasn't much into the art scene.

"From the moment we met, we were almost inseparable. I'm not sure what it was, but something about us clicked. Now, keep in mind, I was living as a Dom at this time. When she found out, she begged me to train her as my sub. She said her best friend was a sub and she knew about the kink world, but had never participated. I jumped at the chance. It was my wildest dream come true, I was training this perfect woman to be my perfect sub. Of course, you know that perfection is just an illusion. There's no such thing."

Andie couldn't keep her eyes off Lennox. To hear him talk about Winifred was captivating. Partially because she knew he shared this story with so few.

"Things started to unravel after a few years. She grew more and more isolated in her studio, but she wasn't selling much. She rarely wanted to have sex and when she did, she didn't want kink. I was frustrated and I'm afraid I didn't handle it well."

He stopped talking and looked beyond Andie to the far wall. His face had gone pale and he was speaking so softly, she had to strain to hear. He didn't want to finish the story, but not only did she want to hear the ending—she had a feeling he needed to tell it to someone even more.

"What did you do?" she asked as gently as she could.

He shook himself and looked at her almost in shock. Had he forgotten where he was and what he was doing?

"You said you were frustrated and didn't handle it well." She paused. "Winifred," she added to help him along. "What did you do?"

"Right," he said. "Winifred. I killed her."

It took her a few seconds to process his words, but when she did, she realized he said it much too calmly for him to have meant he'd actually killed her. But he carried something around with him that made him withdraw from most of the world.

"You'll have to forgive me, Sir," she said. "You don't strike me as the type of person to commit such a crime."

"I could very easily say you don't know me all that well."

"Perhaps not. But Terrence does and Fulton—I mean, Master Matthews does."

He didn't acknowledge her slip. "I may not have been directly responsible for her death, but I know that if it wasn't for me, she'd be here today."

Why was he telling her this story? It made no sense. Was it supposed to help her in some way? Because if so, she couldn't see how. And what type of response should she give him? She toyed with the edge of the bedsheet.

"I knew something was wrong long before she died, but I didn't do anything about it. I think Winnie knew, too. But it was more convenient to stay together. That's not enough to make a relationship work. It only made us miserable and, in the end, she was killed."

He had left a lot of the story out, though she suspected he'd told her more than he shared with most people. But she still didn't know why.

Lennox looked at the clock across from her bed. "Matthews will be back in a few minutes. I suspect Terrence will be by shortly as well." He stood up. "There are two men out there who care deeply about you. One asked you to marry him and one risked his job. You have a choice to make. Choose wisely and for the right reasons. Don't let a little inconvenience stop you."

And just like that, he walked out of her room, leaving her alone with her thoughts.

A NURSE CAME in to check on her and when the door opened shortly after she left, Andie looked up, expecting Fulton, but found Terrence instead. He looked resigned and she sensed a hint of anger as well.

He didn't say anything until he sat in the chair Lennox had recently vacated. Even then, he didn't touch her.

"I wish you'd have told me," he said.

Tears burned her eyes, but she nodded. "I know. I just . . . didn't know myself."

"You knew enough to turn me down. You could have at least told me why."

"I did. I told you the truth. I was having trouble sorting my feelings out. I didn't know what was real and what wasn't. I didn't know if what I felt was him or just because he was the first to bring out that part of me."

Her throat ached and her lungs burned. It was too hard to talk. She lifted a hand to her throat.

"We can't talk about this right now. Not while you're like this." His eyes searched hers. "Do you want me to stay or go back to Chicago?"

"Stay."

"Okay." He gave her a smile and it reminded her why she was drawn to him. Her eyelids grew heavy. "Get some rest. I'll sit here and keep you company."

She closed her eyes and fell into an uneasy sleep.

She was walking through the woods. They were familiar, but she didn't recall ever being in them before. The trees were so tall, surely she would remember if she'd seen trees that tall before. A light rain was falling and she needed to go home before it became heavier.

There were two houses in the distance, separated by a massive ravine. One of the houses was home, but which one? Something told her she had only one chance to get it right. If she picked the wrong one, she couldn't go back. She hesitated.

Maybe she wouldn't pick at all. The woods weren't that bad. The rain wasn't too heavy. She could stay where she was. If she looked around, she might be able to find a cave or something for shelter.

"You can't do that, you know."

She spun around. A beautiful woman with sad eyes stood behind her. "You have to pick one." The woman pointed to the houses. "The woods aren't for your kind."

"Who are you? And what do you mean, 'my kind'?" Andie asked.

"Those aren't the right questions."

"What are the right questions?"

The woman shook her head. "I can't tell you."

"Then can you tell me which house is home?"

"Yes. That's the question you need to ask. But I can't tell you."

"Then what good are you?"

"No, silly girl. I can't tell you because they're both home."

Andie wrinkled her forehead. It's a dream. You just have to wake up. She turned back to the woods.

"No." The woman appeared before her. "You can't go back that way. You have to go forward."

"No. I don't. This is a dream. I'm in the hospital and they gave me a drug I'm reacting to. You're just a figment of my imagination."

The woman reached over and pinched her arm.

"Ouch." Andie batted her hand away. "Stop. That hurt."

"Just trying to prove it's not just a dream."

"Okay. Fine. I'll pick a house. Since you said it doesn't matter, I'll do eenie meenie miney moe."

"Seriously? Is this how you handle things in your world? No wonder everything's so fucked up."

"You're a very strange figment."

"And you're a very strange girl."

"Why do you say that?"

The woman pointed to the two houses. "Because you can't tell the difference."

"I'm sorry I can't see the difference between home and not home."

"Damn it all, this is not what I signed up for," the woman said, looking up at the sky. She sighed and looked back at Andie. "I told you before: they're both home."

"Then there's no difference."

"Yes, there is. One is a better home."

"*They look the same to me.*"

"*Then stop looking with your eyes.*"

Andie rained tiny slaps on her cheeks. "*Wake up. Wake up. Wake up.*"

The woman shook her head. "*It doesn't work that way. You have to pick before you can wake up. Now stop looking with your eyes and look with your heart. One house is perfect and the other is almost perfect, but not quite. You can be happy with almost perfect, but not quite, but you won't be completely satisfied. What you have to decide is if that's enough. Or will you always wonder?*"

"*This is the strangest dream.*"

"*You think so? You should try living here.*"

"*I did. You said I couldn't.*"

The woman laughed. "*You're a breath of fresh air. He's going to have his hands full with you.*"

"*Who is?*"

"*The man waiting inside for you.*"

Andie looked again at the two houses, and it was faint but there was a difference. Then both front doors opened and a man walked out of each. The one on the left was comfort and safety while the other man was . . . not.

But her choice was made and she took a step in his direction, eager to be in his arms again.

"*I knew it,*" said the woman behind her and there was hint of sadness in her voice. "*Live well, Andie. And live happy.*"

"*I will.*" A thought struck her and she turned back to the woman in the woods. "*What's your name?*"

"*There you go asking the wrong question again.*" She made a shooing motion with her hands. "*Go on now. Off you go.*"

Andie felt so light and happy, she almost giggled as she turned and jogged to the future that was waiting for her.

Andie woke with a start and it took her a few minutes to remember where she was. The hospital. Her dream began to fade away, but she remembered bits and pieces. She remembered being held at the end and a pair of strong lips descending onto hers.

A movement from the corner of the room caught her attention. She looked that way, expecting Fulton, but finding Terrence. Of course it would be Terrence; he had been in the room when she fell asleep. A quick look at the clock told her she hadn't been asleep much longer than an hour.

"Where is everyone?" she asked.

Terrence turned around. "You're awake."

She nodded.

"By everyone, I assume you mean the guys from the academy," he answered.

She winced. He wasn't going to make this easy on her, but then again, she really didn't expect him to. "Yes," she replied. "Fulton and Lennox." She didn't add that she wanted to know because she wanted them to be far away when she said what she was going to say to Terrence.

"They had some things to take care of with the boats and the police." Terrence walked to the chair beside her bed and sat down. "You really made a mess of things when you decided to take off like you did. What were you thinking?"

It had been stupid to take the boat out. And, truth be told, she'd known that at the time. But her need to get away from the academy had overshadowed her common sense.

"It would have been fine if the storm hadn't come up like it did," she said.

"No, it wouldn't have. You would be better and not in the hospital, but the other issues would still be here." He looked like he'd aged since the last time she saw him. There were bags under his eyes.

"I was going to call you when I got to Portland," she said.

"And what were you going to tell me?"

She took a deep breath. She could do this, and it was better to do it in person anyway. "I was going to tell you that I quit the academy."

"Lennox didn't say anything about you quitting. Why would you quit?"

"Because I can't afford it on my own and it's not fair for me to ask you to pay for tuition when I'm not sure about us anymore."

She saw the hurt in his eyes and she hated that she'd put it there. It had to be done, though, and it was much kinder to tell him the truth than to leave him hanging.

"When did you start having questions about us?" he asked.

"After about two weeks, if I'm being honest."

His eyes widened at the shock of her statement and she knew what he was thinking. She'd had doubts the night he proposed, and while she had told him the partial truth, she hadn't told him the whole.

"I didn't lie to you. I was still trying to sort everything out."

"Is everything sorted now?" he asked.

"It's becoming more clear." She couldn't keep the tears from falling as she spoke.

"Yes, I suppose it is." He took her hand, and turned it over in his palm. "This is where I'm supposed to gracefully bow out. When I tell you that I'm happy for you and I only want what's best. But, Andie, I can't. I don't want you to be with someone else. I want you to be with me."

There was a part of her that agreed with him. The part that didn't want to give him up. He'd been such an important part of her life for so long and she wasn't ready for that to change. But it would. As soon as he walked out the door.

It would have been easy for him to stay. All she would have to do is tell him she was wrong and she wanted him. He would forgive her and they would move on the way they'd planned. Life with Terrence would be almost perfect.

But not quite.

She looked up. Had someone said that out loud? No, it was only Terrence in the room with her. And she knew that easy wasn't what she wanted.

"I have to do this," she said. "I have to see if something's there with him. I can't explain it. I really wish I could."

His smile was sad. "I know. Deep down, I knew as soon as I saw the way you looked at each other." He squeezed her hand. "I'm going to go back to Chicago. I hope you're happy. I do want that for you. And while part of me hates him, if he's the one, he's the one. But if he's not, I'll be here for you."

It was more than she'd expected from him and her heart broke because he was truly a great guy. "Thank you," she whispered.

He stood up and kissed her forehead. "Be sure to tell him that if he breaks your heart, I'm kicking his ass."

After Terrence left, Andie waited with a mixture of excitement and anxiety for Fulton's return. For the first time, she'd be completely free and unattached in his presence. She almost felt giddy, and wondered if it wasn't partially due to the medication they'd given her.

There was a knock on the door about two hours after Terrence left and she was glad to see Fulton was alone. It wasn't that she minded Lennox, but she wanted there to be only two people in the room when she told him about Terrence.

"I see you're awake," Fulton said, pushing the door open.

Was it her imagination or did he look even better than he had mere hours ago?

"It's hard to get restful sleep in here."

"The doctor was outside at the nurses' station. I spoke to him briefly. He said if you're doing this well tomorrow, there should be no reason for you to stay another night."

"That's the best thing I've heard all day."

He crossed the floor to stand by her bed, but didn't sit. "I saw Terrence leave. Is he getting a hotel or something?"

"He's heading back to Chicago." *Ask me why.*

"A movie set waits for no one, I guess."

"He didn't go back because of the movie," she said, and he raised an eyebrow.

"Oh?"

She nodded. "He left because I told him I couldn't be with him. And he figured out that I have feelings for you."

He grimaced. "I bet that didn't go over too well."

"No," she admitted. "But it's okay—it had to be done. And the best part is now none of those reasons we couldn't be together in Portland apply anymore. I'm going to quit."

He smiled, but she couldn't help noticing that his eyes weren't. He was hiding something.

"What?" she asked.

"I didn't say anything," he said.

"No, you don't have to. Your expression says it all. What aren't you telling me?"

"Nothing concrete, I promise. Just a premonition."

He wasn't looking her in the eyes when he talked. Something was going on. She frowned and picked at the edge of the sheet covering her. "Will you tell me what it is?"

"No," he said, without putting much thought into the question. "What if I'm wrong? I think you've been through a lot today and I'm not going to put any additional burden on you at the moment. You need to rest."

He spoke it as if to say, *That's that.* Like she would blindly obey what he told her to do. Well, he could think again. He wasn't her instructor anymore and they sure as hell weren't in the playroom.

"Where's Lennox?" she asked.

"Checking in with the school. He'll be here in a few."

Andie tried to hide her disappointment. It looked as if Lennox was going to be here after all. Sure enough, not two seconds after Fulton spoke, Lennox knocked on the frame of the open door to her room.

She gave him a halfhearted "Come in."

"How are you feeling?" he asked as he walked inside.

"Better." She wondered if Terrence had told him he was leaving.

"Good," he said. "I have a few things I'd like to discuss with you."

Fulton turned to head to the door.

"With both of you, Master Matthews." He pointed to the chair. "Have a seat."

Fulton looked as if he'd rather be anywhere other than in the hospital room with her and Lennox. She wondered if the coming conversation was related to the premonition he'd admitted to having.

"Andie," Lennox started. "I got a text from Terrence telling me, among other things, that he was going back to Chicago."

"Yes, Sir."

"Where do you plan to go after you're released from the hospital tomorrow?"

This was what he wanted to discuss? Really?

"Andie?" Lennox asked again.

"I hadn't thought about it." Damn it, originally when she'd left the academy, she'd planned to get a hotel room in the city. "I guess I'll get a hotel room."

"I don't believe that will go over well with your doctors," Lennox said. "I don't think they're going to want you to be by yourself."

Shit. That put a kink in her plans. She worked her brain, trying to see if there was anyone in the area she knew of who could either stay with her or had a place she could crash at.

"That's an awful lot of thinking going on," Lennox said.

"Give me a minute. I'll think of someone." And she would, because the other option was to go home and she wasn't doing that.

"I believe I may have a solution," Lennox said.

"I'm willing to listen to it," she told him. "Because my other option is probably to head back to the East Coast and I'd rather not."

"Would you like to finish the summer at the academy?" he asked. Even Fulton, who had appeared to only be half listening to the conversation around him, sat up.

"I don't have the funds." She shook her head. "I thought I'd explained that."

"Outside of the money issue," Lennox added. "Would you like to finish the summer program?"

"Yes." She didn't even have to think about it. "I would."

"Then I have what I hope is a mutually beneficial proposition."

"Tell me."

"Ms. Claremont came to me yesterday and submitted her resignation. Apparently, her oldest is expecting and is due next month. She's moving to Texas to be near her family. I'm thrilled for her, but it leaves a vacancy in my kitchen."

Andie held her breath. He couldn't possibly be thinking . . . Was he going to . . . ?

"I would like to offer the position to you, Andie," Lennox continued. "It comes with room and board and, since you'd be helping me out big-time, you can finish your training, tuition free."

She couldn't believe her ears. All her problems solved. Just like that. Plus, she got a job she'd love and she could continue at the academy. It sounded too good to be true.

"Wow," Andie said still in awe. "That is an amazing offer. It's beyond anything I ever thought possible. Thank you."

"Will you take it?" Lennox asked.

Andie looked at Fulton, trying to catch some sort of expression that would tell her how he felt about the position she'd just been offered. Unfortunately, his face was entirely neutral. Wasn't he happy? This would mean she wasn't a student. Not entirely. She would also be on staff. Surely that would mean that there would be no problem with them having any sort of relationship.

"How long is the position good for?" At Lennox's confused expression she explained further. "Would I only be able to be the chef while I'm in training this summer? Or would you expect the position to continue beyond that?"

Lennox nodded. "I see. You're concerned about the time and the possible limitations. Are you looking for something more permanent? Or do you just want something for the summer?"

She thought about the position waiting for her at the restaurant in Seattle and then she looked at Fulton. "I have a position waiting for me in Seattle this fall."

Lennox thought for a second. "How about this: you work through the summer, or what's left of it, finish your training, and we will reassess in August? If you enjoy the work in the environment, we can look into making it more permanent. But if you don't, you can leave, no hurt feelings, and I'll write you a letter of recommendation."

Andie knew that a letter of recommendation from him would get her into just about any restaurant she wanted. He was a very successful man in the non-kink world as well. She smiled and held out her hand. "It's a deal."

Fulton was still quiet. That was odd, she thought. Why hadn't he said anything? Did he not want her working at the academy?

"What else is there?" Fulton finally asked. "What aren't you telling us?"

Lennox's lips tightened into a thin line. "I didn't want to do this here."

Do what? Andie wondered. What did both men know that they weren't sharing with her?

"Might as well go ahead and do it," Fulton said.

"You're suspended without pay for the rest of the summer," Lennox said. "There will be a meeting of the board later to determine your future at the academy."

"What?" Andie asked. Surely she had heard wrong. She had to have. There was no way they could suspend Fulton. "But why?"

"I think you know why," Fulton said. "I can't imagine it's allowed anywhere for a teacher to be involved with a student."

"But we didn't do anything. Ever."

"It doesn't matter," Fulton said. "The intent was there. On multiple occasions, I might add."

"It's because we believe you didn't do anything that this is only a suspension at this point and not something more permanent." Lennox now looked exactly like the headmaster he was. The calm, easygoing gentleman that she had been speaking to for the last few hours had been replaced by a cold, ruthless businessman. She didn't like him.

"That's ridiculous," Andie said. "If nothing happened, there shouldn't be any kind of ramifications. I mean, even if we had done something, we're both adults."

"This is one of the reasons I didn't want to do this here. Andie, you don't need to get upset. You need to rest. The bottom line is, there are rules in place for a reason. Over the summer, those rules were pushed, if not outright broken."

"I understand," Fulton said.

Andie crossed her arms. "I don't."

Would he even still be on campus? If she didn't see him, did she still want to take the position?

"The lighthouse needs a tenant," Lennox said to Fulton. "If you would like, you can move in there until everything's determined."

"What happened to the person who was staying there?" Andie asked.

"It was Ms. Claremont."

Andie felt better. If Fulton moved into the lighthouse, at least he'd be near campus. Funny how the chef quitting could open up opportunities for both her and Fulton.

"No one else wants it?" Fulton asked.

"I had a few people who were interested in it, but I think you're the best candidate. We talked about it once before and you indicated you would like to live there if the opportunity ever came up."

"Yes," Fulton said. "I'll move in as soon as possible. And you won't see me until the fall semester."

"Very good." Lennox stood up. "Now I believe we should go. Andie needs to sleep—she had a very trying day."

Andie felt as if she had slept all day anyway. She didn't want Fulton to leave. She wanted to talk to him, to see how he felt about things. To see if they had a future. But the medication they'd given her made her tired, and as she drifted off to sleep, she decided it would be best to wait. After all, she knew where Fulton would be. And he would have plenty of time to talk to her.

ANDIE WAS DISCHARGED the next morning, with strict instructions to rest for at least three days. And she had to come back for a checkup in a week. It was also strongly suggested that she keep a rescue inhaler on her person at all times. She agreed without arguing. The incident on the boat had been an eye-opener and she didn't ever want to experience anything like it again.

Fulton wasn't there to take her back to the academy. Lennox took care of everything. She thought about asking him where Fulton was, but decided against it. From the conversation the night before, she got the impression things would be more difficult for Fulton if they were involved with each other.

No, for now she would bide her time and take things slow. She planned it all in her head as Lennox drove her to the boat that would take them both back to the academy. She knew the chemistry between her and Fulton was real. And she was pretty sure that he would like to explore it as well.

And, she realized, if Fulton was no longer an acting teacher, there would be no reason for them not to explore that chemistry.

She could hardly wait.

CHAPTER

Fifteen

F ulton didn't wait at the docks when he arrived back at the
academy. Lennox would be arriving with Andie within the hour
and he wanted to be out of everybody's way when that happened.

He walked down to the lighthouse. There wasn't a key to the
house; rather, Lennox had installed a touchpad. While he liked
the idea that anybody could access the lighthouse in case of emer-
gency, he didn't want just anybody to walk in on his living space.
He would have to see about getting the locks updated to something
more private.

He let himself inside and noted that Ms. Claremont had already
packed up most of her belongings and only a few boxes were left.
It wasn't raining, so he opened up some of the windows, hoping to
alleviate the musty smell that permeated the entire house.

It was a small house, but tidy. The furnishings looked comfortable, if somewhat dated. He could see himself here. A few

touches to make it his and it'd be perfect. He planned where he'd put the woodcarvings his grandfather had made.

He'd have to go get his things before too long, but for the moment he just wanted to be outside, near the sea. Of course, seeing the ocean again brought back memories of Andie and how close he'd come to losing her. When he'd heard that she left Terrence, he'd been elated. Though he knew by the end of the summer he could be let go permanently, he couldn't help but imagine spending more time with her.

He shouldn't want to. The woman had almost gotten him fired. She still might get him fired. But he wanted her and if she wanted him . . . ? Well, he couldn't help but think it wasn't just a coincidence that Lennox was moving him into a space removed from the prying eyes and curious minds at the main building.

He wondered if she'd come to the lighthouse. And if so, how long it'd take her. Since he was on suspension, he wasn't supposed to be near the main building too much. If she didn't come, though . . .

He'd cross that bridge when he got there.

As it turned out, he didn't have to wait long at all. In fact, it was a mere few hours after he arrived that someone knocked on the door to the lighthouse. He lifted the delicate lace curtain, making a mental note that he needed to replace them, and saw Andie standing at the entranceway, carrying a huge box.

Damn it. She shouldn't be doing that.

He jerked the door open and took the box from her arms. "What are you thinking? You shouldn't be carrying things. You just got out of the hospital." The box was ridiculously light. He peered inside. "Why are you carrying an empty box?"

She was completely unaffected by his outburst. "And a good afternoon to you as well, Master Matthews."

"Tell me you at least have your rescue inhaler with you," he said, ignoring her snark for the moment.

"In my pocket." She patted her front pocket.

"Aren't you supposed to be resting?"

"I tried, but everyone kept coming into my room and when Maggie stopped letting them in, they still knocked." She looked around the lighthouse. "I thought maybe things would be quieter here, but I didn't want anyone to be suspicious, so I brought the box. I figured if they thought I was bringing something to you, they'd leave us alone."

She looked up at him with the biggest blue eyes he'd ever seen and he didn't have the heart to tell her no. The fact that they should go slow and not do anything to arouse suspicion danced on his tongue. But she was already here. What would it say about him if he sent her back?

He glanced behind her. The sky was getting darker and it looked like they were going to get more rain. He smiled and pushed the door to let her inside. That solved that. There was no way he was sending her back outside in the rain.

"You can stay here for a bit, on the couch. As long as you can ignore the old lady smell, that is." He waved her toward the living room.

"This is such a cute little house." It was obvious she wanted a tour, but all he needed was for her to have a relapse under his watch.

"I'll give you the grand tour after you rest for thirty minutes."

"Deal." She went and sat down on the couch. But instead of lying down, she picked up a lace doily. "I never pictured you as the lace type."

He snorted. "I haven't really had a chance to make the space my own yet."

"I think you should keep the lace."

"And now I know who won't be helping me decorate."

She stuck her tongue out at him. He tried not to think about what he really wanted her to do with that tongue.

"Rest," he said and made himself walk into the kitchen so he wouldn't be tempted to do anything to keep her from doing so. In fact, he told himself, for the next half hour, he was going to make a list of things he needed to do around the house. And he'd write it in the kitchen. Far enough away so he couldn't touch her, but close enough so he could see her.

She made herself comfortable while he pretended not to watch. Though he couldn't hold back laughing when she sneezed.

"I must be allergic to old lady," she said. "Seriously, do they sell that scent?"

The smell actually reminded him of his grandmother and home-made cookies and sitting with his grandfather. They'd be on the porch and he'd have a snack while watching his grandfather work a piece of wood with his knife.

He opened his mouth to tell Andie, but when he looked her way, she was curled up on her side, sleeping. Obviously, she was more tired than she'd let on. As the first few drops of rain fell, he knew she was where she needed to be.

She slept for over two hours and he would hesitate to mention to anybody how much of that time he stood watching her. She woke up slowly, stretching slightly as she did so, looking this way and that as if trying to remember where she was.

She spotted him watching and he gave her a smile.

"I see you decided to wake up finally," he said.

"What time is it?"

"You slept for about two hours. No one's come looking for you, but you probably have the rain to thank for that."

In fact it was still raining rather hard. He was starting to feel just a little bit uneasy about her being here. What if the rain didn't slack off? Would she have to stay in the house all night? That would not go over well with Lennox. No, he decided, if the rain kept up, he would find some way to get her back to the academy.

"Looks like we should build an ark," she said.

He laughed in spite of himself. "That might not be a bad idea. Either that or grow fins and gills."

"I think I'll pass on the fins and gills."

"You don't want to be a mermaid?" he teased. "I thought that was every little girl's dream."

"I'm pretty sure every girl's dream is to be a princess. Not a mermaid. At least not this girl." She sat up, unable to hide the wince as she did so.

Fulton stood up immediately. "Are you okay? Is something wrong?"

"I'm still just a little sore from everything," she said. "Nothing major."

"Would you like some aspirin or something?" It was then he realized he wasn't in his normal space and he didn't know if Ms

Claremont kept anything like aspirin in her medicine cabinet. And if she did, she might have taken it with her already. Dammit.

"No," she said. "I think I'll be okay without anything. I just need to stretch. Thanks for letting me crash here. That nap felt like heaven."

She stood up gingerly, slowly stretching and working her muscles. He wasn't even able to pretend not to watch. She was stunning and the way she moved was hypnotic. He was utterly mesmerized.

This was insanity. She was *stretching,* for fuck's sake. He shook himself and turned his attention to the half-finished list he'd been working on. He was going to have to make another trip to Portland. Typically he enjoyed getting away to the city, but somehow he knew it wouldn't be the same without Andie with him.

She let out a sexy moan as she finished up, and he gripped the pen in his hand so tightly that it almost split. *Jesus.*

Andie didn't seem to have any idea of what her actions were doing to him. She strolled over to him. "Since it's still raining, can I take you up on that tour?"

"Sure." It wasn't like he was getting anything done with the list he had been working on anyway. "Let's see, you've seen the living room. This is the kitchen."

He took a step back so she could pass him and enter the small area.

"Probably a bit too quaint for a chef." He tried to imagine the space from her viewpoint. Very little counter space, only a few cabinets, and an avocado-colored refrigerator and oven that looked like they had come out of a catalog. From 1973.

Andie spun around slowly. "It needs some updating, true, but it has good bones."

"Really? How so?" He wasn't sure why he ca[...]
been into renovating anything, but for some reason[...]
see what Andie's vision of the kitchen looked like.

"For starters, I'd do away with the half wall betwee[...]
area and the kitchen. Make it all one big flowing space, yo[...]w?
Whenever people come over, they always hang out in the kitchen.
Might as well make it inviting."

She continued, pointing out where she'd add a window and
possible ways to extend the countertop. He barely listened, honestly.
Instead, he allowed himself to get caught up in her joyful manner.

Fuck, she was sexy as hell, standing in his kitchen, suggesting
things to improve it.

Suddenly, she stopped talking and put her hand on her hip.
"Are you even listening to me?" she asked.

And he was caught. He decided to be honest. "Yes" he said,
but shook his head as if saying no.

She tilted her head. "What kind of an answer is that?"

"An honest one."

"How is it honest when it's contradictory?"

He took a step closer to her, for all intents and purposes cor-
nering her in the kitchen. "No, I wasn't listening to your words.
But yes, I was listening to you."

She chewed her bottom lip. "That doesn't make sense."

"Then let me show you." He reached out and lightly stroked
her cheek. "I was listening to your body. The way your hips sway
as you walk from one side of the room to the other." His fingers
brushed her hips. "And I was thinking that would be almost the
exact way they'd move if I had you on your back, fucking you, with
your legs wrapped around my waist."

She flushed a lovely shade of pink.

"And I watched your mouth move as you talked and every so often you'd lick your lips." He ran his thumb over her bottom lip, biting back a moan as she licked it and drew the tip of it into her mouth. "I imagined you doing something like that, but not with my thumb. With my cock."

Her eyes grew dark with desire and she tried sucking his thumb in deeper. He held it just outside, though, only letting her take the tip.

"Not right now, not today, probably not even this week, but one day soon." He leaned in and nibbled on her earlobe. "One day soon, you'll have my cock in your mouth and I'll have you on your back. I promise you."

She surprised him by lifting her arms and wrapping them around his neck. "Kiss me." She shivered in his arms as his lips and teeth found a sensitive spot. "Please."

How could he deny her a kiss? He pulled back and brushed his lips against hers in the lightest way possible. She groaned in frustration and fisted his shirt in her hands, trying to pull him closer.

"Oh no, Andie," he said. "You don't call the shots here."

He took her wrists and held them to her side. Her eyes flashed with frustration and he couldn't help it—he smiled.

"Patience," he said.

She huffed. "I'm tired of being patient. I'm always patient."

"Really?" He took a step back and crossed his arms. "Were you being patient when you took a boat out on the water and got caught in a storm?"

"That's the one time I wasn't patient."

"It was a doozy of a way to make your start." He dug his fingers in her hair and pulled them through the long strands. "Believe me, I want this as badly as you do. But you were in the hospital today and you just took a two-hour nap on my couch. I want you to be completely well and healthy."

She couldn't argue with anything he said and she knew it, he could tell from her expression. "Fine," she said. "But that doesn't mean I like it."

He was getting ready to say something when his phone rang. He looked at the display and frowned. Lennox.

"Hello, boss," he said, keeping his eyes on Andie.

"Matthews," the headmaster sounded winded. "Tell me Andie's with you. No one can find her. Apparently, the last time anyone saw her was hours ago."

"She's here," he got out and before he could say anything else, Lennox jumped in.

"Thank goodness. But I have to be honest: her being there with you probably isn't going to look good to the disciplinary board."

As his boss talked, he took in Andie's thin frame and the shadows under her eyes that the nap hadn't quite removed. And the more Lennox talked, the angrier Fulton become.

"Just a minute," he finally interrupted. "Let me set a few things straight. Andie came over here to rest because people kept coming to her room and she couldn't sleep. So yeah, I get that it looks bad, but I didn't want her to overexert herself. And I'll have you know, she's been asleep for the last two hours and has only now woken up. I was going to get her to the main building after the rain slacked off and she had a snack."

He paused to take a breath and waited for Lennox to say something, fully expecting him to say he was fired.

"I'm sorry, Matthews," Lennox said, instead. "You're right. I should have done more to ensure she wasn't disturbed this afternoon, and of course you did the right thing in letting her stay."

"No need to apologize. I'd just like to think you know me better than to think I'd take advantage of someone who's recently been released from the hospital."

Andie had been listening to his side of the conversation. She stuck her tongue out at the statement he made about taking advantage of her. He wished he wasn't on the phone with his boss because he'd love to give her ass a good swat.

"Of course I don't think that," Lennox said. "How is she? Do I need to come get her?"

"If you want to lay eyes on her to convince yourself she's okay, yes, you can come get her and take her back. Or you can wait for it to stop raining quite so hard and I'll take her back." He resisted the urge to roll his eyes at Lennox. It would be disrespectful of him and he wouldn't do that, especially in front of Andie. Plus, he knew at the heart of the matter, Lennox was only concerned about Andie.

Which probably meant he should keep his hands and all other body parts away from her until after she graduated. But he didn't want to wait that long. Hell, she'd broken up with Golden Boy partially to be with him. But the fact remained, he was going to be living under a microscope for the remainder of the summer and as such, he needed to walk the straight and narrow.

He ended the conversation with Lennox and turned to face Andie. His expression must have told her everything, because her sexy and playful look had been replaced by resignation.

"I'm sorry," he said. It was the only thing he could think of to say, and he knew it wasn't enough.

"We're not going to happen, are we?" Her lower lip trembled.

"We are," he tried to assure her. "We will. Just not before you graduate."

She nodded, but a lone tear snaked its way down her cheek. He wanted nothing more than to pull her into his arms, hold her tight, and tell her everything was going to be okay. He sighed, knowing he couldn't. If he took her in his arms now, he wouldn't let go.

"I really fucked everything up," she said.

"No, but we need to play it cool for a little while," he replied, but he knew he'd hesitated a moment too long before saying it. She turned away from him. "Andie?"

She shook her head. "I think the rain's lightened now. I can walk back."

"Damn it," he said. "You're not walking back."

"I'm fine."

"Look," he said, trying not to let his irritation show. "I'm already in enough trouble. Lennox would have my ass, and rightfully so, if I let you walk back. There's a golf cart in the storage building outside. Let me get that and I'll drive you back."

She held back. "I want to see the lighthouse."

"You mean the top?"

"Yes."

It'd been a long time since he'd been up there. He assumed it was safe, but there was no way he'd go up with her unless he was certain. Even if it was safe, she wasn't in any shape to walk up all those stairs.

"Another time."

"But—"

He lifted an eyebrow and she sighed.

"Yes, Sir."

HOURS LATER, FULTON sat on the back deck of the lighthouse, looking over the ocean and wondering if he had the strength to do what needed to be done.

Earlier in the evening, after he'd driven Andie back to the school, he'd stopped by his office to pick up some papers and fill a box with the contents of his desk drawers. He'd been needing to weed through the material for some time. Since he didn't have anything else to do at the lighthouse, he decided that now was as good of a time as any to deal with all the papers he had.

He'd been making some relatively good progress through the papers at home, especially with everything scattered on top of his kitchen table, when he saw it. The letter he had never gotten around to throwing away. From Phoebe, his last attempt at a long-term relationship.

He reread the letter a couple times and as he did, all the memories came back. All the reasons why he had sworn that he'd never try the relationship thing again. They always left. Always. Andie would too eventually. And where would that leave him?

Alone. Unemployed. Basically about as miserable as he could imagine.

The call from Lennox should have been a wakeup call. From here on out, he would always be known as the teacher who had an affair with a student. It wouldn't matter that she wasn't anymore. She had been and that was enough to condemn him in a lot of people's eyes.

Which was why he was going to do what he now knew had to be done. He'd thought through every possible outcome. Every possible way not to move forward with what he had planned.

Even though he knew he had no other choice, he still hesitated. He was going to hurt Andie and he didn't want to. He knew she wouldn't understand. At least now, maybe with time she would see he had to do this to ensure they both had a future, even it wasn't together.

He wasn't going to go find her, though. If he knew her, and he thought he did, it would only be a matter of days before she returned to the lighthouse. He only had to be patient.

He told himself he wasn't a coward for not seeking her out, but he wasn't sure he believed that. The reality was, he hoped that by the time she came to see him, he would have changed his mind.

But a week later, he spied her coming his way and he knew his time was up. Today was the day he ended things with her. For good this time.

She was all smiles when he opened the door to her knock. She was so beautiful and happy. But he held firm. This had to be done.

She must have picked up on his mood and her smile fell. "Is this a bad time? I can come back."

He held the door open for her. "No, come on in. There are a few things I wanted to talk to you about."

"Sounds serious," she said, walking into the living room.

He wanted so badly to sit down with her and just talk the afternoon away. Ask about how her classes were going. If she was learning anything new. If she'd started in the kitchen yet. He couldn't though. Not with what he was getting ready to do.

He took a seat across from her. "It's not a good idea for you to be over here."

She was smart enough to know something was up. "I miss you. You don't come to the main building."

"I've been suspended. I'm not supposed to be there."

"I'm sure it would be fine for you to stop by for just a minute to say hi." She looked around the room. "What do you do all day here by yourself anyway?"

"Lennox gives me plenty to do. And no, it's not a good idea for me to drop by just to say hi."

"Because they haven't made a decision on your suspension yet?"

He nodded. "Among other things."

"When will they decide?"

He remembered the call he'd had with Lennox earlier in the week. The decision he'd told his boss he'd made. The headmaster repeatedly asking him if he was sure this was the way he wanted things to be.

"Officially after the summer session ends."

She wrinkled her nose. "Officially? What does that mean?"

"It means the official decision won't be released until after the summer session is over."

"So, *unofficially?*"

"Unofficially, I'll be reinstated for the fall term." She gasped in excitement at his words, but before she could become too excited, he added, "Conditionally."

Her smile dimmed a bit. "What's the condition?"

He took a deep breath, hating what he was getting ready to do, but knowing it was for the best. "That I have no romantic involvement with you."

It only took a few seconds for the meaning of his words to completely wipe the smile from her face. "Why would you agree to that?"

"I need this job, Andie."

"I know, but I . . . I thought. . . ."

"We don't even know what we have or if it's going to work out or anything." He could hardly stand to look at her, because he saw how much his words hurt her. "But I know I need a job."

"You're picking your job over me?" It sounded a lot harsher when she said it as opposed to him thinking it.

"It's not like that."

"The hell it's not." She stood up. "I gave up everything for you. Everything. And when things get a little hard, you don't even try. You just give up."

"Everything? How can you stand there and say you gave up everything? You gave up a boyfriend who willingly passed your training off to strangers so he could go make another million dollars."

"How dare you try to make Terrence look bad? At least he . . ."

"At least he what? Fought for you? No, he didn't. He wanted you when it was convenient for him and you know it. Hell, he couldn't even take the time to train the woman he supposedly loved, *just a little,* in his lifestyle. You should thank me for helping you get rid of him before he could suck the life out of you."

"Right, because it's obvious you wanted to be the one to do it. I was worried about being in second place after his job, but I never considered you should be the one to worry about. Tell me, is this some sort of game for you? Getting a student to fall for you? I bet it is. I bet there's an office pool somewhere to see who can get the most submissives."

"You were never a game, Andie." Fuck, how could she think that? Couldn't she see that he had to do this?

She crossed her arms and turned away, but not before he saw a tear slip down her cheek.

Damn it, he'd made her cry. "Andie, don't, don't cry. It's better—"

"I'm not crying because I'm sad, asshole. I'm crying because I'm mad as hell."

"I know it sounds bad now, but after you get some distance you'll see that this is the right thing to do."

"I thought after the talks we had, you wanted to be with me. I thought we were going to try to be together after I graduated." She sniffled. "Were you lying the entire time?"

He thought back to the kiss they'd shared and how good she felt in his arms. Like she was meant for him to hold. How could she think he was lying when he whispered to her how beautiful she was when she came from his touch, even if it'd only been during a class scene?

Maybe it'd be better if she thought it was a lie. It was wrong and it was cruel, but it would accomplish what he wanted it to. But if he did it, there would be no going back.

"Yes," he said, hating himself more with each word he spoke. "I was only saying what I thought you wanted to hear."

She spun back around to face him. She was clearly pissed. "You . . . you . . . I can't think of a word bad enough for you." She stomped to the door and jerked it open. "You disgust me."

He waited until she was gone before he dropped into the chair. The weight of what he'd done, how he'd treated her, felt like two hundred pounds of guilt especially created for him. It hurt to breathe it ached so bad.

He buried his face in his hands. He disgusted himself, too.

CHAPTER

Sixteen

Andie made it back to the main building before her tears started to fall in earnest. She wiped them away and hoped she didn't run into anyone on the way to her room. But as soon as she opened the door, she heard voices and footsteps on the stairs.

Without giving it much thought, she ran down the steps to the class playrooms and entered the first one she found with an open door.

She slumped in a corner, remembering the time she'd waited for Fulton and how he'd spanked her. Then the second time, when it had felt so good and she'd had the most amazing orgasm of her life.

She couldn't believe he'd been lying when he made her play with herself while he watched. She'd felt so awkward, but he'd whispered over and over how beautiful she was until she believed it herself. Had that been a lie? Something he told her because he thought it was what she wanted to hear?

She didn't believe it.

She pulled her knees to her chest, just wanting to be alone and in the dark for a little while longer. For some reason it seemed easier to think here than it did in her room.

Once her emotions were under control, she replayed the conversation she'd had with Fulton just an hour ago. She felt certain he didn't feel the way he said he did. So why would he be untruthful about how he felt for her?

She started to get up, but just as she did, footsteps echoed in the hallway and she sat back down. Damn it. Hopefully whoever it was didn't want to use this room.

A dark figure walked past the door and she recognized the profile of Master MacLure.

Perfect! She'd ask him about Fulton and his *conditional* job. She'd get it straight from the horse's mouth. In the hospital, Lennox hadn't seemed all that against her and Fulton together. Maybe if she relayed the conversation she'd had with Fulton, he'd be shocked enough to talk some sense into him. She rose to her feet again only to freeze completely when she heard a woman call out, "Lennox!"

Damn. Damn. And double damn. It was Mariela. Seeing either one of them individually was one thing, but having them both together was something else entirely. Besides, there was something in the way Mariela said his name that made it seem a lot more intimate than a chance meeting in the hallway. She knew she should get up and announce herself, but she was frozen in place.

"Marie," Lennox said. The grief in his voice caught Andie off guard. Had something happened she hadn't heard about? And why had he called her Marie? She didn't know of anyone who called her that.

"I . . . I thought maybe you shouldn't be alone tonight." Her adviser's voice held a note of grief as well.

"I'm alone most nights. I assure you, I can do this one, too."

"You are the most stubborn, thickheaded man I've ever known. When are you going to come back to the land of the living?"

Lennox laughed, but he didn't sound amused. "Can you blame me for being less than thrilled to spend time with you when you talk to me like that?"

"Treating you with kid gloves doesn't work. Heaven knows everyone else seems to think it will."

"Leave it be," Lennox said.

"I can't leave it be. Not with you continuing to live like this."

There were footsteps as Lennox moved farther down the hall.

"Yeah, walk away." Mariela sounded pissed now. "Just like you always do. You seem to forget that I loved her, too."

Andie's breath hitched. Were they talking about Winifred? How was Mariela involved? And why was the world filled with people who only seemed to be able to hurt each other?

She didn't have any answers. And though she was curious about the issues between Mariela and Lennox, she didn't have the energy to dwell on anyone else's problems at the moment.

IT WAS TWO weeks before graduation and longer than that since Fulton had last seen Andie. He decided to visit the home today in the hopes that it would lighten his spirits. Usually, there was nothing like playing with the kids there to put him in a good mood.

"Didn't work today, did it?" Barbara asked. She was an older woman with graying hair. She had been working at the home when he was there as a resident, and he considered her something of a grandmother.

Even still, he winced at how fast she picked up on his mood. "Am I that easy to see through?" he asked.

"Only to those who know you well." She pointed out to the yard, where several boys were playing ball. "They didn't pick up on anything."

He was glad to hear that. For the last several hours he'd been playing with them, as well as teaching the older ones a little bit about carving wood. It helped to clear his mind, but the truth was nothing was going to completely remove Andie from his thoughts.

"Have to say," Barbara continued, "I don't think I've ever seen you like this. Woman?"

He snorted.

"I'll take that as a yes," she said with a smile.

"I had thought to bring her by one day, but I messed up."

He wasn't sure why, but he told her most of the story—leaving out the parts she didn't need to know. She knew he was a teacher, just not what kind. And he left out Terrence's name. By the time he came to the end, she was nodding.

"Yes," she said. "You fucked that one up. So, the question is, what are you going to do about it?"

He gaped at her in shock. Not because of the language—he'd heard her use such words before. It was the "what are you going to do about it" question that took him off guard.

"I don't think there's anything left for me to do."

"Did I ever tell you how Michael and I met?"

Michael, her late husband, and cofounder of the home. The one Fulton had called Grandpa. "No."

"It was a different time then," she said. "Of course, some things never change. Like love."

"Grandma, I—"

"Don't interrupt me. I'm old and won't be around forever. I might never get a chance again to make sure you don't royally screw up." Her eyes grew misty as she patted his leg. "Does my heart good to know you found someone. You've always been a loner."

He was ready for her to go back to the story of how she met the man she'd marry. That was much more palatable than talking about him.

"As I was saying, when I met Michael, I had plans to write for the newspaper. It wasn't common then for a woman, but I thought if I had a pen name, it wouldn't be an issue. No one would know I didn't have a—"

"Stop." He covered his ears. "Don't say it."

"Degree," she said with a smile and a roll of her eyes. "But something happened on my way to worldwide fame as an award-winning writer. I met Michael. And he turned me upside down and inside out and all those other ways you don't think us old farts know about."

He did not want to hear this.

"I knew after spending time with him that I could have my byline in every newspaper in the world, but without Michael, it would be meaningless. We got married and decided to start our family."

He knew how that went. Two stillborns and a miscarriage made it very clear that Barbara and Michael weren't meant to have children. At least not biological ones. They took their pain and grief and used it to make something beautiful.

She leaned back and looked over the expanse of yard, smiling at the sound of the boys, her boys, playing. "I have more time behind me than before me and I can see all the mistakes I made. But the one thing I did right, if I got everything else wrong, was when love found me, I grabbed onto it with both hands and refused to let go. I wouldn't let it leave me."

But he had. He dropped his head.

"So, I ask you again." She took his hand. "What are you going to do about it?"

CHAPTER
Seventeen

The night of the ball, Andie's last official night of her training, she dressed carefully in the white gown she'd picked out. It was linen and had a flounced skirt, much like the one she'd worn in Portland when she danced with Fulton. She ran her hands down the front, telling herself she wasn't going to think about that or him.

Maggie was getting ready with her and while her roommate's nonstop chatter drove her batty, she knew this was the last time she'd hear it. Maggie was going home tomorrow and Andie would have to decide if she wanted to continue on as the academy's chef or if she wanted to move to Seattle.

The last few weeks she'd loved working in the kitchen. The staff was friendly and she enjoyed the interaction with students. The energy of the academy was amazing. Everyone was excited about both the graduation of the current students as well as the new class that would be arriving in a few weeks.

But when the new class arrived, someone else would as well, and Andie wasn't sure she could handle working around Fulton.

His absence was painful, but she thought his presence might be worse. She'd debated for days the pros and cons of staying, and she still had no clear direction. Maybe after the current students left and everything calmed down a bit she'd be able to decide.

"Andie," Maggie said once Andie had the gown on. "You look incredible."

Andie brushed her hands over the smooth, silky fabric. "Thanks." The gown had been a bit pricey, but she loved the way it looked and felt. Not to mention that the way the full skirt swayed would be perfect for swing dancing. Not that she would be swing-dancing, not without *him*, but still.

"Ready to go?" Maggie asked.

"Might as well." Andie checked her makeup one last time in the mirror and smoothed down her hair. Tonight, collared or otherwise, attached submissives would wear their hair up. Those who were single would wear it down.

If she were still with Terrence, he'd be here and her hair would be up. Maybe he'd have offered her his ring again. Thinking about Terrence, though, didn't hurt. She knew she'd made the right choice to break things off with him.

There was only one man whose memory hurt and she wasn't going to think of him tonight. Tonight, she was going to put on a smile and have a good time. *He* wouldn't be at the ball, and she planned on dancing with all the graduating Doms as well as the male staff members, so she wouldn't have time to miss him.

She wondered what he was doing tonight.

"Come on," Maggie said from the doorway. "You look fantastic."

Andie thought she looked passable, but it'd have to do. She plastered a smile on her face and said, "Let's go."

From the ballroom's entranceway it appeared as if they were among the last to arrive. The room was packed with students and faculty members, as well as friends of the staff who were in the lifestyle. Though she knew Fulton wouldn't be there, Andie glanced around the room to see if he'd shown up.

"Miss Lincoln," David Nader said. "You look beautiful."

With Fulton on suspension, Master Nader had taken over the majority of her training. He was nice and rather good-looking, but he didn't teach like Fulton did, and she often found her mind wandering during class. Not to mention that when he touched her during a physical scene, she didn't feel anything. In fact, it felt so clinical she wondered if she'd just lost interest in sex.

"Thank you, Master Nader," Andie replied.

"Perhaps later you and I can go for a spin around the room."

"I'd love to." She suddenly wished Fulton had shown up at the ball, just so he'd be jealous. She still didn't believe the things he'd said to her that day in the lighthouse. There was no way he could have meant them.

David bowed and said he'd catch back up with her later. She watched him disappear into the crowd, then turned back to Maggie.

"I wonder if Master MacLure will dance?" Maggie asked. The man in question was devastatingly good-looking in what appeared to be a custom-made suit.

Maggie took a bacon-wrapped scallop from a passing tray. The academy had hired a catering company for the evening, since Andie would be too busy attending the ball as a graduating student to perform as a chef. She was grateful because, in doing so, they took away her ability to go off and sulk. In fact, it almost made it impossible for her to do anything other than dance.

"I don't think Master MacLure dances," Andie answered.

"I don't think he does much of anything," Maggie said.

Andie looked over at the bar, where the headmaster stood. Every so often he'd risk a quick glance across the room in Mariela's direction.

"I think there's more to the man than he lets us see," Andie said, remembering the night she had overheard him and Mariela.

Maggie raised an eyebrow, suddenly acutely interested in what Andie was saying. "Do you have the inside scoop on Master MacLure?"

It would have been so easy to gossip, to tell Maggie what he'd shared in the hospital and what she'd overheard downstairs. She'd finally have someone to talk with about it. But her conscience wouldn't let her. It wasn't that he was her boss; it went much deeper than that. She knew for a fact that he rarely shared personal information with anyone, yet he'd shared with her, and even though he didn't ask her to keep their talk confidential, she felt like she should.

"No," she said. "I just believe it's true of most people. Don't you?"

Maggie didn't appear to be so sure Andie didn't have dirt on the headmaster. "I guess so."

Fortunately, Andie was spared from any further questions by one of the student Doms—Maggie's partner, actually.

"Hello, ladies," he said. Andie couldn't help but notice that even though he included her in the greeting, he only had eyes for Maggie.

"How are you, Sir?" Maggie asked, adding the "Sir" for the first time since he'd recently completed training.

"I'd be doing better if you'd join me in a dance," he said.

Maggie's only response was "Bye, Andie" before she went off to the dance floor.

Andie walked slowly around the room, enjoying being part of the overall energy of people gathered in the ballroom. Several students had paired up with one another, including one recent Dom graduate who'd found the nerve to ask Mariela to dance.

Andie checked again for Fulton, but he was nowhere to be found. The ache in her heart made her admit that deep inside, she'd hoped he'd attend tonight.

"Who's that with Master Nader?" a woman standing to her left asked the man she was with.

"I've never seen her before. Must just be a date."

A date. Andie shivered at the thought of one day seeing Fulton with a date. It was bound to happen if she stayed. She swallowed the cry that threatened to escape as she tried to picture him entering the ballroom with a date at his side. She couldn't do it. Wouldn't be able to bear it.

She was going to have to turn down the chef position. She looked toward the bar. Lennox was still there. She took a step in his direction, and as soon as she did, she realized she didn't want to tell him her decision tonight. For one more night, she'd enjoy this place, this setting, without the burden of numerous good-byes hanging over her.

Her rumbling stomach reminded her it'd been much too long since lunch. There weren't very many people at the food tables. Now would be the perfect time to snag a bite or two to eat.

As she made her way to the buffet, someone tapped her on the shoulder. She turned around to find Lennox looking down at her.

"Miss Lincoln."

"Master MacLure."

"I was hoping I could talk you into a dance," he said, holding out his hand.

Andie hesitated only a minute. Why shouldn't she dance with him? Sure he was her boss, but he was also a very good-looking man. She looked around the room, trying to find Mariela. Not seeing her, she placed her hand in his.

"I would love to dance with you, Sir."

He led her to the dance floor and slipped one arm around her waist, holding her hand with the other. The song was relatively slow, which gave them a chance to talk. Andie was pleased he didn't ask about the job or her decision, one way or the other.

"A lot of people here tonight," Andie said. "Is it always like this?"

"Typically, yes." As he spun her around she saw both Maggie and Mariela watching. "It's a very popular event."

He went on to talk about previous years, but Andie's attention was on the crowd around them. Everybody seemed to be looking at them.

"Excuse me, Sir," she said, when he stopped talking for a minute.

"Yes?"

"Why is everyone looking at us?"

He looked over her shoulder. "You'll see."

Right as he spoke, there came another tap on her shoulder.

"Andie?"

It sounded like . . . but it couldn't be. She wanted more than anything for it to be Fulton.

Please. Please. Please.

She turned her head and staring back at her were the eyes that had haunted her dreams and fantasies for the last few weeks.

He had come.

"Excuse me, boss, but I'm cutting in."

Lennox didn't act the least bit surprised. In fact, it was almost as if he'd been expecting Fulton to show up.

Which seemed even more likely when Lennox replied, "Took you long enough," and stepped aside, turning her over to Fulton.

It felt odd to be in Fulton's arms again. And she was suddenly very much aware of all the eyes on her.

"What do you want?" she asked, unable to keep the bitterness out of her voice. "Did you think if you came up to me here that I wouldn't make a scene in front of all these people?"

"I'll admit the thought did cross my mind."

"I wish you hadn't interrupted Lennox and me. I was just getting ready to tell Master MacLure that I'll be stepping down as chef. I'll work for the next few weeks, but after that, no more. I'm moving to Seattle, or maybe Portland. Probably Seattle." She couldn't think of Portland without thinking of *him*.

"Why?" Fulton asked. "Why would you do that?"

"What reason do I have to stay?" She waited for him to give the answer she wanted. The answer she needed. The one answer that would make her change her mind.

But he was silent and she'd had enough. She dropped his hand and pulled away. "That's why."

"Andie," he called, but she was already off the dance floor and headed for the door.

Hot tears burned her eyes, but she wouldn't let them fall. Not here. Not with everyone watching like they were in a freak show. Leaving the ballroom behind, she headed outside. She needed air.

She walked until she came to the dock and boathouse. It had rained earlier in the evening and a fine fog had settled, casting shadows everywhere. It was particularly breathtaking with the faint light of the moon falling across the water.

"Andie, wait!" Fulton wasn't far behind her.

"Are you sure you want me to? I mean, someone might see us and report back to Lennox. I'd hate to be responsible for you losing your job the second time."

"I don't fucking care about the job."

"Really?" She crossed her arms. "Because it sure was important when I got out of the hospital."

"I was wrong."

"Too late." She tried to sound cool and indifferent. "I told you, I'm moving to Seattle."

"That's fine," he said. "Move to Seattle or Portland or even New York, but hear me out first."

"Why?" she asked him, growing more and more angry with each passing second. "Tell me why I should listen to you when you walked away from me and told me everything you said was a lie. That you'd only told me what I wanted to hear. Give me one reason why I should waste any more of my time listening to anything you have to say."

"Because I love you." The moon gave just enough light for her to see his face and the sincerity of his words.

The wall she'd built around her heart when he'd left threatened to crumble to dust, but she held firm. Clenching her fists, she forced the words out. "If that's the case, I'd hate to see how cruel you are to people you dislike."

He looked as though she'd hit him in the chest, and she hated that she'd hurt him, but damn it, he'd hurt her first.

"I deserved that," he said.

She crossed her arms and lifted her eyebrow. *Tell me something I didn't already know.*

"You have every right to be angry and pissed," he continued. "And if you want nothing to do with me after we talk, I promise I won't stop you. I'll let you walk away and you won't have to see me again. Just please." He took a step closer to her. "Give me twenty minutes."

She sighed. What the hell? She could hear him out. She knew it wouldn't do any good, but after she listened, she could walk away and, even though thinking about it was painful, that would be that. No more Fulton. "You have ten," she threw back.

"Ten isn't enough."

"Do you want to waste all your time arguing with me? Because now you're down to nine."

He cursed under his breath. She tapped her foot.

"Don't you think you're being a tiny bit unreasonable?" he asked.

"No. Unreasonable would have been for me to give you five minutes."

"How is five unreasonable and ten isn't?"

She'd had enough and poked him in the chest with one finger as she spoke. "Because I knew you'd spend at least five arguing with me. Therefore, if I only gave you five, that's all you'd have time to do." She looked down at her watch, even though it was too dark to see. "And, surprise, surprise, I was right."

"Damn it, Andie," he said. "It wasn't supposed to go like this."

"You actually pictured it going a different way? In your version did I swoon at your words of love and let you gallantly sweep me off my feet to live happily ever after?"

"I expected more from you."

His words hit their mark, but she refused to show how much they hurt her. "Then I guess it's a good thing you're finding out about the real me now as opposed to later when it would have actually hurt to break up."

"This isn't you." He held out his hand like he was going to touch her, but she shrank back, deeper into the shadows and away from his touch. "Where did the Andie I know go?"

"She left the day you told her everything she believed about you was a lie."

"I'm trying to apologize."

"Yeah, well, you suck at it."

She couldn't see him all that clearly anymore—a cloud now covered the moon—but she could sense his anger building and she was glad. Glad because she'd be damned if she would be the only angry person at the moment.

His voice was eerily calm when he spoke. "You better be glad you aren't mine because if you were, I'd take you over my lap and by the time I finished tanning your ass, you wouldn't sit down for a month."

"Figures you'd say something like that, you damn Neanderthal. You don't know how to discuss anything like a reasonable adult."

"Forgive me. Would you be the reasonable adult here? Because to me you sound like a bratty four-year-old."

All the anger she'd bottled up came spewing out of her. He

thought she was four? Fine, she'd be four. She rushed at him—he was so close to the water; it wouldn't take much for him to fall in.

But he anticipated what she was going to do and grabbed her, right as she reached for him, swinging them away from the water.

"Oh no, you don't," he said roughly.

She tried to jerk away, but his hold was too tight. "Let go of me."

"Not until I'm certain you aren't going to dump me in the damn ocean. Do you know how cold it is?"

She pulled her arm again and it didn't budge. Worthless. "I don't care."

"Well, I do."

She dug her heels in the ground and tried one more time to get away. He pulled the other way, trying to get them farther up the beach. She took a step in the opposite direction, but her feet got tangled up and she fell, bringing him down with her.

She shut her eyes as the impact took her breath away, but that was nothing compared to what she found when she opened them back up.

Fulton was on top of her, his dark eyes looking down with mirth and something else she wasn't ready to name. Apparently, their arguing had turned him on because his erection pressed against her belly. He held her hands down with his, one on each side of her head.

But it was his smile that scared her and turned her on in equal measure. Wicked. Seductive. "This is certainly an interesting twist, wouldn't you say, Miss Lincoln?"

She pressed her lips together, determined not to show how much she wanted him in that second. God, his weight felt good pressing her into the ground.

"Run out of snappy comebacks?" He was relentless in his presumed victory. "That's okay. I have a better use for that sassy mouth. And from this angle . . ." He rolled his hips so she felt every inch of his erection, and she couldn't stop the moan she gave in reply. "I can tell you are definitely not four years old. You are all woman. One hundred percent fuckable woman. And the only question remaining is: do you want me to take you here, like the damn Neanderthal I am, or should I pretend to have an ounce of civility and at least carry you to bed before fucking you senseless?"

CHAPTER
Eighteen

Andie's blue eyes blazed at him and he recognized he was probably going a bit too far, but damn it all, she'd tried to push him into the ocean and then she'd tripped. Technically, he figured, that made it *her* fault that he currently towered over her, with her soft and sensual body under his.

"Neither," she said in a calm voice at odds with the way she'd moaned just seconds ago. "I pick neither. I'm going to go back to my room and use my vibrator. Thank you very much."

Like hell she would. "You're not allowed to use vibrators here. It's a rule." But holy hell, what the visual of her in bed with a vibrator did to him.

"I graduated today, which means I'm no longer a student. I can make myself come as often as I want. In fact . . ." She began grinding her body against his. She arched her back and moaned. "Oh, yes. Now *this* feels good."

His cock strained against the confines of his pants, desperate to be freed. He gritted his teeth in an effort not to do just that as well as hiking up her skirt and giving his cock exactly what it wanted.

"Stop it, Andie."

She closed her eyes and continued humping him.

"I mean it."

She didn't even slow down.

"Very well. Neanderthal it is." He took both her wrists in one hand and dropped his free hand to the hem of her gown, shoving it up to her waist.

Her eyes flew open and she stilled. "What are you . . ." Her words drifted off as he teased aside the tiny silken scrap of her panties and found the slick flesh underneath.

"You know how to stop me," he said, hoping to hell she didn't use a safe word. His fingers slid along her slit. "Besides, I believe it's perfectly clear what I'm doing. But just in case, let's get one thing straight: there will be no vibrator coming near this pussy tonight. The only thing that's going to give it relief is me. *If* I think you deserve to come. And I have to say, thus far, you've been a very bad girl."

He slowly inserted one finger inside her, mindful of the fact that even though she was acting like a sex goddess, she was still a virgin. "A very, very bad girl."

"Fulton." Her hips lifted, trying to get more of him inside her.

He removed his fingers. "For someone who graduated today, you certainly messed that up."

"Sir, Sir, Sir. Please, Sir."

"I don't think so."

Her eyes drilled into him and he could almost see her brain spinning, trying to come up with something nasty to call him.

"Before you let that mouth of yours get you in trouble, I think we ought to move this discussion to the lighthouse." He nodded toward the main building, where he could see people walking around the grounds. "People are starting to leave."

He knew that by the time they made it to the lighthouse, there was a very good chance the moment between them would be gone. Heck, it might be gone even now. Unfortunately, he couldn't let them continue the way they were. The one thing he didn't want was for anything they did to be open to public viewing.

She didn't speak, but pushed herself up to a sitting position. It wasn't until she stood up and brushed off her skirt that she looked his way. "Fine" was all she said.

Hopefully they would both calm down by the time they made it to his house. He really hadn't planned for their first time together to be tinged with anger.

He reached out his hand, a peace offering of sorts, and was pleased when she took it. Maybe all was not lost after all.

They didn't speak as they walked the short path that led to the lighthouse. He wanted to ask her if she was sure she wanted to do this, how she pictured this changing their relationship, and if she'd forgiven him. *Damn it, Matthews, you sound like a woman. If she's fine with it, you should be, too.*

But once they made it to his place and he'd locked them inside, he couldn't keep himself from taking her by the shoulders and turning her to face him.

"Are you sure you want this?" He searched her expression for any sign of hesitation. "We don't have to do anything."

She reached her hand up to his face and lightly stroked his cheek. Then, without warning, she grabbed him by the hair and pulled his head down to hers. "Fucking take me now, Sir. Show me what you do to very, very bad girls."

He almost came in his pants. "Fucking hell, Andie," he said before claiming her lips in what might have started as a kiss but ended up being more of a fight for control.

"You're driving me crazy," he whispered against her lips when he pulled back slightly. "But we're doing this my way, so get that into your head right now."

She nodded and in response, he pushed her against the wall. His lips once more found hers, and this time she relinquished control. Her submission was even sweeter because he'd had to work for it.

Her lips parted at his insistence and he swept his tongue inside, tasting her and committing to memory what he found. She relaxed in his embrace, appearing, for the moment at least, to have yielded to him.

He groaned when she ran a hand down his back and attempted to untuck his shirt.

Her hands felt so good on him. She slid them under the cotton fabric, igniting his skin wherever she touched. But when her nimble fingers reached for his belt, he pulled back.

"Andie, listen." He covered her hand to still it. "I want to go slow, because this is your first time. It doesn't matter how gentle I am—it's going to hurt. But I'm only a man and my control only goes so far. If I tell you to stop, you need to stop. And right now, I need your hands above my waist. Got it?"

"Yes, Sir."

He traced her lips with the tip of his finger and shook his head.

"Not right now. There's plenty of time for *Sir* later, but not your first time. For right now, I'm just Fulton."

She smiled, and his heart melted. It was the first smile he'd seen from her in far too long. He vowed then and there to do whatever it took to keep that smile on her face.

"You know," he said, pushing her hair back from her shoulders. "I don't think I showed you the bedroom when I gave you the grand tour."

"You didn't," she said. "How very negligent of you."

He held out his hand. "Allow me to remedy that."

She nodded and placed her hand in his, but instead of leading her to the bedroom, he scooped her up in his arms and carried her. He expected her to protest, but she surprised him by giggling and burying her head in his chest.

He placed her on the bed and made sure she watched as he stepped back and removed the shirt she'd untucked. He shrugged it off, allowing it to fall to the floor. One at a time, he toed off his shoes, but he left his pants on.

She was definitely watching as he made his way to the bed and climbed up beside her.

He propped himself up on his elbow so he could look down at her while he toyed with the top of her dress. "What are you thinking?"

"That you left your pants on."

"Yes," he said. "It goes back to the control issue. If I have to stop and take my pants off, it'll remind me to take my time and not go at you like a bull in heat."

She blushed slightly, but frowned and looked away.

"Hey." He put his finger under her chin and turned her face toward him. "What's that for?"

"I just realized I don't know what I'm doing." She bit her bottom lip. "And you know everything. And then I thought that's stupid—it's just sex, but it's more than just sex, and then I was back to not knowing what I'm doing."

"You don't have to know anything. I just want you to feel tonight." His words didn't calm her like he thought they would. "Look at it this way: we're not in a scene right now, but you can still trust me. I'll take care of you and if you need to know something, I'll make sure you know it, okay?"

She gave him a timid smile. Quite a change from the woman in the doorway who'd grabbed him and told him to take her. He was going to have to go even slower. He hoped he would be able to control himself.

Acting far calmer than he felt, he reached under her and tugged her zipper down. "Might be best to show you."

She lifted up, so he could slide the gown down. He sucked in a breath as he bared her skin.

"You didn't wear a bra."

Again, he got that timid smile from her.

He'd forgotten how beautiful she was, how her skin looked uncovered. "I've wanted to taste you for so long." His fingertips breezed across her collarbone. He didn't allow himself to touch her breasts just yet.

"I've wanted to feel your mouth on me."

Hearing her words, he gave into his urges and covered one nipple with his mouth.

"Oh." Her back lifted slightly as she offered more of herself to him. "Oh, yes."

He fisted his hand at her response as he understood just how difficult going slow was going to be. If she reacted like that . . .

He moved to the other nipple.

"Shit!" she panted as he both sucked and ran his tongue over it. Her body bucked against his and he took hold of her with both hands, holding her to him while he continued to lick, tease, and nibble his way around her upper body.

It shouldn't have come as a surprise when her hands found his chest. "Can I? With you?" she asked in a breathless plea.

"Not right now," he half growled. Her sexy cries and lithe body were already pushing his control, challenging his ability to remain calm and clear minded. If she touched him too much with those hot hands, he'd lose it entirely.

"Please?" Her thumb came dangerously close to flicking his nipple.

"What did I tell you?"

"But I—"

He stopped her by taking her hand and placing it on his erection. "Do you feel that?" He continued at her nod. "I'm not small. I need you to come at least once, maybe twice before I can even think about fitting it inside that pussy. Do you understand?"

"Yes," she whispered.

"Good. Unfortunately, that means you need to keep your hands to yourself a little bit longer." He took a deep breath. Just talking about his dick fitting inside her made him so hard he could bust. "Grab onto the sheet if you have to because if you can't keep your hands at your side, I'll have to tie you up."

She obediently gathered the sheets in her fist, but looked him in the eye. "Done, but next time I want you to tie me up."

He was going to come if he didn't get his mind on something, anything, else. "Soon," he promised.

Knowing just what he needed to keep his mind off his aching cock, he pulled her dress down and free from her body, leaving her in only her thong. Not bothering to take it off, he simply moved it to the side and licked her, savoring her taste. Beside his head, her white knuckles showed she was fighting just as hard as he was.

"Fulton. More . . . please," she panted while he feasted on her.

"I want you to come like this," he spoke against her skin. "On my mouth. With me tasting you."

He thought she was close. He hoped she was close. He licked her slit, dragging his tongue along it, dipping into her with the tip. She shivered in his arms and whimpered under her breath.

But he wasn't finished. He plunged his tongue in and out of her, mimicking how his cock would soon take her. Her hips lifted off the bed, but he held on to her, not letting her go. He wanted her to come. Needed her to come.

Her body tensed and he redoubled his actions.

"Fulton."

He licked her clit and her body spasmed around him.

"Fulton," she panted. She'd let go of the sheet and was urging him up.

He eased himself back up the bed and stroked her hair. "Yes?"

"I want you. Now." She reached for his pants, but he stopped her hands.

"Not yet. I want you to come again."

"I just came. I'm ready. Take me." She shimmied her panties off. "Please."

He stared at her naked body, his for the taking. "Andie . . ."

"I need you inside me."

His resolve diminished with every whispered plea. He slipped a finger inside her and, finding her wet, added another and stretched her ever so slightly. "Are you sure you're ready?"

"No, but I know that I want you like I've never wanted anything else."

If she wanted him that badly, he wasn't going to wait any longer either. He reached over to the nightstand and took a condom. "Take my pants off, but don't touch my cock."

She hurriedly pushed his pants down and he was pleasantly surprised when she didn't try to disobey him. But even though she didn't touch him, she still eyed him.

"I think it's gotten bigger since the last time I saw it," she teased as he rolled the condom on.

"Having second thoughts?" he asked.

"Not on your life." But she was looking at him as if to say *That isn't ever going to fit.*

Properly protected, he took her in his arms once again and kissed her, wanting to get her back to that frenzied state of arousal. He wanted her so crazy for him and what he could do to her body that she forgot everything else.

She was more tentative with him naked. Almost as if removing his pants made everything more real. And while he wanted her to be aware that he was large, he didn't want her scared.

Little by little, one touch at a time, he began to tease her body. He started with gentle caresses and light kisses, until she was writhing and begging for more. Even then, he didn't give her too much, but just enough to heighten her senses.

It was several long minutes before he slid his fingers back inside her, and when he did, she bucked her hips in an attempt to get more of him.

"Ready for my cock?" he whispered, and bit her ear for good measure.

She yelped, but her muscles tightened around his fingers. "Yes," she said. "So ready."

He drew short circles around her clit. "Come for me one more time."

"Fulton," she said in an almost whine. "Please."

He didn't answer but rubbed her clit harder and was rewarded by a gasp as her second climax built. He positioned himself between her legs, never letting the friction of his fingers stop. When her body began to shudder with her approaching release, he eased the tip of his cock inside her.

His eyes damn near rolled to the back of his head because *holy shit* she was tight.

But he couldn't allow himself to get caught up in how good she felt because he knew the next part was going to hurt and he wanted to minimize the pain as much as possible.

He waited until her orgasm reached its peak before thrusting into her all the way. Her eyes flew open and she gripped his shoulders in a hold so tight, he felt her nails dig into his skin.

"Oww. Fuck!" She panted.

He shook with the effort to remain still until she had grown somewhat accustomed to his size.

"Oww," she said again.

"Sorry." His breath was heavy. "The worst is over."

"You lied."

"What?" he asked bewildered. "When?"

"I think you have the biggest dick known to man."

It was so unexpected, he couldn't help but laugh, but that made him move, and she winced.

"I'm trying to be still," he explained. "But you made me laugh."

She took a deep breath, running her hands up and down his back, until finally he felt her body relax, just a bit, around him. "Okay, you can move now."

He eased out a bit and pushed back in, fighting the almost overwhelming urge to pound her into the mattress. "Better?"

She nodded. "Getting that way. Hold on."

He gritted his teeth and held on, even though every cell in his body begged him to move.

Just when he thought he'd go mad, she wiggled her hips.

"Andie," he half croaked.

"Just seeing."

"Jesus. Just seeing what?"

"If the pain's gone."

"Is it?"

She rubbed her hands down his back. "Mostly."

He wasn't sure how much more he could take, but he was still fearful of hurting her. "I'm going to go slow. Let me know if it's too much."

She closed her eyes and nodded.

"No," he said. "Keep them open. Look at me."

Her eyes fluttered open and he started to move so slow he could have screamed. But eventually her expression grew less strained and more relaxed and he allowed himself to thrust a little faster.

"Oh yes," she said. "This is nice."

"Nice?" he ground out. "Nice?"

263

"Compared to when it felt like you were trying to split me open? Yes, it's nice."

He dropped his head, knowing he wasn't going to last much longer. She was too tight. Too hot. Too much. He worked his hips a few more times and came with a rush.

Exhausted and completely spent, he pulled her into his arms. "Give me a chance to recuperate and we'll try again."

And if she still thought it was *nice*, he'd give up sex forever.

I'M NOT A *virgin anymore.*

Andie almost felt giddy thinking it. *Finally,* she wanted to add. And it had been nice, though for some reason Fulton hadn't seemed to like that adjective too much. He'd gotten up and disposed of the condom. When he'd come back from the bathroom, he'd had a warm cloth he'd cleaned her with.

That had been nice, too.

Though she kept that thought to herself.

Now he rested on his back beside her with his eyes closed. He must have been tired, but she was ready to try again. Especially since he'd given her the impression the second time wouldn't be as painful.

She lifted one leg, experimenting. There was some soreness between her legs, but nothing she couldn't handle.

She glanced once more at the man at her side. She'd been shocked when he showed up at the ball and she probably could have handled it better. But things were looking up and he'd said he loved her. She could almost have wept just thinking about it.

He was magnificent looking, in bed and naked. She lifted her hand to trace his chest muscles, but then stopped suddenly when she had another idea.

She lowered her head and licked his nipple. His eyes flew open.

"Andie?" he asked.

"I decided to reciprocate."

"I'm not so sure that's a good idea."

"Really?" She moved over to his other nipple. She loved his taste and at the moment, his skin was just a bit salty. "Because I think it's one of my better ideas."

He mumbled something she couldn't make out.

"In fact." She sat up and ran her hands down his chest. "I think I could spend *hours* doing nothing but touching and tasting you."

"I'd never survive."

"Nonsense. It's the perfect thing to do while we get ready for round two." She wrinkled her forehead. "There is going to be a round two, isn't there? Because it's not supposed to hurt as much the second time." She nibbled his chest. "And are you going to tie me up this time?"

Quick as a snake, he sat up, grabbed her shoulders, and pushed her down on the bed. "Damn, you're chatty."

"Sorry."

"No, it's okay. I like it. I just want to make sure I answer all your questions." He kissed her cheek. "Let's see. Yes, there's going to be a round two—just give me ten minutes. No, it won't hurt as much and no, I'm not tying you up yet."

"Why not?"

"Because I don't want tonight to be about anything other than the two of us. We have plenty of time for kinky play."

He grew quiet then, but she felt his body tense above her and she lifted her head to see why. "Fulton?" she asked, pressing her palm to his cheek. "What is it?"

"I'm sorry."

"For what?" She wrinkled her forehead, trying to figure out why he was apologizing.

"For the way I acted after you got out of the hospital. I hounded you about Terrence putting his job above you and I did the same thing." He absentmindedly stroked her arm. "But I realized without you, nothing mattered."

She rose up and kissed his cheek. She wouldn't tell him that it was okay, because it wasn't. But she could tell him the truth. "Yes, you hurt me, but I knew how you really felt. Truthfully, you were hurting yourself, too. My only worry was whether or not you'd realize it before it was too late."

"You forgive me?"

She nodded. "Always."

He pulled her tight to his chest. "I don't know what I did to deserve someone like you, but I swear I won't let you down again."

For long minutes they stayed in each other's arms, making small talk, content for the moment with teasing touches and light caresses. But eventually their need grew and the touches became more urgent.

She wiggled against him when he wouldn't do anything.

"You need to stop," he said. "I don't want you to be too sore."

Not ready to give up, she pushed her hips into his. "If I don't, are you going to tie me up?"

"Later."

She held still. "But you're a Dom—don't you prefer kinky sex?"

"I typically enjoy sex when it has an element of D/s in it, but I don't *have* to have it." He traced her lips with his finger. "I enjoyed what we just did and the next time will be even better."

"But we will do the kinky stuff eventually, right?"

"Of course," he said and she felt her arousal grow at the idea of kneeling for him once more. "After all, you still have to pass my final exam."

Silly man. "That's okay, Master Nader gave us our finals. I passed with flying colors." Surely, he knew that. She'd graduated today.

"No, Miss Lincoln, I'm well aware you passed that exam. I said you still had to pass *mine*."

"Oh, fuck," she said as his meaning became clear.

His smile was wicked. "Only if you pass."

A WEEK LATER, Andie prepared for Fulton's so-called final exam in the new staff room she'd moved into days earlier. The day after the ball, she'd gone to Lennox's office and accepted the full-time chef position. Later the same day, he'd reinstated Fulton as Master Professor, with no restrictions.

Though she had her own room now, Andie found she spent a lot of time at the lighthouse. Even after his reinstatement, Fulton had requested to stay in the cozy house, and Lennox had agreed. Andie helped Fulton redecorate a bit, but they were holding off on any major renovations.

Since there was a two-week break before the fall classes started, most of the academy staff had left the island. Other than

Fulton and Andie, the only people who remained were Lennox and Mariela.

Surprisingly enough, she and Fulton didn't have sex at all after that first night. Granted, they'd done it three times that night, and each time had been better than the last. But whenever she'd bring it up or attempt to move beyond making out on his couch, he'd put a stop to it. Needless to say, calling her sexually frustrated was an understatement.

She was hopeful all that would change today. He hadn't told her anything about it, not even where it'd take place, only that she would find out when she needed to know.

Her phone buzzed with an incoming text. **Exam time. Be waiting for me in the lighthouse in twenty minutes. Naked.**

Her heart pounded with excitement. This was it. Time to show him who she really was. And in the lighthouse. He'd never given her the full tour he'd promised.

She typed back a quick **Yes, Sir** and hurried across the academy lawn.

She peeked over her shoulder. Though she didn't see him on the way over, she knew he was nearby. Knowing he'd be joining her soon made her move faster.

THE LIGHTHOUSE TOWER had a separate entrance and she pushed that door open. It took her eyes a second to adjust to the difference in the lighting. She gasped when she saw it fully.

A tall staircase wound upward and on every fifth step was a lit candle. The effect was awe inspiring and she stood staring for who knew how long until she remembered she was on a timeline. She shed her clothing quickly, letting it drop to the floor, and then started up the stairs.

She reached the top and the view took her breath away. While she'd never had a fear of heights, being that high up with that many windows made her a bit dizzy. Though she knew the glass was strong and she wouldn't fall into the rocky sea below, she took a step back from the window.

There wasn't a true middle in the room, but he had left a pillow for her. She knelt on it, wondering how many of her twenty minutes she'd used. She took a few seconds of the peace and quiet to meditate on the fact that, finally, she was kneeling, waiting for the man she loved.

She hadn't told him that yet. She wanted it to be the exact perfect moment.

Thinking about it and him helped her to relax and she felt herself smile when she heard his footsteps approach.

Then they stopped, somewhere near the doorway if she heard right. *Why had he stopped?*

They finally started again, but they were slower. It seemed like forever until he stood before her.

"My god, you're incredible," he said in a hoarse voice. He gently touched her head. "Look at you waiting for me. All mine."

"Only yours, Sir," she answered, the sound of his emotion impacting her as well.

"I never allowed myself to dream you could be mine. It never seemed possible and yet here you are."

Her eyes burned with tears of happiness.

"Stand up for me, Andie."

She slowly rose to her feet. He frowned when he saw her face. "Have you been crying?" he asked, gently wiping a tear away.

"Only because I'm so happy." She took a deep breath, knowing it was time. "I love you."

"Andie," he whispered, gently pulling her into his embrace and kissing her softly. "I love you so much. I don't know what I'd have done if you hadn't forgiven me."

"All that is in the past," she assured him. He'd told her about his visit with Barbara, and they had plans to see her and the home the following weekend. "I want to focus on our future."

"How true." He gave her cheek one last caress. "Are you ready for your final exam?"

"Yes, Sir."

"Move back to your knees." He gave her shoulders a gentle push and her heart began to pound because he no longer sounded like Fulton Matthews. He was Master Matthews, and it had been far too long since she'd heard him.

His hands were not as gentle as they had been just moments before when he cupped her chin and lifted her head. "What are your safe words?"

She told herself he was asking to remind her that she had them— that was all. She hoped. "Green, yellow, and red, Sir."

"Very good." He unbuckled his belt. "I hope you've been working on that gag reflex."

They had practiced on cucumbers in class, which he would know since he had written up the course schedules. But a cucumber was a sorry substitute for what she really wanted, and hearing him talk only made her want to taste him more. She'd attempted to take him in her mouth when they were in bed the previous weekend, but he'd stopped her. He didn't look like he was going to stop her now. He pushed his pants down and she licked her lips at the sight of his erection.

He tapped her chin. "Open and take me deep."

She eased her mouth around his tip, enjoying the feeling of taking him this way. He fisted his hands in her hair and pushed forward, hitting the back of her throat.

"Fuck, yes," he said when she worked to swallow more of him. "I would love to do nothing else than to stand here and fuck that tight throat."

Breathe through your nose.

She shifted her focus from the cock in her throat to breathing as best she could. Right when she thought she couldn't take anymore, when she was mere seconds away from saying "Red," he pulled out.

She didn't have time to catch her breath before he grabbed her hair and lifted her head up to meet his eyes.

"If I wanted to fuck that tight throat, you'd let me, wouldn't you?" he asked.

"Yes, Sir."

"And do you know why?" he asked.

He remembered! She couldn't believe he remembered. She had only mentioned that fantasy once and it had been months ago.

"Yes, Sir. I remember."

"Do you want me to say it?" His eyes searched hers.

He was asking because he wanted to make sure it was still what she wanted. What would make her even more wild for him. And maybe that he wanted to be sure it was the words she wanted from the fantasy and not the man she initially fantasized saying them.

"Yes, Sir. Please."

"You'd let me fuck your throat because you're my little slut, aren't you?"

Delicious shivers ran up and down her body when she heard him say the words. When she'd first had the fantasy, she felt guilty for liking it, but now, kneeling before Fulton, there was no guilt. It felt right. She only felt acceptance. It was what she liked and what turned her on. There was nothing to feel guilty about.

"Yes, Sir," she said, feeling completely free for the first time in a long time.

"Say it."

"I'm your little slut, Sir." She was and she liked it.

"My little fuck toy."

"Yes, your little fuck toy. Your little fuck toy slut loves your cock, Sir." Her hands flew over her mouth. "I can't believe I said that, Sir."

"Why? Was it untrue?"

"No, Sir." It had felt good to say it, and because of that she wasn't sorry after all. "Matter of fact, I take it back, Sir. I'm glad I said that."

"Are you?"

"Yes, Sir. I'm proud to be your little fuck toy slut who loves your cock."

He crossed his arms and looked down at her. "You know what that means, don't you?"

Did she do something wrong? Had she spoken out of turn?

"No, Sir. I don't know what that means." And she was just a little scared to find out.

"Embracing your fantasies. Accepting what turns you on. Not letting fear or self-doubt hold you back." A huge grin spread across his face. "You just made an A on part one of your final."

While she was thrilled to hear he'd given her an A, she wasn't expecting a multipart exam. Just how many parts did he plan? And was he going to fill her in on the requirements? She could ask, but she was fairly certain he wouldn't tell her. Plus, she thought it showed more trust in him if she didn't ask.

She bowed her head. "Thank you, Sir."

He waited as if expecting her to say something else, but when she didn't, he stepped away. She heard something move across the floor and the clanking of chains. Her first real session; she couldn't believe it was finally time.

"Come stand by the window, Miss Lincoln," he said.

She stood up and saw that there were chains hanging from the ceiling, not far from where she'd stood earlier. How had she missed them? As she moved closer to where he waited, it hit her. Heights. Window.

She swallowed and moved to his side.

"We're going to experiment with different impact toys," he said while she walked over. "I have the checklist you completed earlier this week."

After their first night together, he'd asked her to fill out a new checklist. Plus, he'd given her a copy of his. It was the first time she'd seen his list and she'd devoured it, reading every line and trying to commit it to memory.

As he shackled her wrist to the padded cuffs attached to the chains, she tried to mentally compare their two lists, but she was having a really hard time doing so. Maybe if she wasn't naked and being chained to the ceiling, she could think.

"Your mind is working overtime," Fulton said from behind her. "Stop it."

"I'm trying, Sir."

"Try harder." He nibbled on her neck, sending shivers down her spine. "Mmm, your skin pebbled up when I did that."

"It felt good, Sir."

"I'm glad." He took a step back. "Tell me how the crop feels."

"What?" She turned her head to try to see what he was doing, but before she could, the crop landed on her backside with a sharp thud that seemed to travel directly to her clit. "Ohhh, yes."

Her response must have enticed him to continue, because he swatted her ass several times. Each landing brought an initial shot of pain that quickly dissipated into pleasure.

When the leather tail connected with her clit, she heard herself groan, and she widened her stance, needing more.

His chuckle seemed to come from far away. "Greedy little slut."

She was. She was so greedy and needy. Below her and out the window, the waves crashed along the rocks. In her mind, the crop landed at the same moment the water hit land. She blinked and she was a boat, gently swaying with the tide. Back and forth. Up and down. There was a word she needed, but it floated out in front of her and she couldn't grab it. The crop landed on her clit again and her surroundings simmered in the hue she was looking for.

"Green. Green, Sir."

The next thing that landed on her skin was sharp and hit her everywhere all at once. *Yes. Yes. Yes.* It fell over and over and she never wanted it to end. But he seemed to be slowing down.

"Green, Sir," she said, wanting to recapture the feeling she'd just experienced.

"I need you with me for this next one."

Something thin and altogether wickedly painful struck, but this time the pain didn't end with pleasure. It just hurt and it hurt bad. There was no longer a boat and she couldn't focus on the sea. She sucked in a breath, bracing for the next strike and not wanting to fail, but after the second, she knew she couldn't take a third.

"Red," she said, not caring one way or the other as long as it stopped.

Immediately, her wrists were released and Fulton gathered her in his arms. "Andie?"

She blinked back tears. "Sorry. That thing fucking hurt."

He sat down and kept her in his embrace, rocking her slightly while he stroked her hair. "There's nothing to apologize for."

"But I couldn't do it."

"Your job isn't to take anything and everything I dish out, now, is it?" he asked.

"No, but . . ." She trailed off, seeing his point.

"When you wanted more, you used *green* and you're not apologizing for that, are you?"

"No, Sir."

"So don't apologize for using *red*. That's why you have the words." He turned her so she faced him and he framed her face in his hands. "I want—no, I need you to use them without hesitation. That's the only way I can allow myself to dominate you. Understand?"

"Yes, Sir." Not only did she understand, but she trusted him even more now.

"I was going to give you another A for part two of your exam, but I'm dropping it to a B because you apologized for safe-wording."

She nodded. "I suppose that's fair."

He lifted an eyebrow and she picked an imaginary piece of lint off his shirt.

"There's just one tiny little problem," she told him.

"And what is that?"

"I don't make anything less than an A. So I need to ask if there's anything I can do for extra credit."

"Extra credit?"

"Yes, Sir. To bring my grade up to an A."

"Mmm, I'll have to think about this one."

She leaned in close and whispered in his ear, "Think hard. Think really, really, really *hard*."

"Fuck, Andie."

"Works for me."

"Are you topping from the bottom? Because that'll drop you down to a C."

"Who me? You're the one who brought up fucking, I was just agreeing with you."

He gave her thigh a playful swat. "Hands against the glass. You better be glad there are only two other people on the island right now, or else we'd be putting on quite the show." He cupped her chin, lifting her head up so he could look into her eyes. "Or maybe you'd like that? You'd like for the entire academy to watch as I pound you into that window, wouldn't you?"

"Yes, Sir," she replied in a whisper, feeling so empty and wanting him so badly, she ached. She slid out of his arms and turned back to the window, bracing against it as best she could.

He brushed her ass. "We're going to do this my way this time."

Yes, she wanted to shout. Right now.

"So as of this minute, no talking unless I ask you a question or you need to safe-word. No moving unless I tell you to." She heard a zipper being undone and the crinkle of foil. "Understand?"

"Yes, Sir," she managed to get out, and she felt herself grow wet at his words. Finally. She braced herself and waited, knowing her obedience would be rewarded soon.

He didn't acknowledge her answer, but instead pushed her head so her cheek rested on the cold glass. He kicked her legs farther apart. One hand rested at the small of her back, an unspoken reminder to remain still. She hoped she could do it.

When he was satisfied that she wasn't going to move or talk, he rubbed her ass. His gentle strokes gradually became rougher and she bit her tongue to keep from calling out when he pinched a spot that was still sore from earlier.

"Such a good girl," he said.

He leaned over her back, placing kisses down her spine, and she swallowed a moan because it felt so good.

"I think I wanted you from the second I saw you, first thing this summer." He teased her skin right at the juncture of her thigh. So close and yet not anywhere near close enough. "I never imagined I'd be fortunate enough to have you as my own."

This was the worst kind of torture she'd experienced, hearing him talk like that and not being able to reply.

"That day when I thought I'd lost you in the storm was the worst day of my life. Or at least it was until the day I actually lost you due to my own stupidity." His fingers inched closer and she thought her eyes would roll straight back into her head if he didn't touch her, really touch her, the way she needed. "But the day you came back to me and forgave me, that was the best day."

He slipped a finger inside her, maybe to make sure she was ready, and chuckled at what he found. "And to see you now, offering yourself to me, trusting me. I don't need anything else. I found it all in you. I vow to you now to be the same for you."

He took a step back and slowly eased his way inside her. She was pleasantly surprised to find there was none of the pain she'd experienced the previous weekend. There was only the slow, seductive stroke of his body sliding into hers and the overwhelming pleasure as they joined together.

"My new goal in life is for you to know how I feel about you and what you mean to me with everything I do and say." He pushed deeper until he was all the way inside her. "Whether I'm taking you slowly and sweetly or riding you hard for my own pleasure, you will always be my beacon of light and my heart's home."

Tears filled her eyes at his precious words and she made her own vow in her heart and head to be the same for him. She wanted to tell him, but it occurred to her that he'd set this up so she couldn't talk. So she had to listen without the burden of forming a reply, and she silently thanked him for that.

He kept moving with slow, intentional thrusts calculated to wring as much pleasure as humanly possible from her body.

"I need you too much to be slow today," he said. "Come when you want."

His hand slipped between her body and the window so he could tease her clit. At the same time, he started fucking her harder and faster. *Holy shit and a half.* She didn't know it could feel that good. His hands. His cock. His words. The coolness of the glass against her skin. And the warmth of him inside her body. Every part of him whispered to her that she was his and that he would protect her and love her with all he had.

Her release built slowly but steadily until it threatened to overtake her each time he thrust into her.

"Fuck. I'm not going to make it much longer," he panted. "Get there, Andie."

He sped up, pounding her into the window, just like he'd promised. She bit her lip to muffle the scream as her orgasm shook her body. He followed shortly thereafter with one last hard thrust and a groan of male satisfaction.

For long seconds, all she could hear was the blood pounding through her head, but she felt him. The kisses he placed on her shoulders. The gentle caress of his hand ghosting down her side.

"Are you okay?" he asked.

She cleared her throat. "Better than okay, Sir."

He kissed her lower back. "Good. Let me get rid of the condom and clean you up."

He dropped a blanket on her back and disappeared down the stairs. He returned with a warm washcloth he used to clean between her legs. She wanted to tell him he didn't have to do it. But he knew that and she guessed that he wanted to do this for her. It was obvious in the way he touched her.

Before the cloth could grow cold, he threw it in a nearby basket and gathered her close to his chest. He carried her across the short room to a waiting pile of blankets and pillows.

"I meant every word I said earlier. I hope you know that," he whispered.

"I do," she answered. "And I feel the same about you."

He pulled her even closer and she heard his racing heart.

"Andie?" he said and he sounded worried.

"Yes?"

He reached beside her and took a velvet drawstring bag she hadn't noticed. "Look at me, please."

His voice was soft, but she didn't mistake his words for anything other than the command they were. She pulled back so she could see his face. The candles from the nearby staircase caused shadows to dance across his face. Yet she focused on his eyes and the intensity reflected there.

"Will you wear my collar?" he asked. "I know it seems early and maybe I'm moving too fast, but I love you and this feels right."

He was offering her his collar. Of all the things he could have said, she never thought he'd ask that. Terrence had told her he wasn't into collars, and she'd never believed she'd be offered one. Yet seeing Fulton offer her his made her want it more than anything.

It felt right to her, too. "I love you, too, and yes, I will accept your collar and wear it with pride."

He took a silver chain out of the bag. It looked like platinum and was constructed of delicate intertwined circles. He held it up and nodded.

She lifted her hair to give him access to her neck and sighed as he clasped it around her throat.

"I've never collared anyone before." His smile came easy now. "You were worth the wait."

She reached up to touch the chain that marked her as his, and she knew her choice had been right.

"And," he said in the seconds before his lips claimed hers, "you passed my exam."

Nineteen

M ariela opened the door to her apartment, smiling when she saw Fulton and Andie waiting. "This is a surprise. What are the two of you up to?"

As if the fact that Andie was now wearing a collar and holding Fulton's hand didn't tell her everything she needed to know. Ever since he'd chased Andie out of the ballroom, Mariela had been anticipating something like this. It took them long enough.

"We wanted to share our news with you," Andie said, smiling up at the man by her side.

"Come on in, then." She moved to the side to allow them to pass her and she told herself she was going to act like she was happy if it killed her. Truthfully, she was happy. She always knew Fulton was a great guy and just needed the right woman to come along. Not to mention she'd grown attached to Andie and her firecracker personality over the summer.

No, her unhappiness stemmed from the fact that the couple before her had something she feared she'd never have. She'd been patient. She'd waited. And nothing.

"Tell me your news," she said when everyone had sat down in her living room. Fulton and Andie took a place on the couch. Of course, Andie was practically sitting in Fulton's lap. Mariela sat in a nearby armchair.

"Andie has agreed to wear my collar," Fulton said, his voice full of pride as he looked down at his new submissive. Andie reached up and kissed his cheek.

"That is wonderful news. Congratulations!" Mariela snapped her fingers and stood up. "Wait right here; let me go get something."

She had a bottle of champagne she'd been saving, and now was as good of a time as any to bring it out. She rummaged through the kitchen to find three glasses. And there was a tray somewhere. Maybe in her bottom cabinet? She bent down to look.

"We were going to tell Lennox as well, but couldn't find him," Fulton called from the living room. "Do you know where he is?"

Mariela straightened up too fast and banged her head against the upper part of the cabinet. "Ouch. Damn it," she muttered to herself, not wanting to disturb her guests. "Lennox went to Cannon Beach for a few days. He should be back the middle of the week."

And she really didn't want to talk about it. She set the glasses and champagne on the tray and carried it into the living room. Fulton was still on the couch, but Andie had walked over to her mantel and was looking at the pictures displayed there.

"Champagne toast, you two?" Mariela asked.

"Perfect." Fulton reached for the bottle, but frowned when Andie didn't say anything. "Andie?"

Andie turned around and her face had lost all its color. Fulton jumped up and hurried to her side.

"Andie?" Mariela asked. "Are you okay?"

Fulton had his arm around her, guiding her back to the couch.

"That picture of you and the woman at the beach, who is she?" Andie asked.

Mariela didn't have to look at the mantel to know which picture she meant. She pictured it in her head: two young women in front of an old beach cottage. She could almost hear their laughter as the wind blew their hair in front of their faces, making it impossible to see the photographer. "That's me and my best friend, Winnie. She—"

"Died," Andie finished, and though it didn't seem possible, she turned even paler. "Lennox told me. In the hospital."

"Who's Winnie?" Fulton asked.

"He told you about her?" Mariela asked at the same time. "Did you know her?"

It wasn't possible. There was no way Andie could have met her. Yet she obviously recognized her picture and Lennox had talked about her.

"I don't think I know her," Andie said. "I recognized her from somewhere. And I'm trying to figure out where."

"She was an artist," Mariela said. "Maybe you've seen her work?" It was the only possible explanation.

"No. That's not it." Andie chewed her bottom lip. "I was walking with her in the woods. She told me I had to choose." She looked up at Fulton. "And I did. I picked you. She was happy and told me to have a good life."

Mariela rubbed her arms as goose bumps rose up on them. "When was this?"

"When I was in the hospital. I thought it was a dream, but it seemed so real. I'd forgotten about it until now." Andie smiled faintly. "She said I had to pick between perfect and almost perfect but not quite."

"That sounds like her," Mariela mumbled as the chills moved from her arms to her spine.

"I still don't know who she is," Fulton said.

Mariela sighed and looked at the champagne. "Wait here."

She felt the weight of their stares as she walked into her kitchen and to a different shelf. It had been years, but she knew where it was. Her fingers wrapped themselves around the bottle and she pulled it out, grabbing three whiskey glasses on her way back to the living room.

Fulton's eyes grew large when she placed the items on the table in front of the new couple. "Uh, Mariela, that's forty-year-old Highland Park Scotch Whisky."

She didn't need to answer him. He would understand shortly.

It was time to tell her story.

Continue reading for a special preview of

THE
FLIRTATION

Coming soon from Headline Eternal

t was never a good thing when Nathaniel West showed up at your office unannounced. Simon Neal had been a Dom for over ten years with his New York BDSM club and in that time, he'd heard of Nathaniel showing up five times at a club member's office. Not one of the members had ever returned.

Simon tried to think reasonably. Nathaniel wasn't very active in the club anymore, and since Simon ran a temp agency, maybe he need a temp, or he might have just been in the neighborhood and decided to stop by. There was no reason to think he was stopping by on club business.

As soon as Simon opened the door and saw Nathaniel's expression, though, it was clear the man had not stopped by for a friendly chat.

Wondering what the hell was going on, Simon waved the other Dom inside. "Nathaniel, good to see you. Come in and have a seat."

"Thank you," Nathaniel said and proceeded to sit in a chair across from Simon's desk.

"Are you and Abby in town?" Simon asked, taking his seat.

He never wanted to play poker with Nathaniel, as the man had the ability to wipe all trace of emotion off his face. It was a bit unnerving, especially when he turned that blank face toward you, like he was doing now.

"We are," Nathaniel said. "But just for the day."

"I'm glad you stopped by. I haven't seen you since Luke DeVaan's party."

Luke, a mutual friend, had thrown a party at his BDSM club a few weeks ago for the launch of his book *The Muse*. Nathaniel and Abby had been at the club that night. His gut clenched as he remembered who else had been with them. Lynne Ryder.

He tightened his fingers into a fist. He wouldn't think about Lynne right now. He wouldn't think about Lynne, ever. That chapter in his life was closed and he wasn't going to reopen it.

Nathaniel watched him with eyes that Simon knew missed nothing. He wondered what Nathaniel was watching him so intently for.

"I'm not sure you're aware, but Abby and I hired Lynne several months ago as our nanny," Nathaniel said.

Simon's breath came out in a whoosh. "No, I didn't know." *Holy shit, Lynne works for Nathaniel and Abby.* "I'd heard she'd left the city, but I had no idea. She's your nanny?" And why was Nathaniel here? He'd said she'd been with them for months, so obviously, he wasn't stopping by to tell him they'd hired her. "Wait a minute—is something wrong? Is she okay?"

"I can assure you she's fine. Or at least she was when I left her with Abby, twenty minutes ago."

Relief flooded Simon's body. "If I may be direct, what brings you by? I know you didn't stop by to tell me you hired my ex as your nanny. But I get the distinct impression this isn't a social call either."

Nathaniel gave him a curt nod of his head. "You're right. It's not. You see, Lynne wants to go back to school to get her teaching certificate and a summer program opened up at the university that could get her closer to that goal. As it turns out, Abby's blog at the news station is on hiatus for the summer, freeing up Lynne to attend the program."

Lynne was going to be back in Manhattan. Damn, but he was a bastard for how excited that made him.

You're to stay away from her. She's not for you.

No matter how truthful the voice of reason was, it still hurt like hell to hear it echo inside his head.

Simon cleared his throat. "I assume she'll be moving back to the city?"

"She'll be staying in our penthouse. It's safe and near the campus, and will offer her the peace and quiet she needs to study."

Simon nodded. Still trying to figure out why Nathaniel was telling him this. Surely, he could have accomplished the same thing via the phone.

"In the few months she's been with us," Nathaniel continued, "Lynne has become part of our family. The children and Abby adore her and I view her as my little sister."

With those words, Simon knew immediately why Nathaniel decided to stop by his office.

"Nathaniel, I—"

Nathaniel held up a hand. "Let me finish. In the last few weeks, Lynne has expressed a renewed interest in BDSM. She's told us she's going to take it slow. She doesn't even want to pursue membership at the club." Nathaniel's voice dropped and he leaned forward. "She's under my protection, and you know what that means."

Yes, he did. He sure as hell knew.

Nathaniel's eyes flashed with danger. "You are to stay away from her. I don't know what happened between the two of you, but if I find out you've disregarded my request or that you've hurt her in any way . . ."

He didn't have to say the rest. No one crossed Nathaniel West. Not if they were smart.

"I understand," Simon said. He didn't need anyone to tell him that he wasn't the right man, or Dom, for Lynne. Wasn't it obvious that he'd figured that out ages ago? Why the hell did Nathaniel think he'd ended it with her in the first place?

Nathaniel nodded. "I'm sure you do. I like you, Simon. More than that, I respect you. You are one of the few people I've allowed into my playroom and to observe my Abby. But let there be no doubt about it: I will have your balls on a silver platter if you harm Lynne. Mentally, physically, or emotionally."

Yes, he understood completely and it pissed him off that Nathaniel felt the need to threaten him over something he had no intention of doing. But he liked and respected Nathaniel, too, so he kept his growing anger to himself and stood up.

"I assure you my interest in Lynne is over. You have nothing to worry about. Unfortunately, I have a meeting at the top of the hour, so I'm going to have to cut this short."

Simon walked to the door and waited for Nathaniel to stand. Nathaniel looked as though he was going to say something as he walked out, but at the last minute, he seemed to have changed his mind. Simon closed the door behind him, determined not to even think about Lynne.

Discover The Submissive series from
New York Times bestselling author

TARA SUE ME

beginning with

TARA SUE ME

THE
SUBMISSIVE

THE WORLDWIDE PHENOMENON
Before there was **Fifty Shades of Grey**...

Abby King yearns to experience a world of pleasure beyond her simple life as a librarian—and the brilliant and handsome CEO Nathaniel West is the key to making her dark desires a reality. But as Abby falls deep into Nathaniel's tantalizing world of power and passion, she fears his heart may be beyond her reach—and that her own might be beyond saving...

HEADLINE
ETERNAL

HEADLINE
ETERNAL

FIND YOUR HEART'S DESIRE...

VISIT OUR WEBSITE: www.headlineeternal.com
FIND US ON FACEBOOK: facebook.com/eternalromance
FOLLOW US ON TWITTER: @eternal_books
EMAIL US: eternalromance@headline.co.uk